"I didn't think [...]
  Friday would g [...]

Sara dropped into a chair opposite her roommate, Nicole Ellis.

"Why? What happens Friday?" Nicole asked, still feeling confused.

"The opening, you goof," Sara said, referring to her art show. "You should really have your memory checked."

"But you've had that." Nicole had gone to the party afterward. "That was a week ago. Last week."

"And you say that I wake up slowly." Sara frowned in exasperation. "This is Wednesday, but August thirtieth. You're a week ahead of yourself. Say, are you feeling all right?"

ABOUT THE AUTHOR

Laura Pender lives in the Minneapolis, Minnesota region where she works at a local newspaper and lives with her family of two children and her spouse. Laura's spouse contributes heavily to her Intrigues. A prolific writer, she has written for *Alfred Hitchcock's Mystery Magazine*, and many other publications.

Books by Laura Pender

HARLEQUIN INTRIGUE

Déjà Vu
Laura Pender

Harlequin Books

TORONTO • NEW YORK • LONDON
AMSTERDAM • PARIS • SYDNEY • HAMBURG
STOCKHOLM • ATHENS • TOKYO • MILAN

Harlequin Intrigue edition published July 1990

ISBN 0-373-22142-8

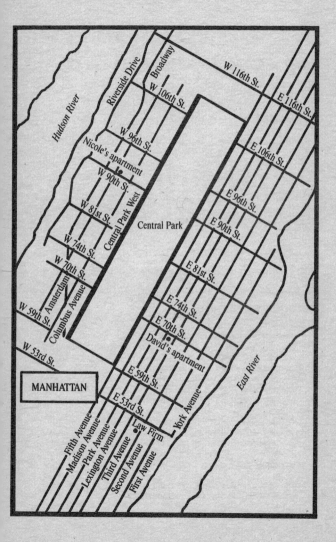

CAST OF CHARACTERS

Nicole Ellis—She was fated to get a second chance.

David Germaine—He held the key—to a woman's life, and to her heart....

Clint Forrester—Did he always have his clients' best wishes in mind?

Connie Wright—She knew what she wanted, and how to get it.

Jerry Brunsvold—All fingers pointed guiltily to him.

Sara Davis—She was a cushion in times of dire distress.

Lance Decker—When he was on his motorcycle, his body was a bullet.

Chapter One

Nicole Ellis looked up from her notes, startled by the raised voices of the two arguing men. Her boss, Clint Forrester, was the normally self-possessed lawyer, who carried out his client's wishes without batting an eye. Now he argued heatedly. Nicole had never even seen him so anxious about his own money, let alone someone else's. Still, from what she knew of David Germaine, the rugged oceanographer seated across from her, he wasn't far off track in his estimate. She watched, mesmerized by the scene.

"I have plenty of money. Besides, I didn't get into this profession to get richer." Germaine's weathered, square-cut face wore an amused cast as he returned the lawyer's gaze. It was obvious he'd gotten this reaction before and had dismissed it with similar ease. "The costs of scientific research have gone so high already that I can't in good conscience take a profit from the scientific community." He glanced at Nicole, then smiled that unabashed look he'd cast her way before.

Nicole felt a blush rising to her cheeks and turned her attention back to the pad. She'd enjoyed the appraisal in his eyes, always feeling a warmth in his presence that she couldn't quite pin down. There was an energy about him, like a net pulling her in. She had felt it a week earlier when he first came to the office.

Nicole had stopped taking notes after the lawyer's exclamation. She'd been Clint Forrester's legal assistant long enough to know what was to be included in the record of his meetings, and this was off the record. Her gaze latched on to the scientist as she sat quietly enjoying the unflappable manner with which he handled Clint's determined objections.

"That's wonderfully noble of you, David." Forrester walked around and took his seat behind the broad mahogany desk, bridging his fingers before him. "And I don't entirely disagree with you. But let me just play devil's advocate for a moment, won't you?"

"It won't change my mind." David spoke with calm resolution, looking again at Nicole as though searching for something in her face.

"No, but it would be malfeasance if I let you go through with it without spelling out your options." Forrester cleared his throat, a stalling maneuver she'd seen him use countless times before as he gathered his thoughts. "You're thinking merely along scientific lines, but there are other considerations, as well."

"I don't care," David Germaine said simply. "My invention was not intended to make money."

"I can think of at least three commercial uses that wouldn't interfere with the goal of the donation, David. You can give the Woods Hole Institute all the free use they want, but then reap the benefits of leasing the research sub out."

"You don't understand me. If the oceanographic institute can make some money renting the device out, I'm all for it. They need the funding. But I've got four generations of trust funds to bank on and I haven't even begun to put a dent in them. I simply don't need the money."

"What about your partner? I drew up the contract giving him a half interest in all properties used jointly in your research. He's got some say in this, too."

"I developed it with my own money, Clint. I didn't use any of our research grants or fees, so it doesn't belong to him. Besides, Jerry thinks the bookkeeping would take too much time away from our work."

"Hire a bookkeeper."

"Face it, Clint, you won't talk me out of it."

"You're impossible." Clint Forrester closed his eyes wearily, then glanced at Nicole. "Don't ever try to talk sense to a scientist. Business matters are beyond them."

"Or below them," Nicole said, smiling. David Germaine chuckled quietly, and the sound of his amusement pleased her.

"You too?" Forrester put his hand to his heart in mock pain, letting a smile fight its way onto his craggy face. "All right. It's not my money, after all. And if you've got my own assistant on your team, I don't stand a chance."

"I do appreciate your concern," Germaine said.

"Yes, but will you still appreciate me when you've gone broke traveling around the world on that ship of yours?"

"Don't worry," the scientist said, laughing. "I'll be sure to remember that you told me so."

"All right then. The papers arrived this morning, so I'll have Nicole get everything ready and you can come back this afternoon and make it legal."

PREPARING THE LEGAL FORMS needed to transfer ownership of David Germaine's property to the Woods Hole Institute was more work than Nicole had anticipated. The oceanographer had seen fit to include a clause specifying that his device was to be shared freely with other scientific researchers, not just for paid commercial use. The man seemed to have thought over his gift more thoroughly than Clint Forrester had given him credit for.

Nicole wasn't entirely sure what the invention at the heart of the matter was. The brief description of it in the contract stated that it was a submergible robotic laboratory vessel—not clear to her at all. All she knew was that it tested conditions on the ocean floor, and when rented out, harvested sizable profits. But David Germaine wasn't in it for the money.

The scientist had been a pleasant surprise on his first visit a week earlier, with his second call only serving to enhance her favorable impression of him. Virile and athletic, he wasn't at all like the stodgy, absentminded scientists found in motion pictures, but an energetic young man whose idealism shone through his rugged exterior like an inner light. Standing slightly over six feet tall with sandy hair and insightful blue eyes, he was the type of man a woman would notice right away in any crowd. He wore an air of confidence and moved with easy grace. Unlike many of the businessmen who crowded Clint Forrester's appointment book, this man didn't vacillate or flinch in the face of objections. He was too sturdy for that.

But there was something more about him—something she couldn't put her finger on...he was different from anyone she'd met, and the feeling that he was more than just another client nagged at her all morning.

Woolgathering wouldn't get her work done in time for lunch, so Nicole fixed her wandering attention back on business. David Germaine seemed like a fascinating man, but after he'd signed the contract that afternoon he'd be gone. There was no point in pondering the possibilities of a man who was just passing through. Besides, he was probably married to a fellow scientist who traveled the globe with him unlocking the mysteries of the deep. The good men are always married.

From what Nicole could see beyond the office window as she put the contract in a file folder, the Manhattan skyline looked like a primordial landscape. Fog shrouded the canyons of skyscrapers, and rain cascaded down from low-slung clouds. September had started off well with a beautiful holiday weekend interrupted only briefly by a short rain shower. But this morning, September sixth, dawned cold and wet as a small taste of the coming fall season. *It looks like the end of the world out there,* Nicole thought.

But rather than the end of the world it was only lunchtime, and she was late by the time she'd finished with the papers.

It must be great to have an assistant, she thought as she made copies and piled all three sets of papers on Forrester's desk. She could only hope the rain would let up before she went down because she didn't relish the thought of being soaking wet in addition to hungry. With only an abbreviated lunch hour remaining before she would be required to be back to witness the signature, a dash to Hoffman's Deli on the corner of the block for a quick sandwich was all she'd have time for.

It was half past twelve. She slipped her tan raincoat over her new paisley-print challis dress and rode the elevator down to the street.

The rain wasn't as bad on the street as it looked from the window, and she pulled her collar up around her neck and forged ahead with a folded paper held resolutely overhead. If she let some rain get her down mid-week, how could she possibly make it to Friday?

At the corner, where the light was against her and a taxi turning close against the curb spattered her newest pair of

shoes with dirty water, she almost gave up and went back
to the office without eating. Almost, but the idea of her
stomach growling through the rest of the day kept her
going. When the light changed, she ran across and down
the block toward the deli.

It looked as if her luck was about to change when she
reached the next corner. The crowd of people standing in
line to order could normally be seen through the front
window of the shop, but today only one man was there,
looking tiredly out at the rain. She might actually get
something to eat after all.

One more street to cross, and she reached the door in
step with a tall man in a dark topcoat who grasped the
door handle and smiled as he began to pull it open.

"Hello again," he said, smiling. It was David Germaine. A dribble of rain ran down one side of his strong
face like a stream winding over a plain of gently weathered granite as he held the door open for her. There was a
sparkle in his eyes, warming her to her toes.

"Goodness, I didn't expect to run into you here." And
she smiled in return, suddenly feeling that it was a nice day,
after all. Maybe fate would be kind, and give her an excuse to extend their acquaintance beyond the office.

"I've been sightseeing," he commented in succinct explanation. "Well, now that we've found each other, we
needn't have a lonely lunch."

"No, I guess not." Her heart increased its tempo briefly
as she looked into his eyes and saw a reflection of her own
desires in them.

But another man rushed up to them before they could
enter the deli. An impatient little man incongruously
wearing sunglasses with his brown raincoat bumped into
Nicole, knocking her slightly to the left and apart from
David Germaine, who was still smiling at her.

That was when Nicole looked down at the arm with which the intruder had bumped her. And she alone saw the squat black gun raised toward the scientist at the door.

The split second after she saw the gun seemed to last an eternity. The man lifted it, his finger tightened on the trigger, as David turned his attention from her to the second man at the door. But Nicole's voice was frozen in her throat. She did the only thing she could think of doing. She lunged at the gunman.

The gunman fired twice in the confusion. They were strangely small pops, nothing sinister in the sounds. Yet they came with the force to thrust Nicole against the open door like a puppet pulled off its feet by two small tugs on its strings. Nicole felt no pain, only a hot, tightening feeling in her chest as she sank to the sidewalk watching the man in the brown raincoat turn and hurry away, confusion stamped on his face. Then someone was holding her shoulders, lowering her to her back, and David Germaine was leaning over her saying something with horror besetting his features.

Nicole tried smiling at him. She wanted to reassure him that she'd be all right. She'd lost her footing, that's all. But no sound came out. She wasn't even sure if she was moving her lips. The only thing she could hear was her own heartbeat. *Ta-thum, ta-ta-thum.* It echoed through her body, a stumbling bass beat. *Ta-thum.* Slower now, leaving an empty space between reverberations. *Ta-thum.* Slower still. And then it forgot to beat again.

Everything was so quiet. She could feel raindrops falling against her face, but she could no longer see them.

Chapter Two

It was raining in her dream. Fat raindrops pelted the pavement beside her as she watched them descend like silvery bullets. A man with worry-etched lines in his strong features was leaning over her. The rain was dripping from a curl of glossy hair that drooped across his forehead. She knew that face but couldn't put a name to it. A nice face, strong and capable and refined, and she decided that she'd just lie here a bit longer and admire him. But then someone was shooting a machine gun into an empty garbage can and the sound was so abrasive that it shattered the man leaning over her. It melted the sidewalk and obliterated the rain.

And the machine gun was her alarm clock and she bolted up in bed with the morning sun in her eyes.

The windup alarm continued to strike the twin bells poised above the clock face. Outraged, all she could do was climb out of bed and curse herself for not being satisfied with the small electronic peeping of her clock radio.

As Nicole threw her covers back, she felt a constricting twinge in her chest. *Get up and stretch the kinks out, girl, it's another day.* She swung her feet out of the covers, and winced. Her chest spasmed again. Fortunately it passed quickly, and she hurried to the bureau to silence the alarm before it woke Sara Davis, her Upper West side apartment roommate.

Nicole showered quickly, thinking of the dream as water cascaded down to warm her willowy body. It seemed so real somehow, and the man in it was awfully familiar. But who was he? And more to the point, why was she lying on the pavement in a rainstorm? She could remember the feeling of concrete against her back and the rain on her face vividly, eerily so. Yet she still couldn't remember what happened before that. It seemed important, somehow, that she remember.

Though Nicole felt certain of rain, the sky outside was clear and the air already warm, so she dressed in a skirt and blouse and carried her summer-weight jacket to the kitchen to grab a quick breakfast of toast and orange juice.

"You have an obnoxious alarm clock." Sara Davis joined her in the kitchen, padding over to the table in her pajamas, scratching at her tangled blond hair. "I think I'll throw it away while you're gone."

"Good morning, sunshine," Nicole said. "I see you're in your usual morning mood."

Sara was Nicole's second roommate since she'd come to work in the city. An easygoing woman with calm humor and a ready smile, she'd easily become Nicole's best friend in the two years they'd shared the two-bedroom apartment together. She worked at the Clayton Art Gallery in the city, and so her work hours had always started later than Nicole's, but all the time she'd put in on last week's opening of their new show had won her a couple days of well-deserved rest. Nicole had hoped to get away without disturbing her.

"I don't think Friday will ever get here," she said, dropping into a chair opposite Nicole with a tired sigh. "I can't take many more days like yesterday."

"Why? What happens on Friday?"

"The opening, you goof," Sara said, referring to the show. "Our big Brent Winston unveiling. You should really have your memory checked, dear."

"But you've had that." Nicole had gone to the party afterwards. "That was last week."

"And you say that *I* wake up slowly." Sara frowned in exasperation. "Get with the program, honey, the opening is in two days."

"But I remember—"

Remember what? Nicole was suddenly unsure of what she remembered, and an icy spasm of fear struck along with the confusion of memories. And as if to further confuse her, Sara walked over to the calendar hanging on the wall by the stove and tore off the top page, her ritual for greeting every new day. The page she revealed proclaimed that it was still August.

"But today is Wednesday, Sara, September the sixth. Isn't it? Isn't it!" Nicole spoke tightly, trying to calm her agitation. It was September sixth today. It had to be.

"No way," Sara protested. "Our opening at the gallery is the first. This Friday. It is Wednesday, but only August thirtieth. Are you feeling all right?"

"But I'm sure that—" Then Nicole laughed nervously and shook her head. "Maybe I should go back to bed and get up again," she said, with self-deprecating humor. "Of course it must be the thirtieth. It's going to rain on the—" What? Again, she was struck with an unnamed fear. Had she lost her mind during the night? "I'd better run or I'll be late," she said lamely as she glanced at her watch, then sat staring at it. "My watch is stopped," she said.

"What did you expect for five bucks?" Sara laughed. "Maybe the battery is dead."

Nicole stared at the face of the digital watch. According to it, the time was 12:41 p.m. "No, if the battery was dead the face would be blank," she said, breathing deeply to try to slow her heart. "But it's just stopped. The little colon between the hour and minutes is still blinking."

"Like I said, it's a cheap watch."

"Must be." Yes, it's broken, that's all. What was she so nervous about? "You'll be at the gallery all day?" Nicole rinsed her glass in the sink and took her coat from the back of the chair, calming herself with mundane tasks.

"After ten, I will. I might even be home at a decent hour."

"I won't hold my breath waiting for you. Bye now." Nicole took her purse and coat, stopping at the closet for her raincoat. No, it was a beautiful August day today so she'd hardly need a raincoat. Again, she was struck by the thought that there wouldn't be any rain till a week from today. September sixth.

A week from today? The day that she had thought it was when she got up this morning? Maybe she'd dreamed that it was the sixth. And maybe she'd dreamed about the gallery opening as well and it had come to the surface of her mind to make her positive it had already happened. Maybe. Her dreams affected her more than she had thought possible if she couldn't keep track of what day it was. But why remember only some stupid dream about lying in the rain? And why jump ahead a week? Nobody gains time when they become absentminded, do they?

No matter. It didn't appear that it was going to rain today, so she left without a coat and took the elevator down from their fifth-floor apartment. In the elevator, she looked at the watch that was still strapped around her wrist. On impulse, she pressed her fingernail against the small button on the side and was surprised to see that it

switched over to the date as usual. But the date was no
more correct than the time had been. The watch insisted
that it was September sixth.

A week from today.

NICOLE ARRIVED AT HER DESK in the anteroom of Clint
Forrester's office at Gilbert, Forrester and Dean feeling
wary of her surroundings. The journey to work had been
laced with a feeling of déjà vu that she couldn't shake. It
was as if she'd done it before. Not just ridden the subway
or walked along the avenue to her building before, which
she'd done every work day for three years, but that she'd
actually lived this particular day before. And the more that
feeling persisted, the more she thought about her dream.
There was still something wrong about that dream.

It was the man in the dream, of course. That was it, the
man had looked familiar though she didn't know him by
name. In fact, she didn't know him at all. So why had she
awakened with the feeling that she *did* know him?

Seated at her desk, an impression came to her of another man. Sunglasses. She remembered a man wearing
sunglasses, though it was an overcast day. What was it
about that man? Nicole closed her eyes, trying to remember him. Was he part of the dream or someone she'd seen
somewhere else? It was no use; the image of the man in
sunglasses slipped from her mind. All she could remember was the gentle face of the man leaning over her in the
rain. Beyond him, the dream was a blank. Still, that man
seemed so real.

It was a strange world where her dreams seemed real but
her memories weren't. She was more sure of knowing a
man she'd never met than she was of attending the opening at Sara's gallery—even though she thought she remembered the opening quite clearly.

The man! She had met him outside Hoffman's Deli. Yes, she remembered standing in the doorway with him and then lying in the rain. Both pieces of a peculiar dream were crystal clear in her mind now but they weren't connected by anything.

My goodness, this isn't an ordinary dream, she thought. *It's more like a memory of a real event.*

And that was wrong, because dreams are hazy things, not open to rational examination. Dreams didn't become more clear with time but grew more murky and didn't leave such intense physical memories as the feeling of rain on her face.

What a strange morning this had turned out to be.

"Nicole."

A voice disturbed her thoughts, and Nicole looked up to see Clint Forrester standing in the door to his office.

"It's in the Dalton file," she said, without thinking.

"Oh, of course." He smiled, rubbing the side of his bulbous nose absently as he turned back to the office. "Thank you."

What was in the Dalton file? Nicole sat stock still for a moment, thinking about that brief exchange. He hadn't asked her anything, had he? She couldn't remember him asking, but she knew he was looking for a set of incorporation papers from something they'd handled a month earlier. He hadn't asked, but she knew what he wanted!

No, he must have asked. She'd been so absorbed by her thoughts that she'd heard him without paying conscious attention.

Nicole felt queasy as she thought about it. Was she going insane? How could she go about her office tasks entirely without thought? More to the point, why had everything that had happened since she'd wakened make her feel so anxious? She wasn't normally a timid person, but everything seemed wrong today and nearly everything scared her.

Before she could get back to her work, she was struck by the thought that Mr. Gilbert's secretary, Jane Lee, was going to come through her door looking for a bottle of whiteout.

No, now you're really getting nuts.

But the office door opened no more than ten minutes later and Jane stepped in.

"Morning, Nicole. Do you have any whiteout?" she asked, striding up to the desk. "My bottle is dry and we're out in the storeroom."

"Yes, but bring it back," she answered. Her stomach tightened a bit beneath her pounding heart.

"I'll have it back in a jiff," Jane said. Then she paused, regarding Nicole with a motherly frown. "Say, do you feel all right? You look pale."

"I'm a little off today." Nicole smiled wanly. "I'm probably coming down with something."

"I hope not, dear, it's going to be a lovely holiday weekend. You don't want to spend it in bed. Well, I'll fix up my mistakes and be right back."

Jane left Nicole seated mutely behind her desk searching for an explanation, and she buried her face in her hands and took a deep breath. She hadn't known they were out of whiteout, but she'd known that Jane would be looking for it just as she'd known that Clint Forrester was looking for those papers. Why?

Jane is coming back, she thought, suddenly. *She's bringing the mail.*

"Mail call," Jane sang out as she bustled through the door to drop a pile of envelopes on Nicole's desk. "It came early and I thought that as long as I was coming back with your whiteout I might as well play mailman."

"Thank you," Nicole said, absently.

What was going on? She was almost ready to grasp at the thought that she was losing her mind, eager to accept even that to explain things. But, if that were the case, why did her watch agree with her first thought that today was the sixth?

"HAVE YOU EVER HAD THE FEELING that you've been in a situation before?" Nicole lay on the couch staring up at the ceiling and gestured casually with the remaining loop of the pretzel she'd been munching on. She hadn't had any more premonitions, and the fear that had all but consumed her during the day had almost faded in her comfortable surroundings. Almost.

"Déjà vu?" Sara asked, looking over from the television screen.

"Yes, but more involved than that, I think. I mean, have you ever known exactly what someone would say in a certain situation even though you had no reason to expect them to say it?"

"No, I can't say that I have. I've read about déjà vu before, though," she offered. "They say it's caused by a mix-up in the signals between your senses and your brain. You see or hear something and your brain registers it as a memory before it experiences it as a present event. I guess it's fairly common, though it's never happened to me."

"Really? You mean such things really happen? They aren't just made up in the movies?"

"I guess so."

"Then maybe I'm all right." Nicole felt somewhat foolish about her fears now. Déjà vu was something she could live with, and it surely beat insanity as an explanation.

"You're saying that it happened to you today?"

"Yes. Today. It was pretty strange." She cut herself off from saying more. "But it's over now."

"Good, 'cause I thought you were nuts this morning. Have you got your calendar straight now?"

"Yes, I—I guess I just dreamed about the gallery opening. I wasn't as awake as I thought I was."

Despite her assurances to Sara, Nicole felt a small tendril of fear beginning to slip through her stomach again as she thought about it. It wasn't right. Nothing was right. But she had no words to voice her fears, no way to explain this unnamed feeling within her.

Later, as she lay in bed, Nicole was disturbed by the growing suspicion that her problem wasn't simply a case of déjà vu and a broken watch. But what else could it be?

And as sleep stole over her that night, the image of the second man finally began to grow in her mind. She remembered sunglasses and two gunshots. That was how she ended up lying on the sidewalk with rain falling on her face. No wonder she hadn't remembered that part of the dream before. Who would want to remember such a thing?

In her dreams Nicole understood the mute warning of her frozen watch. Drifting in the world beyond hard reality and logic, the truth was exquisitely clear. But it wasn't a truth that could survive the assault of logic. It was a dream truth, and she wouldn't remember it in the morning.

Chapter Three

The stars sparkled overhead, undaunted by the glow of civilization so near the research vessel *Katharine* where she lay at anchor in Long Island Sound. David Germaine stood on deck, listening to the waves slapping against the hull of the sleek, expensively outfitted craft and looking up at the stars. It had been a long time since he'd turned his attention to the stars for anything other than navigation, yet tonight they were strangely compelling. Distant and mysterious, they matched his mood.

He'd felt unsettled all day, out of place and unsatisfied as they finished up their survey work for the State of New York. Most unsettling was the fact that his day-long dissatisfaction had been caused by a dream. Or had it?

He'd awakened knowing that he had dreamed, but not remembering anything about it but the image of a face, and the lack of any other memories had upset him. He generally remembered his dreams quite clearly. But this one was different and that made it seem important. All he could remember was that he had been dreaming of a woman named Nicole.

Dreaming about a woman wasn't abnormal, but the woman he usually dreamed of was his late wife, Katharine. Though such dreams had come less often lately, in the two years since her death she'd frequently inhabited his sleeping thoughts. He'd missed her horribly after the accident, after the night when she'd been overdue and his vigil at the window had been ended by a call from the State Patrol telling him that a drunk driver had shattered his life on the highway.

Yes, David had dreamed of her nearly every night after that, carrying her memory into his sleep until he was almost afraid to go to bed at night. And the dreams had eventually forced him to sell their house and take up permanent residence on the boat he'd named after her. His grief had thrown him into his work as never before in an effort to avoid dreaming, avoid living. Time had begun to do its work, diminishing the frequency of the dreams and taking the pain out of them.

But this was the first time since before his marriage that he could remember dreaming about anyone other than Katharine. So why break the routine with a stranger's face? And why name that face Nicole? He didn't know anyone named Nicole.

He leaned on the bow rail and looked down at the glittering surface of the water, imagining the dream face before him. The woman he had dreamed of was quite pretty, with soft brown hair and intelligent hazel eyes. Her lips had been sensuously full and soft beneath the straight line of her nose. He remembered that much, just as he remembered the resolute arch of her cheekbones. But that was all he remembered. No actions, no conversation, just that lovely face and a name that seemed to go with it.

Why wasn't there anything else? It didn't seem possible that he would dream of only a face. Especially a face so dissimilar to Katharine's. There must have been something else to the dream, and he felt it was urgent that he remember more of it. But why? What urgency could there be in a dream?

The water rippled against the hull with a softly hypnotic slapping sound, the ocean's lullaby. He was tired, and the sound increased his languor, but he didn't want to sleep. He wanted to remember. And the waves flowed in even rows, sounding like closely spaced bursts of rain against the boat. Rain.

Nicole's face had been wet. Yes, it was raining on her face as though she was lying on her back in a downpour. He remembered that now, and remembered the sound of the rain falling around them. But as to why they were in the rain, or where they were, he hadn't a clue. What a peculiar dream.

"Are you going to stay up all night?" A woman's voice from the cabin disturbed his thoughts, and he turned toward her as she approached. "You put in a full day. I thought you'd be tired."

"I am." He smiled at the woman in the long terry-cloth robe who joined him at the rail. Connie Wright was his research assistant. But, more than that, she was his sister-in-law. In fact, she had first introduced him to Katharine five years earlier. "I was just enjoying the night air."

"It is a beautiful night, isn't it?" Connie leaned on the rail beside him, her long blond hair wafting on the light breeze as she scrutinized him with her piercing blue eyes. "But are you sure that's all you're doing out here?" she asked, slipping one arm around his waist and settling her body against his side comfortably.

"What do you mean?" He wasn't about to mention his dream to her. It was too foolish a preoccupation to put into words. Besides, he had no way of explaining the effect it had had on him.

"I mean that maybe you're reconsidering your little gift." She spoke softly, but there was a chiding edge to her voice and her determined lips lost a bit of their smile.

"No, I'm certain about that." He frowned. Ever since he announced his plan to donate his research robot to the Woods Hole Institute, Connie had been trying to make him change his mind. Of course, she had more than passing interest in what happened to the *Crab* since she'd been there throughout its creation to lend a helping hand, and he understood that she was only looking out for his best interests, but her concern was beginning to grate on him. "Katharine would have agreed with me."

"Not completely, David. I don't believe she would have wanted you to give up all claim to it." She reached up to squeeze the hand he'd negligently rested upon her shoulder as she leaned against him. "I don't want to seem to be meddling in your affairs, but it seems to me that the Germaines wouldn't have gotten to where they are by throwing money away. You could easily spend everything you've got doing your work, and then what will there be for your—" But she broke off then, dropping her hand with a scowl.

"My children?" he completed, bitterly. "There won't be any children, Connie. Not now. And I don't see any point trying to outscore my ancestors in the game of making money just for the sake of making it."

"I'm sorry." She rested her head against his chest with a sigh. "You still miss her, don't you?"

"Yes. But I think I'm finally out of mourning, if that's what you mean."

"Should I have left, David? Does it remind you too much of her to have me around?"

He smiled then and tightened his arm on her shoulder. "No, I wouldn't want to lose you, too. I have your introduction to thank for the best years of my life, Connie. Besides, how could I give up the only person on board who knows where everything is?''

"I'm indispensable," she said, smiling against his chest.

"We've been working together so long that sometimes I think you know what I'm thinking before I think it.''

"I wish that was true. Then I'd know when to help you fight the blues, and you wouldn't lose sleep staring off into space at night.''

"I'm not blue," he said, carefully. "I was just noticing how beautiful the stars are. And now I'm ready to hit the sack.''

"Tomorrow is another working day," Connie commented, slowly stepping out of his arm. "You have an appointment to give away money.''

"Now, Connie!''

"Okay, that's my last shot," she laughed. "It's not my money, anyway.''

"Knowing you, it's far from your last word on the subject," he said, walking beside her to the cabin of the ship. "I know how stubborn you Wright girls are.''

"Yes, but we do know when to give up on a wasted effort." Then she stretched up to kiss his cheek quickly. "Good night, David.''

"Good night.''

And David lay in the double bed in the master stateroom thinking about wasted efforts. His mournful attitude after Katharine's death had been a wasted effort, too. He knew now that he best served her memory by remembering the joy and getting back into the mainstream of life. The *Crab*, the robot submarine that he'd created and was going to give away, had been the only positive result of that grief. He'd worked hard to perfect the first truly independently operating mobile robot lab, and he was proud of his accomplishment, but the rest of his grief-driven energies had been self-destructive and pointless. He couldn't bring her back by grieving and he couldn't keep up his constant working pace indefinitely. Only when his invention was complete did he fully realize that. Now he was ready to begin anew and treat each day as a new chance rather than a punishment for living while she had died.

Perhaps that's what his strange dream meant. A new face, totally unknown, might represent his new attitude. Yes, it was his subconscious telling him that he could relax a bit, that it was time to move on.

And David allowed that interpretation to lull him to sleep, satisfied that he needn't worry about the dream woman any more. She was just a beautiful face in the rain, after all. And the rain was only in his mind.

HE WAS LOOKING at the highly polished surface of a mahogany door and feeling his fingers curl around the knob. The door swung in on an office totally devoid of furnishings other than a desk in the center of the sun-bright space. A woman was seated behind the desk, and she looked up from her work as he entered.

"May I help you?" she said.

But he was staring at the nameplate before her and didn't answer. There was one word on it in white letters cut into the black surface. NICOLE.

And he was watching a door swing open as the woman in the white room looked up and said, "May I help you?" And the door opened on the white room and the woman looked up, smiling. "May I help you?" she asked when he pushed the door open, and pushed the door open to see her smiling, again and again until the sun-bright room was his own stateroom on the ship and he was awake with the memory of her smiling lips fresh in his mind.

And, as sleep left him, he felt immensely happy.

David sat up and stretched, smiling slightly at the memory of the dream. He'd had dreams before where he was constantly opening doors that only led to another door, and another, but never an exit from whatever dream-room he was trying to escape. But rather than exits, this dream was about entrances. He was going into the room. He was starting something new. And, though details of what lay beyond the door rapidly became lost in memory, he knew it was something good. For the first morning in a long time, this day felt like a new day rather than just a weary continuation of all the past days.

For the first time in a long time, life seemed to be completely worth living.

David's partner, Jerry Brunsvold, was already on deck when David left his cabin. The small, dark man was standing by the rail, smoking a cigarette as he looked toward the Long Island shore. As taciturn as David was outgoing, Jerry wore a habitually glum expression and viewed the world with a suspicious look in his deep-set eyes. Today was no exception, and he looked over the Sound as though daring it to be a nice day.

"Change your mind about the convention?" he asked, without turning around. The World Ocean Sciences Conference was being held in New York all of the next week, an event that David had vowed to miss.

"No, I've read the journals covering most of what they'll be saying, and I don't have anything to add myself. I'll let you represent us, partner." David leaned on the rail beside Jerry and watched him smoke. Jerry wasn't coughing yet, so it was probably only his third or fourth cigarette of the day.

"They'll all want to hear about the *Crab*." Jerry smiled thinly. "Everybody will want to shake hands with someone so noble as to give away thousands of dollars in fees for the sake of science."

"No, they'll have more fun talking about the dumb rich bastard who shows off his money by giving his fees away."

"Now, that might be fun," Jerry said, allowing a hint of mirth to break through his visage.

"Do you think I'm foolish, Jerry?" David said, seriously.

"I don't know. The money might be nice, but the bookkeeping involved would be a headache. I vote to give it away and be done with it."

"Really? You don't object to my depriving the partnership of income?"

"We've got income, David. What I want is more time, and I don't want to waste any more time on the *Crab*."

"It's done, then." David slapped his partner on the back with a broad grin. "I'll get our lawyer started on the paperwork today, and that'll be the end of it."

The end of what? As David went about his business that morning, he felt unsure that anything was actually ending. Something was wrong. Something was going to happen.

IT WAS HOT in the city when David left his car in a parking garage and walked the couple of blocks to Clint Forrester's law office. New York had always had a strangely mixed effect on him, both energizing and depressing him as he walked along the crowded streets beneath the towering buildings. On one hand, he could appreciate the massive city as a symbol of human achievement and the potential for greatness in future achievements. But he also saw the city as a giant cage, a rat's maze where human potential was turned into pollution and pain. Today, he was feeling more invigorated than in the past, more willing to see the greatness of the city and overlook its short-comings.

And as he drew closer to his destination, David felt a growing sense of anticipation, a strange mixture of excitement and strange fear that seemed to have no source. He merely felt it, and the feeling grew as he entered the offices of Gilbert, Forrester and Dean and was directed to Forrester's door. The door. What was it about that door?

He opened it.

AND NICOLE ELLIS LOOKED UP from her desk to see her dream man walk into the office.

At first, her breath caught in her throat and she stared at the man who, in turn, froze momentarily just inside the door. Yes, it was him. It was the same rugged outdoorsman's face, the same thatch of sandy hair and same keen blue eyes that had been haunting her from the dream, and he was there in front of her desk, holding a briefcase in one hand as though he didn't know what to do with it. All she could do in response was to stare at him in disbelief, as though he had come in clothed in a loincloth.

After an embarrassingly long silence, she forced herself to speak. "May I help you?"

"David," he said, pausing to moisten his lips. "David Germaine." He spoke awkwardly, his own expression a mirror of Nicole's confusion. He glanced down at the nameplate on her desk and then he stepped forward and thrust his hand out for her to shake it, letting a smile slip onto his face.

Nicole shook hands with him, feeling an almost electric shock of recognition at his touch. She released his hand quickly, eager to escape the feeling, and pushed the intercom button to announce his arrival. "Ah, Mr. Germaine is here," she said, acutely aware that the man was staring at her.

"Send him in," Forrester replied. "You come, too."

"Through there," she said, indicating the door to Clint Forrester's office.

"Thank you." David Germaine turned quickly and walked to open the door. Then he paused in the doorway, turning to study her once more before entering the office.

Nicole slumped back into her chair with a shocked sigh. David Germaine was definitely the man she'd dreamed of. But, if he was a client of Forrester's, then she'd probably met him on an earlier occasion. Of course, and she couldn't expect to remember every client who stopped in at the office during her tenure there. She had no clue why she would have incorporated his face into a dream at this point in time, but that was obviously what she'd done. That was all. Wasn't it?

It was a convenient explanation, one that allowed her to catch her breath and slow the pounding of her heart, but it wasn't enough to remove all of the dread from her thoughts as she took her pad and pencil into Clint's office. With everything else she'd experienced in the last couple of days, she felt there had to be a better explanation.

As the meeting went on, Nicole became increasingly nervous. Something about the man's attitude, the words he said and the tone of his voice affected her deeply. It was as if she were in touch with him on a subconscious level, beyond words or appearances, beyond logic, and the feeling of communion with the man created a pulse of conflicting emotions within her. The base feeling was of excitement and anticipation, but the mere presence of such strong emotions was disturbing, frightening. So she spent the meeting on the edge of her chair, struggling to capture the pertinent information on her pad and still maintain her composure.

It might have been pure imagination, but it seemed to Nicole that David Germaine was paying a bit more attention to her during the meeting than might be expected, too. He seemed distracted, and glanced her way several times with a probing look. But whether his attention was simple attraction or if there were deeper motivations, she didn't know. All she knew was that even when he wasn't watching her, she felt that he was thinking about her.

Not that she would object to his thinking of her. On the contrary, she was strongly attracted to the man and would have liked to think the attraction was mutual. But that attraction seemed to be connected to the other feeling, the frightening feeling of communion she had with him, and so it was suspect. How could she trust any of her feelings when they all left her so unsettled?

"That's it, then," Clint Forrester said, pushing back from his desk. "We'll draw up the papers and contact the Institute for you, David."

"Great. I'd like to get everything finished up so we can put back out to sea." The scientist stood, glancing at Nicole as he spoke. "We've got a contract to survey shrimp beds in the gulf."

Clint laughed. "It's so terrible that your work forces you south with winter coming on. And where next?"

"Australia, if we can swing it. Jerry is studying coral formations, and he is desperate to check out the Great Barrier Reef. All we need is a paying customer to get us down there."

"So your work isn't pure research?" Nicole said on impulse.

"No, we do what we can to make ends meet. In the end, everything adds to the total of knowledge we have about the oceans, whether it's pure research or a commercial assignment."

"And it never hurts to have someone else pay the freight, right?" Clint said. "We'll take care of this, you take care of Australia." Then, turning toward Nicole, he said, "Prepare a transcript of the meeting. We'll want everything documented on something like this. I imagine you'll have to dig the file out of storage to update it. It's been—let's see, about five years since David was in last."

"Six," David corrected him. "Since Jerry and I set up the partnership."

"Six years. I'm sure that file has been sent down then, Nicole."

Six years? Nicole felt an icy lump of fear in her stomach. She'd only been there three years, so she couldn't have met David Germaine before. There was no way she could have known him!

"I'll see you in a week." David extended his hand to the lawyer.

"Nicole," Clint said. "Set up an appointment for next Wednesday, the sixth."

"The sixth? I'll do that." Nicole moved woodenly through the door to her desk, paging through the appointment book in a mockery of normal business procedure. A week from today.

"Will 10:00 a.m. be all right?" she asked the oceanographer when he came out of the office. Her voice sounded tight and nervous.

"That's fine." He stopped before her, smoothing the tips of his fingers over the polished surface of her desk. "Nicole, is it?" he said. "Nicole Ellis?"

"Yes, why?"

"Sounded familiar," he said quietly, looking at her with direct but friendly scrutiny. "But we couldn't have met before. Could we?"

"No, I don't see how."

"Well, it was very nice meeting you." Clutching his briefcase, he took a slow step back from the desk as though unwilling to leave just yet. "I'll see you in a week."

"I've always been curious about the ocean," Nicole blurted out as he began to turn away. "It must be interesting, living on board ship and studying the sea as closely as you do."

"I've always thought so," he said. Then he stepped back to her desk. "If you're really interested, you could come out over the weekend. We're always willing to show people around."

"I might take you up on that." She returned his smile nervously, drawing back from her impulse to accept his offer right then and there. "It is a long weekend."

"You have my number. Give me a call."

"I will." Nicole returned his direct gaze with equal interest for a moment, then demurely looked away. "That is, I'll see what's happening over the weekend."

"Right. Well, I hope you can make it."

And then he left her alone with a fluttery feeling growing in her chest. But it was a warm feeling, quite the opposite of the icy incomprehension she'd felt for the past two days. Whatever was wrong with her, this man seemed to be part of it.

NICOLE DIDN'T TELL SARA about the strange feelings that had assailed her that day. She didn't want to inhibit the mood of almost giddy anticipation that Sara was in when she got home from the gallery. The next day's opening was the first one where she'd had some say in the arrangement

of the exhibit, a milestone in her career. The last thing
Nicole wanted to do was distract her attention with her
own confusion.

"I bought a dress for the opening today," Nicole said,
determined to concentrate on pleasant thoughts.

"A new dress? My, you're really getting into the spirit
of the event, aren't you?" Sara had showered and was
wrapping a towel around her hair as she came out to the
living room. "Do I get to see it, or are you planning a
grand entrance?"

"It's right here." Nicole went to the front closet where
she'd hung the garment, still wrapped in plastic from the
store. There was a faintly musty odor in the closet that she
hadn't noticed before, but she dismissed the scent in her
eagerness to show her roommate the new dress.

"Oh, that's nice." Sara rubbed one hand over the fabric when Nicole pulled off the protective wrap and held it
out toward her. "And it's not too dressy for the office,
either."

"It cost too much to use for only special occasions,"
Nicole said. "I saw it in the store window and just had to
have it."

"You? I don't believe you, of all people, would be
turning into an impulse shopper." Sara laughed.

"No, but I'll admit that this particular dress seemed to
have my name on it. Do you like it?" Nicole held it up before her, pulling the blue paisley-print challis fabric in at
the waist and swaying slightly from side to side.

"Sure do. When do I get to borrow it?"

"Oh, I suppose that if you beg and plead I'll let you
wear it someday," Nicole said, laying the garment over the
back of the couch. "I bought a pair of gray heels to go
with it, too."

"A dress and shoes in one day? So little Miss Make Do is finally loosening up the purse strings. Good, now you can be poor but well dressed like the rest of us."

"I'm usually well dressed," Nicole protested happily.

"Yes, and I've always been annoyed that you can look so good and spend so little. Even now, you managed to be practical."

Yes, Nicole was practical. And, as she hung up the new dress and prepared for bed later, her practical nature was again at a loss to explain the events of the past couple of days. No matter how she looked at everything, she couldn't force it to add up. Her strange awareness of certain mundane events like Jane's need of whiteout and the fact of her dreaming about a man she'd never met just days before meeting him should have practical explanations, but they didn't. She was always a woman who believed in what she could experience directly, and, while she liked to keep an open mind, she wasn't willing to just leap into acceptance of unexplained events.

The eldest daughter of a lawyer and a teacher, she'd come by her rationality naturally. In both law and mathematics, the truth was what could be proved. All else was mere conjecture. And her parents had seen to it that both their daughters were practical girls who wouldn't take every claim at face value.

So she felt compelled to explain the dream and ferret out the meaning of her anxiety since awakening from it. But the more she thought about the matter, the more anxious she grew. It didn't make sense, and yet it had happened. It had happened to her.

"So is that why you practically threw yourself at a stranger?" she thought. "Are you so desperate for a solution that you'll throw your sense of propriety away on a whim?"

And what reaction would she get if she mentioned her dream to the amiable oceanographer? He'd think she was crazy, of course, as any sensible person would. And she didn't relish the idea of being thought crazy. So she resolved to avoid visiting the ship. The invitation had come about as the result of a strange whim, anyway, and she was no longer in a whimsical mood. She'd find an answer somehow, without involving anyone else in her dilemma.

But Friday morning came with a feeling of trepidation that weighed upon her heart like a storm cloud obliterating the clear morning. She'd only been at work for half an hour before the phone was in her hand and she was dialing David Germaine's number. She told herself she didn't have to talk about the dream or mention the strange urgency she felt when in his presence to find out if there was any connection—logical or not—between her strange experiences and the oceanographer. And it seemed like an awful shame to waste the opportunity she'd been given to visit him. But then she'd only be fooling herself if she counted that as her sole reason. She was strongly drawn to the man, and no matter what the circumstances, she'd have felt this same desire to be with him. After all, she didn't meet so many interesting men that she could afford to ignore one for whom she felt such instant desire. But, of course, the most important reason now was that she was afraid that something bad would happen if she didn't accept his offer.

"Hello?" A woman answered the phone, and Nicole was stricken by fresh doubt. What if he was married? Might it look improper for her to visit his boat like this? And, if he was married, did she really want to bother visiting?

"May I speak to Mr. Germaine, please?"

"Yes." The woman spoke abruptly and in a cool tone. "May I ask who's calling?"

"Nicole Ellis," she said, adding, "Mr. Forrester's assistant," as though to give a sense of propriety to the call.

"Hello, Ms. Ellis." David Germaine came on the line quickly, his voice a cheerful contrast to the sober woman. "Have you decided to take me up on my offer?"

His voice calmed much of her irrational fear, soothing her heart to slacken its pace. And she was happy to note a hint of eagerness in his voice, or, at least, she imagined she did.

"Yes, if it's still all right."

"I'd love to have you. I'm not busy at the moment, so there's plenty of time to show you around and what not."

"Fine. When should I come out?"

"I imagine you're busy today, so first thing in the morning would be great."

"That sounds good."

"Bring a bathing suit," he said. "You can stay for the weekend, can't you? Maybe we'll take a short cruise."

"I'd love that, if it's no bother."

"No bother at all. I'll be waiting."

Nicole hung up the phone feeling contented, but it didn't last. As the minutes crept along to become the hours of her day, she became more and more apprehensive. A knot of anxiety filled the pit of her stomach, and the clock became the focus of her attention. When she thought of David, her stomach would calm somewhat, but never enough to allow her to relax into her normal routine. The same sense of foreboding that had greeted her on rising clung to her for the rest of the day, weighing her down as though to squeeze the breath out of her. Something was happening, something horrible, and she felt herself in the midst of it.

She finally gave up the pretense of working, content to merely hang on till the day was done and she could begin the weekend. She let her mind ponder the question of why it felt so important to go to David Germaine's ship. Yes, to follow the incredible track of her dream, but as a practical woman, Nicole had to admit to herself that was only part of her decision to accept his invitation. She found the man handsome, his life-style interesting, and in saner times no other reason would have been needed to accept his friendly offer. But these obviously weren't sane times and she wouldn't be suffering such an anxiety attack just for the sake of a physical attraction. There was no explanation for that.

And when she looked at the useless wristwatch that she'd habitually put on that morning, she couldn't help seeing his face in the rain. And she couldn't avoid the thought that she'd forgotten something very important about that dream. Illogical as it might be, the memory of his worried eyes looking down at her scared her.

There was something bad at the core of things and she could feel it creeping up behind her as surely as time moved on.

Chapter Four

Nicole pulled her car into Saturday-morning traffic just before ten the next morning. She had awakened early, anxious to be on her way despite the late hour she'd been at the gallery the night before. She'd packed her suitcase hurriedly with an increasing sense of nervous anticipation and had nearly run to the parking garage where she kept her car. On waking, she had had the unaccountable thought that she was going to visit her mother at her home near Boston. It seemed as though she'd dreamed of going, but the thought of making the trip was more like a memory than a dream, feeling much as the other dream had. But there was no urgency connected to the impulse, and it remained simply a misplaced thought.

It was going to be a beautiful Labor Day weekend with only a small chance of rain, but the weather barely entered her mind as she drove away. Her only real thought was a driving desire to see David Germaine again. More than desire, it was an absolute need based on her instinctive feeling that he could in some way resolve her recent problems and calm her agitated nerves.

And then there had been a strange incident at the opening the night before, which served to reinforce her sense of wrongness in her life and drive her out on this bright Saturday morning. It was more than apparent that her life wasn't going to get back to normal on its own.

The opening of the show at Sara's gallery had been an apparent success, and Nicole's roommate had been ecstatic when they'd gone home afterward. Several of the more important art critics had been there and expressed favorable opinions of both the artwork and the setting designed to display it. Though Nicole was distracted and mainly passed her time wishing it would soon end, things went well for Sara, and all the hard work she and the rest of the gallery staff had put into the show had paid off handsomely.

But Nicole had suffered a personal mishap about halfway through the evening and the circumstances of the disaster increasingly pressed on her mind as she drove through the city toward Long Island. She'd just finished talking to an acquaintance on the gallery staff and was making her way to the buffet when she saw a man in a dark suit walking toward her. He was with a woman and gestured with his wineglass as he spoke. Nicole was absolutely certain that he was going to bump her and soil her new dress with his wine. It hadn't been merely an impression that he *might* spill his wine but full-blown foreknowledge. She treated the thought seriously and took steps to give him a wide berth as they passed. But, just when she felt safe, he turned to call out to a third party, knocking his hand against a post and dropping his glass. The red fluid splattered out across the hem of her dress. The location and seriousness of the spill weren't as she'd recalled, but it was a wine stain nonetheless.

Nicole was initially shocked into immobility by the incident, amazed to find yet another impression played out in fact. Then she hurried to assure the red-faced man that all was well and the stain would come out, trying to make everything seem normal. But she had the cold feeling that the wine spill was an event that was ordained and could not have been avoided even if she'd run in the other direction. It was a strange thought, and it grew in her mind as she dabbed club soda at the small spatters on the paisley fabric. It was almost as though she'd suffered through the same incident before. More déjà vu?

The stain was minor, and what didn't come out was disguised by the pattern of the dress, but the incident itself was more important than the stain. Even now, on a beautiful, hot Saturday morning, it was contributing to her feeling of dread at the time it was taking her to get out of the city, the time between her and David Germaine. Time was important. Every second mattered greatly to her and was lost with regret. She felt that she should have gone out the night before, finding some excuse to thrust herself upon the scientist, welcome or not. That she would even consider such a breach of manners was a sure sign of how greatly affected she was. She felt herself slipping over the edge of a great precipice with nothing to grasp at but a hand in the rain.

How could this be happening? And what *was* happening? She'd imagined a wine stain and received it, dreamed of a man and met him, and the two events had to be related by more than the fact that they were both coincidental in nature. But how they were related and why she should feel they were was beyond her at the moment.

So she drove out of the city with a mindless sense of dread. Strange as everything had been nothing dangerous had happened, so there was little reason to feel so intense. Yet she did. She felt it just as surely as she felt that David Germaine was the only one who could quell her feeling.

Did he feel something strange, too? Why else would he have extended this unexpected invitation to her? He didn't appear to be any more likely to invite a stranger as a weekend guest than she would to accept such an invitation. Still, he'd asked and she'd accepted. The words had jumped out before she'd even thought of what she was agreeing to or how out of character it was for her. Some kind of instinct had told her it was all right, that he wasn't a threat, that he might even be the solution.

In a situation as crazy as this, it seemed prudent to pay some attention to her instincts. They had told her to go, and so she was going.

The thought of David Germaine was a pleasant one. Exactly what thoughts she should properly have about the handsome oceanographer, she wasn't certain, but she felt warmer and more secure whenever he entered her mind. She hadn't allowed herself much opportunity for a social life lately. And, though she wasn't sure how it had happened, she'd fallen into the bad habit of just going home and vegetating after work every day. She wished that this visit was only a social call, a time to enjoy a new setting and new company, but she hoped for much more than that, much more than she even knew.

DAVID GERMAINE SAT in a canvas chair on the deck of the *Katharine* and watched gulls circling the clouded backdrop of sky. Jerry had already gone into the city, and Connie had gone ashore on a personal errand, so David was left alone with his thoughts and an unclear sense of dread knotting his stomach as he waited for his guest to arrive.

Why did you invite her here? he wondered again, and still had no answer. He'd been second-guessing himself since Thursday but had come no nearer to explaining his impromptu invitation. Perhaps the most confusing question on his mind this morning was why he felt such a compelling need to explain himself at all. He was attracted to Nicole, and that should be reason enough. But it wasn't. And he didn't know why.

All he knew was that he'd dreamed of this woman and would have found some way to see her again even if she hadn't offered him one herself. He wasn't a superstitious man but, with the dream preceding their meeting as it did, he couldn't help but feel their acquaintanceship was important. So never mind that she was lithe and lovely and spoke with intelligence and poise, there was something beyond simple attraction between them. David Germaine desperately wanted to know what it was.

But, one thing was certain, he wasn't about to mention any of these feelings to another living soul. The slightest hint of mental instability could provoke a court battle over his grandfather's money. His cousins had tried to contest the will before and failed, and he felt they were only biding their time. It wasn't his fault that he'd been the only one to share his grandfather's love of the ocean. And he hadn't asked to be rewarded for that love. Their only use for the sea was to impress their friends on yachting excursions, polluting the depths with garbage. And for that reason they had coveted the ship and tried to stop him when he began converting it for research. They'd failed once, but that didn't preclude their trying again.

No. He smiled ruefully. He would never mention the way a woman like Nicole had walked into his life.

The sound of a motorcycle entering the harbor parking lot startled David from his reverie. A helmetless rider wearing denim roared up to the end of the dock and killed the motor, kicked the support leg down, and, dismounting, strode toward the sleek vessel where David was rising from his chair.

"What do you want?" David shouted, before the man from the bike could start up the gangway.

"You owe me money, Doc," the newcomer said, smiling. He was a small-shouldered man who wore his dark hair cropped close. He was boyishly good-looking, but his features were a bit narrow, his eyes wily. Now he stood with a thumb hooked into a belt loop as he shifted his weight to his right leg and squinted up toward the scientist. "I've got a week's pay coming."

"I don't owe you any money, Decker." David spoke with firm conviction, but not in an unfriendly tone. "I made sure of that when you left."

"No, Doc, because I went over my hours and I'm a week short on pay. I wouldn't gripe about it, but hell, you kinda put me out looking for a job unexpected-like and I've got to have it now." He frowned, cocking his head to one side as he regarded David. "I gotta eat, you know."

"You put yourself out of a job," David said, leaning on the railing. "And I think that what we've paid in on unemployment should cover your food bill till you find another job."

"Come on, man, I wouldn't be here if I wasn't owed the money." The young man scowled then, sheltering his dark eyes with one hand to look at David more directly.

"Yes, you would." David laughed. "You just figured it was worth the trip out to see if you could con me out of some money. You've got gall, Lance, that's for damn sure. But you don't have a leg to stand on. We can go over the books, if you'd like."

"Well, if you're so damn sure, I guess I can't argue with you. But I still say I'm getting a raw deal here." He crossed his arms, scowling.

"You always think you're getting a raw deal, Lance. But the fact remains that nobody owes you a living. Certainly not me."

"Okay, okay." Lance shrugged, half turning, then he looked back up at David. "Is Connie on board?"

"No. I'm not so sure she'd want to see you, anyway."

"Doesn't hurt to try," he said. Then he turned and walked away with a slight wave of one hand.

"Yes you certainly do try, don't you, Decker?" David said to himself as he watched the man get back on his motorcycle and roar away.

If Lance Decker had tried as hard to do his job as he had done to avoid doing it, he might still be employed on board the *Katharine*, David thought. But he'd proved to be one of those people who'd been getting by on their smiles rather than their abilities. Eventually, those people run into a situation where a smile isn't enough, and that situation for Lance had come aboard the *Katharine*. True to form, he was greeting his lesson in life by blaming others for his dilemma.

David had been watching for a cab to deliver his guest, but a blue Buick Skylark entered the harbor parking lot just after Lance departed. Watching it park, he felt certain that it was his guest. And, when she emerged from the car carrying a small case, a warm burst of eagerness swelled within his chest.

"Come aboard, Ms. Ellis." David met her at the head of the gangplank. A sense of joy lifted him as he watched her approach.

"Good morning." She smiled as she walked up to meet him, a sense of relief flooding in at seeing him there even as the image of rain on his face intruded on the sunny scene. It felt good to breathe freely again. "You have quite an impressive little boat here," she said, shaking off the chilly thought of wet concrete.

"It does the job for us," he replied, reaching to take her suitcase. "We'll take this below and give you a little tour." Her nearness in his own domain gave him a heady feeling, a sense of great possibilities for the two of them. But he backed away from the feeling, restraining himself with a conscious effort to maintain a friendly but detached tone.

And Nicole felt an equally intense happiness to be with him, almost as intense as the dread that had driven her to him, but the strange thoughts bred of her dream and her experiences in the past few days served to temper her feeling with wariness, tightening her smile somewhat. "Yes, I want to see everything." Because the ship, too, was important. Something about it or the man with her was at the source of her feelings; she knew that as surely as she knew her own name. She wanted to see everything in the hope that something might spark the flame of knowledge.

The *Katharine* was a sleek vessel that had been a yacht before David had her refitted to accommodate his research work. Now the decks were packed with various scientific instruments and clusters of antennae crowded the air overhead. Inside the main cabin, as well as below deck, the ship retained most of its original design. The stern door opened onto a surprisingly spacious salon outfitted with various electronic equipment. There was a galley amidships, and a narrow hall ran along the port side to the bridge. A spiral staircase led down to the crew accommodations from the hall. Everything was new to her and held no sense of being seen before.

"Small but tidy," he said. And Nicole detected a touch of nervousness in his little laugh as he guided her along the central hall running forward between cabins. "We normally sail with five aboard, but most of the crew is away right now. Connie will be back, though, so you needn't worry about being chaperoned.''

"Connie?" She spoke abruptly, nervously, then smiled to cover it.

"Connie Wright. You spoke to her on the phone." He stopped outside a narrow door to their left and pushed it open. "She's my research assistant. My sister-in-law, too, for that matter. Your cabin adjoins hers, and you share a bath.''

Sister-in-law? She knew she shouldn't be shaken by the idea that he was married, but the thought jarred her nonetheless. Though she hadn't spent much time considering it, all her thoughts had been based upon his being a bachelor. Could it be that she'd assumed too much?

She followed him into the cabin as he laid her suitcase on the narrow bunk fixed to the outer wall. There were two bunks in the cabin, with a built-in closet-and-drawer combination with a writing table connecting them at the feet. A second closet stood at the head of the outer bunk opposite the hall door, and a second door beside it opened onto a small bathroom. There was nothing unusual here, either.

"Would you like to continue the tour, or would you prefer to freshen up after your drive?" He slipped around her and stood by the door, the light flooding through the porthole accenting his features with warm shadows.

"Should I change clothing? I mean, will we be touring the engine room or crawling through the bilge?" She laughed, thinking that maybe she should allow herself to relax a bit and let the weekend happen.

"No, unless you'd like to. I think your clothing will be safe enough.''

"Then I'm ready to go." Nicole followed him back into the hall, taking note of the position of her door in the line of similar doors. "How many cabins are there?"

"Seven. We could sleep fourteen in a pinch, though one cabin is pretty much filled with spare gear. Yours is our only official guest room. I'm afraid it's the smallest, though." He walked to the end of the hall, where a door opened toward the bow. "This is the master stateroom." He opened the door, giving her a glimpse of a double bed on one wall of the wedge-shaped room with a built-in bureau and desk.

"Who sleeps here?" But she knew, of course, that it was his room, and she couldn't help look for signs of feminine occupancy. There were none that she could see.

"It's mine by virtue of this being my family's yacht to begin with." He looked at her then, seeming to search for something beyond what was visible to the eye.

"Your family yacht? But I thought you just used it for research." Nicole let her gaze catch his, feeling a harmonious current between them, then she returned her eyes to the cabin, feeling self-conscious under his scrutiny.

"We do. I'm the only Germaine who still takes to the sea. The ship came down to me through my grandfather's will."

"That was handy." No, there was no stray clothing indicating a woman in the room nor any toilet articles atop the dresser. "So, this is all sleeping quarters down here?" she asked, to avoid her increasingly probing thoughts.

"The fore section is. The aft has storage and the engines. Come on, I'll show you around topside." He closed the door and walked back to the staircase.

As she followed him, Nicole felt a strange shifting sensation that she couldn't attribute to any motion from the waves. The deck seemed to tremble slightly, the air waver before her, and then she felt the clear sensation of a hand stroking her cheek. For a moment, she found herself surrounded not by the narrow hall and rows of doors but by the master cabin they'd just looked in on, and filling most of her strange vision was David Germaine's smiling face, his hand moving up toward her cheek as he drew closer. Then the vision was gone, and she found herself standing in the hall, looking dumbly at David, who was waiting for her at the foot of the stairs.

"Are you all right?" Concern knotted his brow as he watched her resume her stride. "You look a bit pale."

"Do I? I feel fine." But she felt far from fine as she followed him up. The anxiety that had begun to clear was back with a vengeance. What had she been seeing back there? And why? She felt ill at the memory of how real the hallucination of David stroking her face had felt. It seemed that he'd been ready to kiss her. What kind of strange daydream had that been?

She'd hoped today would break her free from the strange turn her life had taken in the past week, but it seemed intent only on making it stranger. Now she followed him past the galley and the dining area, the small library and the bridge with only half her attention committed to his words. The rest of her mind was occupied by rain and spilled wine and an incident of supposed passion that had never happened.

"So that's all there is to the ship." David leaned against the control console before the window looking out over the bow of the ship lying quietly at anchor. "I hope you're not disappointed."

"No, though I'm more than a little bit curious to see this robot that you're giving away." She spoke more to cover her own nervousness than to carry on their conversation, smiling and talking as though it was just a normal sunny day while her life was crumbling about her.

"Sure. But maybe you'd like a bite to eat first. We've got plenty of time." Then he stopped, smiling awkwardly. "But I'm assuming that you're planning to stay the weekend. You are, aren't you?"

"I had planned to," Nicole said. "If your wife doesn't mind," she offered, tentatively.

"My wife?" A look of distress passed over his face for a moment.

"But then you said that your sister-in-law would be here," she said quickly, startled at the transformation in his features. "Is your wife away?"

"Oh, I see." A smile slipped onto his lips, loosening his expression again. "I'm afraid that I gave you the wrong impression. My wife is—well, she died two years ago. A car accident."

"I'm sorry." Nicole's cheeks flushed with embarrassment as she blurted out her apology. "I didn't know. I mean, that your file didn't have anything about a wife at all, so when you mentioned your sister-in-law, I just assumed."

"My fault." David's smile broadened as he placed a comforting hand on her arm. "Don't worry about it."

"People shouldn't make assumptions, should they?" Nicole smiled now, warmed by his touch.

"No, I suppose not. Come on, and we'll—" A sound from the doorway cut him off, and he turned away from her. "Connie," he called.

But when Nicole looked at the door she didn't see a woman but a thin man in jeans and a work shirt wearing thin leather gloves. And sunglasses.

"Who—" she began, startled. But then the man was gone, replaced by a trim red-haired woman. No! she felt like screaming, it can't happen again! I can't be seeing these things! But she had definitely seen a man for a split second, not the slim young woman standing there now. The only similarity between her and the man Nicole had thought she'd seen were the jeans and blue blouse the woman was wearing.

"Nicole Ellis, this is Connie Wright." David stepped toward the newcomer. "Connie, Nicole called the other day."

"Hello." Nicole took a deep breath and approached the woman, fighting past the shock of her second hallucination of the day. "Pleased to meet you."

"Yes, I'm glad to meet you, too." But the smile on her pale lips was only the thinnest of superficial formalities and there was a hard look of dislike in the green eyes above the smile. "I hope David is able to explain things adequately for you."

"He's done all right so far." Nicole's tone hardened in response to the hostility she felt from the other woman, and she withdrew her hand quickly. "I expect it will be a very pleasant weekend."

"I do hope so." Then Connie turned to David, her smile brightening. "Were you discussing lunch?" she asked.

"Yes, you're just in time. Let's all go raid the galley."

But Nicole accompanied them with mixed emotions. Had she been correct in her impression of Connie Wright's greeting, or was she just confused? And, if she was correct, why on earth would the woman feel such instant dislike for her? Why, indeed?

THE AFTERNOON WAS WARM and pleasant, and the three of them took advantage of the weather by changing into swim wear after a light lunch. Connie lightened up as the day wore on, losing the hardness Nicole had detected at the start. But she reserved her full warmth for David, always keeping Nicole at a distance.

"I hope you don't mind my being here this weekend," Nicole said to her when they were alone in the galley. She'd gone to help her bring out chips and sodas while David made some adjustments on his robot vehicle in preparation for a short demonstration. "It didn't occur to me that you folks might have other plans when I accepted his invitation."

"Why should I mind?" Connie smiled broadly, and somewhat indulgently, Nicole thought. "We have guests quite often."

"But I don't suppose most of your guests are scientifically illiterate legal assistants, are they?"

"Well, no." Connie laughed. "But maybe our guest list could do with a few, to even out the flow of boring workaholic scientists who normally come aboard."

"So then not all his colleagues are as interesting as he is?"

"None of them are," Connie said, seriously. "I'd have gotten out of the oceanography racket years ago if I were working for anyone else. But David is special, I think. He's not so absorbed in his work that he ignores other people. He makes it a point to pay attention. Of course, my opinion is biased."

"I suppose so, being his sister-in-law," Nicole commented, taking three soda bottles from the galley refrigerator as Connie lifted the tray of chips and dip. "It must have been horrible to lose your sister that way."

"Yes, but then I don't see where that's any of your business." Connie turned abruptly and strode out to the salon, the friendliness of a moment before gone like a candle extinguished by a gust of wind.

Nicole decided it might be best to let Connie pick the topics of conversation to avoid further blunders like the one she'd just made. The woman was obviously sensitive on the subject of her sister.

"Ready for the big show?" David was standing beside a power winch that fed cable through a davit extended over the side and down into the waters of the Sound.

"All set!" Nicole called out, sitting on a deck chair and putting the bottles down on the table where Connie had placed the chips.

He'd already shown her the mechanism in question. It looked rather like a torpedo mounted on tank treads, except of course for the mechanical arms folded against the forward half of the five-foot body. TV cameras and various small doors and instruments also broke up the sleek lines of the vehicle.

David ran out cable until it was noticeably slack, and then turned a television monitor with a long sun hood extending over the picture toward them. "The TV will show us what the crab sees," he told her. "The numbers at the bottom show the depth and water temperature."

The black-and-white picture was that of a sandy sea bottom with plants growing up toward the dappled light from above.

"It's only in twenty feet of water here, so we're using the natural light. In deeper water, we'd switch on the lights on the machine. The battery is low now, so I won't bother with that."

"It runs on batteries?"

"Yes, it can. It's designed for several modes of use. It can be freestanding and run independently from the ship, so it's provided with batteries for that purpose. Or you can run power down through the cable. That would be the most normal mode, of course, since nobody would want to risk losing an expensive piece of equipment. We hadn't planned to send it down again, so we've already disconnected the power."

"You didn't have to make a special run just for me."

"Sure I did." David grinned, walking over to take a chair beside hers. "It's always much better to show something than explain it. Now, here's the remote control," he said, leaning to hand her a fat metal box with buttons and switches on it. He pointed to a control in the center like a joystick from a video game. "Move the lever right here to make it move."

"Me? What if I get it stuck?"

"You won't. Just pick a direction and go." He placed his hand on hers and gently eased the lever ahead.

Nicole was rewarded by a slight lurch of the TV picture and then a steady movement through the weeds on the bottom. "This is fun," she said, smiling at her host. She commanded it to turn right, watching its response avidly on the screen.

While David led Nicole through a series of movements, Connie moved from her seat to take a position kneeling between them. "Of course you can't operate the arms with this control," she said.

"No. This is just a remote box," David said. "It takes two people to run it at full capability. Connie is our resident expert at operating the arms, aren't you?"

"I had a good teacher," the woman replied, her voice soft with admiration as she spoke to the scientist. Then she turned toward Nicole, losing the warmth in her tone. "Maybe I'll give you some pointers on them while we've got it down there," she said.

"I'd love to have you show me the ropes," Nicole said, returning her appraising stare.

"Not today, however," David cut in. "The batteries are too low. I'll charge them up overnight and you guys can play tomorrow."

"I'd like that," Nicole said.

"Yes, Dave, then we'll see how she cuts it as your assistant." Connie maintained an air of playfulness over the sarcastic tone of her voice, playing both sides of her audience artfully as she looked at Nicole through narrowed eyes.

"I could never replace you," Nicole said, calmly.

"You'd better not," the woman said.

Now Nicole knew what Connie had against her and would always have against her, no matter how hard she might try to be liked. Connie saw her as an intruder and a rival for David's attention. Connie Wright was jealous.

"We'd better bring her up now." David stood and walked toward the winch. "Switch it off, Connie."

Connie took the control from Nicole, pressed a switch down and the TV picture decayed into noise. "Playtime is over," she said.

Nicole took her soda and stood at the rail looking out at the water beyond their mooring. The sky was a cloudless canopy of blue, the waters spread beneath it like a moving carpet of deep green and the air was warm and comfortable. But it wasn't as perfect as it had seemed when she first arrived at the ship. Now she had Connie Wright's jealous maneuvering to contend with, and that put a damper on things. But then her visit had never been social, so she needn't be flustered by yet another unpleasant event in a week full of them. Nicole hadn't come to the ship to claim a man. She'd come to reclaim control of her life.

"The party is over." A man's voice, harsh and de-
manding, spoke in her ear. "You shouldn't have stuck
your nose into this," he said, in a thin whisper.

Nicole turned her head, gasping in surprise to see the
thin-faced man standing not more than a foot away. The
sun gleamed on his dark glasses.

"Shouldn't have come out here," he said, lifting the gun
up toward her.

"No!" she exclaimed, frozen at the railing.

"What's that?" David called out from where he was
lowering the crab down to the deck from the winch. And
the man disappeared, leaving only the sun and sea and her
congenial host.

"Nothing." Nicole managed to get the word past her
trembling lips, but no more than one word. She felt faint,
terrified by the aura of disaster that suddenly seemed to
hang over the ship. The man with the gun had been the
same man she'd imagined seeing when Connie came into
the wheelhouse. And Nicole was beginning to feel that he
had been in her dream as well.

"I'm going to go down to my cabin for a while," she
called out, when she'd mustered sufficient breath to speak.
"Too much sun, I think."

"I forgot you're an office type," David laughed. "You
go ahead and relax. I'm going to start this beast charging
and then see about supper. Any preferences?"

"Whatever you like." Nicole was already walking away,
afraid to stay on deck any longer for fear of embarrassing
herself completely. She set her bottle down on the table
carefully, afraid her trembling fingers might upset it, and
then continued into the salon.

"Are you all right, dear?" Connie stood by the door, a
sour smile on her face. "You look pale."

"Us office types are always pale," Nicole said wanly. "I'm going to freshen up."

"Well, I suppose you can try," the woman replied, walking away.

Nicole knew now that if she wanted to get to the bottom of her strange hallucinations, she'd come to the right place. The sheer volume of occurrences on the ship told her that much. But did she really want to find an explanation? No, the truth was that she'd be happy if it would just stop, explanation or not, but she didn't think it would. And it seemed obvious now that the man she'd imagined seeing was the source of the dread she'd been feeling. Was she making the prophecy of her feelings come true by letting them bring her here? Or was the danger unavoidable, like the wine stain at the gallery opening?

As she entered the tiny cabin, Nicole felt again that something bad was going to happen. And there was nothing she could do to stop it.

Chapter Five

Nicole eased the door of her cabin shut carefully, as though afraid it might shatter if handled roughly, and stood within the room for a long moment before moving.

As before, she felt herself at the center of something, an ethereal turning point in her life, and perhaps David Germaine's as well, and she had no idea how to proceed safely. Whether she liked it or not, she'd have to abandon any pretense of logic in pursuit of answers. There was nothing logical about what was happening to her, and to find the reasons behind it, she'd have to give in to the illogic of the emotions that were driving her. But now that an explanation seemed to be struggling to come out, she didn't know how to interpret it.

She'd hoped to be able to explain the near chaos of the last week as merely a few random flashes of insight and disorientation brought about by stress or lack of sleep or some other mundane reason. And despite her unease and sense of catastrophe, she'd fervently hoped to have an uneventful weekend to prove it. But the weekend was already far from uneventful. Now she was left with the unpalatable task of admitting the possibility of a more occult explanation. And that wasn't an admission that she relished making.

Taking a deep breath, she turned and opened her travel case and removed her wristwatch from the pouch in the lid. Still frozen at 12:41 p.m., the numbers on the watch face were like malevolent hieroglyphics that she lacked the skill to decipher, the colon blinking in silent acknowledgement of the passage of time.

Everything else that had happened was entirely subconscious, errant thoughts and visions with no basis in physical fact. But the condition of her watch was physical and confirmable—Sara had seen it, too—and so seemed to be totally unrelated to anything else. She might very well be going crazy, but it wasn't possible for her watch to go crazy with her.

Therefore, she wasn't crazy. And, if not crazy, there must be a discernible reason for her flashes of precognition and her feeling of having been to events such as the gallery opening before. And there must be some reason for her to have known what David Germaine looked like without having met him.

She threw the watch back into the bag in sudden frustration and threw herself onto the narrow bunk in near despair. What did she have to do to come out from under this cloud? There was something she was supposed to do.

The boat was rocking gently with a comfortable reassuring motion as she lay staring up at the ceiling. It was a feeling she felt she could easily grow used to. Relax, it said, don't fight it. Rock on the waves rather than plow through them. And when nothing is logical and common sense is shattered, admit that new reality and live with it.

Yes, she thought, roll with the waves. It must be nice to relinquish oneself to these peaceful waves. What was life on board ship like? Did they ever feel trapped in their small world, or was the ever-changing vista of the ocean around them liberating? What a wonderful life he must lead, she thought.

There'd been something subtly out of place about David Germaine when he came to the office, as though he didn't quite fit there. It wasn't any unsureness on his part, but more that the world was in some way unsure of him. Once she'd seen him on the ship, she knew why she'd felt that about him. His place was aboard a ship at sea, just as surely as Clint Forrester's place was in his office. They were both fated to fill the niches they'd chosen for themselves.

Fate, she thought, *is a strange thing.* And what was her fate in the grand scheme of things? What was life's plan for her? As the slight rolling motion of the ship lulled her into semiwakefulness, she wondered if her fate was to end up in an asylum somewhere, or be entwined with David's. Nicole realized, with the clear vision that is sometimes obtained in a totally relaxed state, that a future tied to his brimmed with promise. And at that moment she felt a desire for the man that was physically debilitating.

It was foolish lying alone like this. The incident on deck reflected the mystery that drew her to the yacht in the first place. The only way she'd ever get an explanation was to get back up there and act. Roll with the waves.

"SHE'S NO KATHARINE, is she?" Connie was saying, as Nicole approached the salon.

"I'm not looking for another Katharine." David replied defensively.

"You've sure provided a beautiful day to be on the ocean," Nicole said, entering the room. What had she interrupted there?

"We aim to please," David said, with a somewhat forced casualness. He'd been sitting at the center table with

Connie, and he stood quickly to step toward Nicole, with what appeared to be relief in his broad smile. "I hope you're enjoying your visit."

"I love it here." Nicole smiled up into his eyes, wishing she could just fall into their gentle gaze. Behind him, Connie stood and walked out on deck without a word, and a profound sense of relief swept over Nicole. "I hope I'm not intruding," she said.

"Never." David placed his hand on her arm in gentle punctuation to the serious tone in his voice. "I want you to be here."

"Why did you invite me?" Nicole stepped toward the window, feeling awkward with her own question. Did he feel awkward with the situation, too? Did he have questions, just as she did?

"I had the feeling that you wanted to come," he said simply, matching her movement to stay near her. "Didn't you?"

"I did. But—" How could she begin to ask the questions she had inside? He'd think she was insane if she mentioned even one of the occurrences that had plagued her that week.

"But what?" He leaned against the window frame and returned his hand to her arm as though he couldn't help touching her, while he smiled his encouragement for her to speak.

"But I thought you might have something better to do." She couldn't, not now. It was still possible that he had nothing to do with her strange experiences, and she didn't want to dampen the feeling she saw growing behind his eyes by making him think she was a nut. "I'd hate to be in the way."

"Not at all. And I've got nothing better to do that I can think of. It feels good to have a new face on board again."

A serious look came over his face, and his eyes held hers with a questioning stare. "I've had a good time. It's been so long that I don't know what to make of it."

"You've been hurting a long time, haven't you?" Nicole spoke with compassionate insight, putting her hand gently on his tightly muscled shoulder. Touching him worked like a powerful drug to alleviate her tension and fear. "It's terrible to lose a loved one," she said, allowing herself to enjoy the stolen contact.

"Yes, but it may be even more terrible to throw away a life in mourning. I feel as if a storm is just passing overhead. The rain is lessening, the wind dying down, and I can see sunlight on the ocean beyond it." He spoke in a poetic murmur, grasping her hand in his gently, as though afraid his touch might break her. "Thank you for coming out this weekend," he said, squeezing her hand.

"Thank you for inviting me."

Nicole could not remember ever feeling so consumed by the desire to hold someone as she was right now. His hand on hers was strong and lightly callused from outdoor work, but capable of great tenderness and affection. And his eyes seemed to echo her desire even as he released her hand. Another woman might have given in to the impulse to throw her arms around him. Even Nicole, under different circumstances, might have given in. But these circumstances were far too different, her state of mind still too confused to trust the primitive emotion that surged through her. She didn't know the man except as a character in her dream, didn't know what his thoughts would be if she expressed her interest. And Nicole wasn't at all sure of what her interest was. She had to find out before she did anything to further confuse the situation.

So she swallowed her desire and took a breath to slow her suddenly stammering heart and took a step away from him.

"I'll get started on dinner," David said.

"Can I help?" Some mundane culinary task was just what she needed to focus her concentration just then. She'd managed an invitation to the ship in order to find answers, so it was about time she took advantage of the opportunity she'd been afforded.

"Everyone earns their own way on ship, Nicole, and guests are no exception. Come on."

David led the way to the galley, laughing, as Connie Wright stood on the deck watching through the window. The wind whipped her blond hair across her narrow face and into her eyes, and she shook it away roughly as she turned to look toward the mainland. She rubbed one balled fist across her eye, scowling as she glanced back through the window. Then she walked along the outer rail with purposeful strides and descended to her cabin and locked the door.

THE SUN SET with a fragile strawberry-and-orange hue, bathing everything in comforting warmth as Nicole and David sat on deck that night. A brief storm had been forecast, but even though clouds were building rapidly overhead the seaward breeze was warm and gentle, in perfect sympathy with the light, promising a beautiful evening. They'd pulled their chairs close together after Connie retired to bed, and now they spoke in low tones.

Again, his presence was a balm to her frayed nerves, the only calm point in a storm-tossed world, and she was taking advantage of her feeling of ease to learn more about her host.

"I love the ocean," David was saying, trying not to stare at her. He badly wanted to touch her, and his hand, resting now on the arm of his chair a few tantalizing inches from her hand, had maintained its own steady rhythm of movement toward and away from hers. Just hold her hand, he thought, it's no crime to hold her hand. But he didn't feel right about presuming so much and didn't want to risk displeasing her, so he kept calling the hand back and struggling to hold up his end of the conversation. "It can be a hard place, suddenly violent, yet safe as houses if you know what you're doing on it. There's so much variety beneath the waves, so much to be learned. I want to study it and protect it for as long as I live."

"You have a big challenge before you," Nicole replied. The admiration she felt for him and his heartfelt devotion to the sea only enhanced the desire that danced within her. Listening intently to his words, she still couldn't help watching his hand and wondering if she wanted him to take hers or not. She wanted to avoid becoming emotional but the emotions wouldn't fully release her to her task. They would only consent to be contained somewhat by conversation as she struggled to find a way to broach the subject that had brought her to this night.

"It's not as though I'm alone in this work." He laughed, self-deprecatingly. "But you're right about it being a big challenge. But then, why take up a task that isn't a challenge?"

"That's a good point," she said, thinking of the challenge she faced this weekend. "And I agree with it."

He was looking at her closely and smiling as though he enjoyed the sight of her in the sunset that still shone past the gathering clouds. "What about you?" he asked. "Do you find your work challenging?"

"No, not at all," she confided. "Though it was a challenge at first, it became routine all too soon."

"Are you satisfied with that?"

"What do you mean?"

"I didn't mean to imply anything about your work," he said, quickly. *Now she'll think I look down on legal assistants or something,* he thought, embarrassed by his inept phrasing. "But I'm curious about your plans for the future. It certainly doesn't sound as though you plan to remain a legal assistant all of your life."

"I had planned to return to law school in the fall. My father died, you see, and I quit school to help out."

"Making money instead of spending it." He nodded his head in appreciation, finally letting his hand move to grasp hers.

"Exactly."

The clouds had moved overhead in force now, covering the stars and blocking out the last of the sunset. David watched them for a moment, a dizzying sense of unease passing through his mind briefly as he contemplated the idea of rain.

"But it sounds like you're not sure about going back. Aren't you interested in law anymore?" He spoke carefully, ignoring the strange wariness he'd felt and enjoying holding her smooth, delicate hand in his. He wondered why he'd been restraining himself all night.

"I don't know." And she was suddenly aware that she really wasn't sure anymore. It had seemed like a clear career choice mere days ago. "After working for a lawyer for three years, I've begun to think that the world already has plenty of lawyers."

"To tell the truth," he said, laughing, "I've always thought that." He turned slightly toward her, unembarrassed now to look at her as he continued to hold her hand.

"The law schools keep pumping them out, but Lord knows where they all find employment."

"Oh, they find it. I just don't know if I'm interested in joining their ranks. I feel as though I've already spent enough time in an office. Time is flying, and I'm spending it sitting still." Why did she say that? She'd never felt so aware of time as she had in the last few days, becoming increasingly aware and regretful of its passage.

"Yes, it is." He looked slightly puzzled, then shrugged it off with a smile. "Have you decided on an alternate career?"

"No, but I'm looking."

The first raindrops were fat and cold, falling as solitary scouts in advance of the coming onslaught. Nicole and David both paused, waiting to hear the next heavy plop on the deck with similar feelings of dread.

"Rain," Nicole said, thoughtfully. "I hope it doesn't ruin the weekend."

"No, it is supposed to pass through overnight." David squeezed her hand, reassuring himself with her physical presence. "If anything, it'll be hotter tomorrow."

"Good." Nicole shuddered as a raindrop hit her neck and another struck her knee. "I used to like rain."

"A distant rainstorm on the ocean is quite a sight. You can often watch the whole thing from miles away, the clouds black and heavy on the bottom, pouring gray streaks of rain into the sea while their tops are still nearly white and shining in the sunlight above them. It's quite a thing to see."

David spoke calmly, thoughtfully, but his tension was evident in the increased pressure of his hand on hers. Holding on for dear life, she thought. And the worried grasp of his hand combined with the approach of rain brought back the inner dread their conversation had almost erased. A storm was coming. Thunder could be heard in the distance, though she hadn't noticed any lightning yet. Fear slipped into her stomach, cold and heavy, freezing her to her chair.

"It sounds quite majestic," she said, thinking how foolish it was, the way human beings habitually covered their feelings with polite conversation. What she wanted to do now was run for shelter well in advance of any actual storm, but since she had no rational excuse to move, she covered her impulse with words and hoped it would pass. "But what happens when the storm moves to strike you, too?"

"You ride it out," he said, looking at her again. "All you can do with a storm is ride it out." The same look of worry and concern that Nicole remembered from her dream was in his eyes now. Then a flash of lightning ripped through the sky over the island, illuminating him in ghostly light as the explosion of thunder compelled him to action.

"Come on," David said, jerking to his feet. He pulled her from her chair and it seemed as though he would have dragged her inside if she hadn't gained her footing and run with him. Inside the cabin, he stood against the door without saying anything, a look of deep thought tightening his brow. "I, ah, I didn't want to get wet," he said, softly. Then he smiled. "Sorry to have moved so quickly."

"That's all right. We came in just in time," Nicole said, nodding at the hammering wash of rain striking the window beside him. "I had almost decided that it was going to pass us by."

"Sailor's instincts for a storm, I guess." He laughed, but it was unconvincing, and Nicole felt an echo of her own trepidation in the sound. "Maybe we should call it a night."

"I think so. I've had a lovely stay so far, you know."
This time she took his hand, seeking the reassurance she'd
found there before. She wasn't disappointed, for his touch
washed away the edge of fear built up by the storm. "But
I am tired."

"Salt air will do that to you," he said.

"Yes, so I've heard." She felt like a teenager struggling
to find a parting line at the door after a first date. "Good
night."

"Good night." He released her hand slowly and stood
there, watching her walk through the salon to the hall,
feeling all the while like a foolish child afraid of a storm.

She must think I'm a complete idiot, he thought. The
lightning had actually scared him, sending him scurrying
like a rabbit to get away from a bit of water. The least he
could have done was walked at a respectable pace rather
than dragging her along like a rag doll. What was getting
to him today?

But he'd felt strange since waking and it all seemed related to a beautiful woman's presence on his ship. Seeing
her, and especially touching her, made him feel a swell of
euphoria that had no recent parallel, and her short ab-
sences were times of equal unease. He was constantly
fighting the urge to take her into his arms and hold her
close, to never let her go. He felt himself off course from
his normal life, drifting at the whim of his attraction to
Nicole.

That attraction was normal enough, he supposed, but
tonight, when the rain began falling, his sense of balance
had gone off kilter again. Each of the few, slow drops had
fallen like a bullet, and each increased his nervousness.
And then came the lightning, and for a moment he'd seen
her drenched with rain and staring up with unseeing eyes
as rain washed blood away from her lips. It had only been

a brief impression illuminated by the lightning flare, but it had filled him with a terrible fear for her safety on deck. And that made no sense at all. The lightning wasn't going to strike her and rain couldn't harm her, so why had he become so convinced that she was in danger?

What was wrong with a little bit of rain?

Chapter Six

The rain fell heavily for nearly an hour and then was gone as quickly as it had come on, leaving a brilliant moon and its attendant stars to occupy the clear sky over the Sound. David went out on the deck as soon as it stopped, standing by the chairs they had occupied, lost in thought as the small sounds of civilization winding down for bed drifted in from the town beyond the marina. What was so important about rain?

He couldn't have slept and so didn't try, but stayed in the salon with a cup of coffee and his thoughts. Scattered images tried to enter his mind only to hang back beyond the borders of full recognition. Small images like the one of Nicole in the rain, like the smear of blood on her lips, seemed to be pieces of the dream he'd had, though he couldn't say why he felt that. He'd only retained a name and the vague image of a face from his dream, and he usually remembered his dreams. Now it seemed finally to be coming back.

Rain on her face and blood on her lips and a strange empty look in her eyes. It was an image of death, and it frightened him to think of Nicole dead.

His feelings for Nicole were the central fact of his current confusion. He'd been unaware of when they'd started, but his faint attraction had exploded into absolute desire sometime during the day. And it was a desire more complete and consuming than simple need for her lithe body. It was concern and hunger and intellectual engagement all striking in a hammer blow of emotion. At another time in his life he would have called it love and been happy with that. But love had been a dead emotion for him for so long that he wasn't sure he knew what it was anymore. All he knew was that he wanted to sweep her off her feet, impress her and protect her and keep her at his side forever.

So why would he have dreamed that she was dead before he'd ever met her?

NICOLE LAY IN BED staring at the darkened ceiling of the cabin. *What do I do now?* Her stomach tightened at the question. She didn't know what she should do. Didn't know what was right.

But she did know what she wanted to do. She wanted David to weigh anchor right now and take her away to sea. She wanted never to return to anything that was real before she met him and create a new reality with him. That's what she wanted to do.

But it was raining on the streets of New York and David had just opened the door of the deli for her when a small man in a raincoat and sunglasses came up to them with a gun. The weapon went off at point-blank range, knocking Nicole out of her bunk to the floor. "Oh, God!" Not yet awake, she stumbled to her feet, threw open the door and ran blindly into the hall. "My God." The gunshots echoed in her head, and the heat from the gun seemed to burn at her chest as she ran to the stairs.

"No, no!" Her voice sounded distant and small, and she realized that she was crawling along the hall toward the main salon. "No." Why was she here? How had she gotten here? Then she remembered the gun and cried out in fear as she regained her feet and burst into the salon to stand shivering with the realization that it had been a dream—only a dream.

"Nicole? What's wrong?" David had seen the movement from the deck and ran in to see her standing there, only just waking up from her interrupted slumber. He paused uncertainly for a moment in the door and then ran and gathered her to him, allowing his arms to hold her close and his lips to graze her forehead lightly as he tucked her head in against his chest. "Are you all right? What happened?"

"I had a dream," she sighed against him. "Somebody was shooting and then I woke up here." She put her arms around him, listening to his heartbeat as she clung to him.

"You're all right now. You're awake." David was all too aware of her, physically, as he held her. And, though it was covered with sturdy white cotton from her neck past her knees, the fresh-scrubbed light of the moon had silhouetted her body when he'd first seen her. Now, as he held her close to him, his need for her was so strong that he felt like crying and he stroked her hair, hungry for any touch that might satisfy the feeling.

"I feel like a fool," Nicole admitted. The muscles of his back were taut beneath her hands, and he held her with such strength that she was tempted to give some sign of her desire for him so that she might have some reply. But she held herself in check and was content with only taking security from his arms.

"That's all right. But you might have walked off the deck." The smell of her hair was intoxicating, and he had to break free of his emotions before he made a regrettable mistake. "My cousin once went sleepwalking and ended up in the pool."

"I'll bet that woke him up." Nicole laughed, pushing away slightly so that he released her.

"Yes, but he was lucky to have fallen into the shallow end." David was smiling, but his eyes were serious, almost sad, as he continued to look at her. "Are you sure you're all right?"

"Yes, embarrassed but fine."

"Good." David couldn't take his eyes off her, and couldn't think of a thing in the world to say except all the wrong things.

"The storm cleared off quickly," she commented, aware of how banal the conversation was becoming, but unsure of how to broach the subject that had forced itself to the fore again. The direct approach might be the best after all, she decided, for she'd already made as much fool of herself as she could. "David," she began, "I wanted to talk to you."

"No." He cut her off, shaking his head. His surging pulse roared in his head, washing away coherent thought in a flood of emotion. "Not now, please?" He took a step back, smiling wanly. "I can't."

"What's wrong?" A protective urge swept over her at the hurt in his eyes, and she had to do something to wipe that look away.

"You're so beautiful," he said, softly, sadly. "I— Good night." Then he turned abruptly and strode out of the room.

Nicole sat down at the table and stared at David's abandoned coffee cup. What had she done to send him running from her?

"Don't push him." Connie spoke icily from the outer door.

"What?" Nicole started at the sound of her voice, looking toward the woman standing with her hands on her hips and scowling at her. "What are you talking about?"

"He's not ready for you," Connie said. She walked in and sat across from Nicole at the table. The moonlight cast black shadows across her eyes, giving her a malevolent look. "His wife is dead, and here you come trying to snare him."

"I'm not—" *No, don't let her pull you into some stupid argument,* she thought, *stay calm.* "She's been dead for two years, hasn't she? He seems to have recovered."

"Maybe, but I know him better than you. Don't push him."

"I'm not pushing anything."

"Really? You come out here, dressed like that, pulling some nightmare shit to get him feeling all fired up and manly, and you say you're not pushing?"

"I'm not. It's a cotton nightgown."

"And a very bright full moon," Connie said disparagingly. "What are you looking for? Money?"

"That's enough of that!" Nicole stood up angrily and glared down at the other woman. "I don't suppose you can help your jealousy, but you could at least try to avoid embarrassing your guests with it."

"Jealous?" The woman seemed genuinely shocked. She probably hadn't been aware that her feelings were so transparent. "You're crazy. I'm just looking out for David."

"David can look out for himself," Nicole said. And, with that, she turned and walked from the room.

"DON'T START WITH ME AGAIN, Robert. I'm not going to change my mind."

David's voice was hard, straining to remain civil as he spoke on the telephone Sunday morning. Nicole stood in the hall, unsure of whether she should venture into the main room or go back to her cabin till his conversation was finished.

"It'll be a cold day in hell when I sell anything to you," he was saying. "And I don't care what kind of offer you cook up for me. You can't pull your usual crap, either, since it's not a public company."

Nicole's course was decided for her by a slight creaking sound behind her. Connie was coming up the stairs to the main deck. Nicole didn't want to be caught appearing to eavesdrop on David's conversation, so she walked resolutely into the room with him.

"You must be in hock up to your eyes if you're coming back to me," he said. He turned in his chair when he noticed her entrance, then smiled and motioned for her to sit down. "What's wrong? Did those worthless bonds you put out go sour on you?"

The other party must have hung up, for David let the phone slip away from his ear and replaced it carefully, working a smile onto his face. "I have a cousin who likes money more than it likes him," he said. "Always trying to pull something to get richer."

"The sleepwalker?" she said. She sat on the edge of the table by him, smiling.

"Yes, that's the one. Robert Philips."

"Robert Philips is your cousin? He's a client of ours." Robert Philips was a junk-bond manipulator one or two levels below the big names in the racket, and he had brought Clint a steady stream of deals to draw up in the time Nicole had worked there. "Why do you say money doesn't like him?"

"He never seems to have enough of it." David laughed, wryly.

"He seems to do all right for himself, though," Nicole mused. "He's a fairly shrewd manipulator."

"Who is?" Connie was wearing a skirt and blouse this morning, and walked in casually munching on a slice of toast as though nothing had happened between her and Nicole the night before.

"Robert. He called."

"You should let me talk to him," she said, seriously. "All he ever does is make you mad. What did he want?"

"Albany Manufacturing."

"Again? You know, it wouldn't harm you to hear him out once. Especially when he's offering so much for it. You said yourself he was offering more than the market value."

"Yes, he is, and there has to be something shifty going on for him to make the offer. Besides, I don't like the way he does business. My only major asset is a small tool-and-die company in Albany," David explained to Nicole. "Robert seems to think he should own it. He says I'm a lousy manager."

"Are you?" Nicole asked, playfully.

"I would be." David laughed. "But I own it, I don't manage it. And as long as I own it, the company will stay in business. If my dear cousin gets it, he'll expand operations until he can sell at a profit, and the new owner will probably have to sell off the assets to pay Robert's old debts. But that's just family laundry." He stood and stretched, working his neck around in a slow circle. "Shall we take a short cruise today, ladies?"

"I'm going to town," Connie said, quickly. She glanced at Nicole as if to emphasize her willing absence during the day. "You two go ahead if you wish."

"What's going on in town?"

"Nothing, but everyone else is taking advantage of the break. I could use one myself."

"Will you be back tonight?"

"I think so." She finished her toast and brushed the crumbs from her fingers. "You two have fun today. I'm going to run."

"'Bye," David called as she walked away.

"See you later," Nicole said.

"You might." The woman smiled back at them and then walked out and down the gangplank to the dock. Nicole saw her pause halfway along the dock and look back at the ship before continuing to the parking lot.

"I hope Connie isn't leaving on my account," Nicole said, impulsively.

"Why would you think that?" David asked in surprise, unaware of the tension between the two women the day before. "She's just eager to be off the ship, is all."

"I don't know," Nicole mused. "I don't think she was very happy to have me here. I think she's jealous."

"Jealous? Connie? Of what?"

"Of me, I think. I got the impression that she thinks you're interested in me."

"And that would make her jealous?" He pursed his lips in thought, making no comment on the matter of his interests as he grasped the uprights of one of the canvas chairs in the salon and leaned on it. "No, not Connie."

"I might be wrong about that, but not about her feeling toward me."

"I don't know what she thinks of you," he said. "But she surely doesn't have interest in me. In fact, she and one of the crewmen were getting quite serious not too long ago."

"Then she's spoken for?"

"Not really. They had a bit of a falling-out. We fired Lance when we got to New York a month ago."

"You fired him because of the argument?"

"No, we fired him because he was a lazy bastard. Lance Decker is a natural-born con man. Unfortunately, he talked himself into a job without thinking that he might actually have to work at it. I think he expected to have a nice leisurely world cruise."

"I see."

"Should I talk to Connie?" he asked, earnestly.

"No, don't make waves on my account. It's just a weekend."

"Well, I didn't invite you here to be treated badly." No, the last thing he wanted to do was give her an unfavorable impression.

"I'm fine," she said with a laugh.

"So, should we cruise?"

"Can we, with only two of us?" Nicole turned back toward him. He was wearing a blue polo shirt, white shorts, and deck shoes without socks and looked like anything but a scientist proposing that they take his research vessel out for a pleasure cruise. His ruggedness sent thrills through her.

"The only hard part without a crew is docking," he assured her. "But we don't have to worry about that until we return."

"I'm game if you are. Why don't I work up some breakfast first, though?"

"Great. I'll take a quick look-see and then give you a hand."

As she began preparing a light breakfast for two, Nicole was struck by the ease with which she'd accomplished the awkward task of waking up as the guest of a relative stranger. She'd never been especially comfortable as a houseguest before, always struggling to be of help and generally getting in her host's way. But David was a different kind of host, or maybe she was a different kind of guest this time, but she was definitely more in tune with the rhythm of his life than she'd ever been with any friend or relative she'd ever visited. She'd have thought that after the confusion and awkwardness of the previous night there would have been more tension between them, but there wasn't.

She noticed, too, that her own inner tension was lessened today. Not gone entirely, but the raw fear and worry had slackened to a faint nagging at the back of her mind. It felt as though something had clicked overnight, allowing her a respite from distress.

Or maybe it was just the lull before the storm.

THEY CRUISED SLOWLY up the coast, navigating from the flying bridge above the wheelhouse proper. The wind blew Nicole's long hair back like a pennant, giving her a feeling of recklessness and strength. No use holding back and waiting for answers to drop into her lap, no sense in being petrified by doubt. She'd come for a purpose other than merely enjoying his company, and it was time to get down to it with the same directness she'd resolved to use the night before.

"David, I have to talk to you about something," she said, raising her voice slightly to be heard above the wind.

"Yes, you said so last night." He cut the engines down, letting the ship slow itself against the waves. "I should apologize for cutting you off like that."

"No, I understand. I think I do, anyway." Nicole was somewhat embarrassed by what she thought she understood about the night before. She didn't feel at all prepared to talk about that particular incident.

"I didn't mean to make an ass of myself like that," he told her. He turned, squinting against the sun as he regarded her with a serious smile. "I'm not used to, you know, women. New women, I mean. I was taken off guard by your entrance."

"Anyone would," she laughed. "I don't remember getting from my cabin to the salon at all."

"Must have been one hell of a dream." His smile broadened, as though relieved that she was allowing the conversation to move away from the reason for his apology.

"It was." A tinge of disappointment flickered through Nicole's mind that he wanted to get to a different subject so quickly. She had thought she'd seen genuine interest in his eyes the night before, but it seemed to be gone now. Its passing saddened her more than she would have thought. "The dream is what I want to talk to you about. I've had it before."

"I don't know much about dreams," he offered. "Except that they never seem to mean anything."

"I would have agreed with that not too long ago." The civilized shore of Long Island was passing slowly, and Nicole watched it slip by while she gathered her thoughts to make a good presentation of things. "Before I first had this dream, my dreams were all whims. But this is different."

"How so?" He was turning the ship slowly to follow the coast up and around to the Atlantic.

"Because you were in it." There, it was out. There was no going back now.

"I was?"

He appeared shocked. She'd anticipated interest or likely laughter, but not shock.

"Yes, you were. And what's weird is that I dreamed it before I ever met you."

"Come on, now." David's face lost much of its color and he licked his suddenly dry lips with a furtive motion of his tongue. "You must have seen my picture in the paper or something."

"I don't remember it. It happened two nights before you came to the office. I didn't remember much at first, but it's been coming back more strongly since then. All I really remembered was your face. And it was raining."

"Raining?" David almost shouted at the mention of rain. A face in the rain again, but his face this time. What kind of dreams were they having?

"What's wrong, David? You look like you've seen a ghost." Nicole rubbed her hand up his arm to the shoulder, grasping him gently as he stared at her in bewilderment.

"I had a dream, as well," he said slowly. "I dreamed about you. And I dreamed it was raining, Nicole."

"I'LL CONCEDE that coincidences occur all the time, David. But I've never heard of any like this." Nicole tapped one long finger on the edge of her coffee cup and regarded David seriously. She'd briefly outlined her experiences to him as he brought them back to their berth, and now they were seated at the table in the salon trying to make quiet sense of the situation. "What does it mean?"

"I don't know," he said. "You know, there's no proof that people don't share dreams. It might be quite commonplace. We don't know what is normal."

"Don't be so scientific." Nicole smiled. He was remaining within the structure of his profession by insisting on looking at every angle before committing to an opinion. But Nicole had already gone through every logical answer she could think of and had found none. That must be the answer. "This isn't logical or scientific, David. But it seems that we did."

"At least part of one." He leaned back and combed his fingers back through his tousled hair, grimacing at the question before him. "It was so strange," he said. "I woke up remembering your name and a vague image of your face. It bothered me all day, clung to my mind so my thoughts kept coming back to your name. But I couldn't really remember anything else—not at first. But last night the rain seemed to bring much of it back."

"That's why you were in such a hurry to get in?"

"Yes." He sat forward, reaching to take Nicole's hand instinctively, but stopping himself. "The lightning scared the hell out of me. And I had a very clear vision of you lying on a sidewalk."

"In the rain?"

"In the rain. And there was blood on your lips."

"Blood?"

"Crazy, isn't it?"

"I'm scared, David."

"You don't have to be," he said, with far more conviction than he felt. "We're in this together now, Nicole."

"I've been scared since I first woke up after the dream," she admitted. "And every minute that passes seems to bring more fear. The worst thing is that I don't know why I'm afraid."

"Nothing bad has happened, has it?" He wished he could will away the confusion and fear that welled up in her eyes. But he didn't know how, and felt as helpless as a lamb in this unfamiliar inability to take concrete action about something.

"No, nothing actually harmful has happened. But I can't shake the feeling that something bad *is* going to happen. Something very bad. And it isn't just a feeling, it's stronger than that. Just as I knew that man would spill wine on me no matter how I tried to avoid it, I know something bad is coming."

"You can't know that."

"I couldn't know about the wine, David. I couldn't know what a secretary at the office would say before she said it. But I did. And I'm afraid of whatever is coming."

"I'm here for you, Nicole. Whatever you want me to do, just ask."

"That's why I came here," Nicole admitted. "Whatever is going to happen concerns you. In fact, I think you're the key to everything."

"Me?"

"Yes. I don't know what, or why, but I know you play a big part in it."

"Because I was in the dream?"

"Yes." Everything seemed so unclear again. The strange dream that had sent her running from her cabin that morning had faded into jumbled images, losing the clarity and purpose it had when she first woke from it. "I remember it was raining. You were...yes, you were opening a door for me and another man joined us. Then there was a gunshot, I think. But I'm not completely sure now."

"But it ends with you lying on the sidewalk in the rain," David finished for her, nodding as he pondered his own memory. "You had blood on your lips in my vision."

"I don't know about that. I remember you looking down at me." Then she laughed, despite the awful scene the dream depicted. "When my alarm clock went off I just wished it could leave me alone so I could stay with you in the dream. I didn't want to leave you."

"What was I doing?"

"Just looking down at me. It was just that I felt so good being with you there that I didn't want the dream to end."

"I'm glad I made a good first impression. Actually, by the time you heard your alarm clock the dream was over, anyway. It was only a memory then."

"That's what it felt like, too. A memory. It was very clear at the time—what I did remember of it—like a memory rather than a dream. And I remembered Sara's gallery opening like that, too."

"But that was a dream."

"Must have been, though I don't remember dreaming about the gallery."

"Did the actual opening conform to your expectations?"

"I'm not sure. By that time everything had gotten all jumbled up. But when that guy came toward me with his wine it sure felt as if I remembered him."

"Remembered dreaming about him."

"Just remembered. Whether it was a dream, I don't know."

"I'm totally at sea on this, Nicole," David admitted. "I have never believed in occult experiences. And, to tell the truth, if you were anyone else I'd think you were crazy and let it go at that. But I can't. We dreamed of each other on the same night—before we ever met. That can't be coincidence. It just can't. But, if it isn't, then what the hell is it? When I walked into Forrester's office and saw you sitting there, I felt like someone had clubbed me over the head."

"How do you think I felt? I wanted to pinch you to see if you were real. And I couldn't let you get out of there without making some kind of connection. It was very strange, but I was desperate to stay in contact somehow.

Your invitation to come out was exactly what I wanted. I just didn't know *why* I wanted it."

"So that's why I invited you for the weekend. You willed it." He laughed then, shaking his head. "I didn't know what made me ask you to visit. I'm not usually that forward with women—even ones as beautiful as you—but the invitation just popped out."

Beautiful? Nicole basked in the warmth of that word, unwilling to fight the pleasure of knowing he thought she was beautiful.

"But what did it accomplish?" she asked, still tingling with happiness but keeping her mind on the matter at hand. "Neither one of us knows why this is happening. Not even what is happening. It's so frustrating."

"I hate to bring it up, but we still can't be entirely sure that we aren't both just plain nuts. Even if we allow for some kind of ESP, how do we know there's any reason for it? Maybe we just decided to go insane together."

"Do you think we could get a group discount with a shrink?"

"I hope we don't have to find out."

"Wait!" How foolish she'd been. She'd entirely forgotten about her broken watch. "I might have some proof. My wristwatch was broken that morning. It's stuck at 12:41 on September sixth. That's not normal for a digital watch. They usually just go blank when the battery dies or they malfunction. They don't—" Then she stopped, seeing the horror-struck look on David's face. "What's wrong?"

"Your watch? My God!" Then he was up and hurrying out of the room.

"What is it?" Nicole ran after him down the stairs and along the hall into the master cabin. "David? What's wrong?" Nicole stood just behind him, waiting for his reply.

"Your watch," he said, throwing open a top drawer in his dresser and digging through the clothing inside. Then he stopped abruptly, his shoulders tensing beneath the taut fabric of his shirt. He took something out and turned with it in his hand. "Look at this."

He was holding a gold Rolex in his hand. The watch proclaimed that it was twelve forty-one, its sweep second hand moving casually over the numbers.

"It seems to be running all right," she said, though she felt a chill in the pit of her stomach.

"But it says 12:41. And look at the calendar window," he commanded urgently, pushing the watch closer to her. "I can't budge it away from that time! The same time as your watch!"

The same time *and* date, for the numerals in the gold-framed window set in the upper left side of the watch face claimed the date to be September sixth!

Chapter Seven

Nicole and David responded to the evidence of his frozen watch with mute awe. No words came, no coherent thought, only a shared moment of very real terror. And then Nicole broke the silence with a cry of frustration and anger.

"What the hell is going on!" Shouting to the sky, her eyes darting about the room as though searching for a clue in the furnishings, she balled her fists impotently and slammed them against her thighs. "We're living a damn *Twilight Zone* episode! There's no way any of this can have any purpose. It can't even be happening!"

"But it is happening, isn't it?" David laid the watch aside on the dresser and reached out to grasp her fists, bringing them together and smoothing the tension out of them as he held them to his chest. "I can't believe it any more than you, but I have to. Our watches are stopped at exactly the same time."

"You can't set it, but does the watch still wind?" She wouldn't allow herself to give in to anger or self-pity. She would strive toward an answer if only to keep sane in the quest.

"I don't know. In fact, I haven't wound it at all, but the second hand is still moving," he said, looking at the watch with increased wonder. "It should be wound down by now."

"Just like the little dots that keep blinking on mine," she mused. "When did it break? Wednesday morning?"

"Sorry. I didn't put it on till Thursday when I was preparing to see Clint. I'd ruin it in daily wear. But, you know, the second hand was moving then, too, though it must have been a week since I'd last worn it."

Fear, like an icy knife, slipped into Nicole's stomach and threatened to drive her to useless anger again. She fought the fear by laying her cheek against David's chest and seeking the solace of his presence that had worked before. "So how do we find a reason for this? How do we escape it?"

"We ride out the storm, I guess." David lifted her chin with two fingers, dropping his head to catch her rising gaze. "We tie everything down and hold on." *So beautiful,* he thought. *So near.* The numbing fear that had assailed him was gone now, replaced by a more pleasant feeling, harder to control. The desire that struck at him in sporadic raids surged through him now as he looked down at the determined sparkle in her hazel eyes. He wanted to claim some hold on her emotions and tap the resources of her intelligence and drive. He wanted to experience the heat that was attested to in the warmth of her hands and the fire in her eyes. But he couldn't allow that masculine beast to be his master, couldn't presume to take what wasn't offered or take advantage of the confusion in her life. *Say something, please. Break this spell so I can get away from these feelings.*

But Nicole was wrapped in her own contemplation. *Ride out the storm,* she was thinking. *Roll with the waves.* Beautiful words—David's own—to describe their situation. No, she couldn't let things carry her where they would. It was important that she fight the flow, fight through to her own conclusion. And so she pushed back the fear and confusion to find light.

Though she wanted to savor her growing feelings for this man, she knew that the circumstances that drew them together were more powerful than simple attraction. The situation warped their feelings, making them suspect. Would she have felt anything under different circumstances? She didn't know. And she couldn't be sure that he had any corresponding feeling for her even now, so it was best to swallow the emotions to avoid disappointment.

"Do you remember anything else from your dream?" She spoke slowly, as though coming out of sleep or deep contemplation.

"Just pieces." David let go of Nicole's hand. "I remember you lying in the rain mostly."

Nicole turned and picked up his wristwatch, holding it carefully and seeing the second hand turn around past the immobile hands on the watch face. "When you woke up, did you feel as though it was some day other than what it was? September sixth?"

"I don't remember anything like that. The dream wasn't clear at all in the morning but only became so over time."

"I was thinking that maybe that date was important to deciphering the mystery, but it seems that I'm the only one who was affected in that way."

"But you've been affected more strongly in every way," David pointed out. He couldn't resist the impulse to touch her, placing one hand on her shoulder as she stood looking at his wristwatch. "I haven't had any strange visions, only a dream. That date could still mean something."

"I just wish I had a better idea of what is actually going on. Is this some kind of clairvoyant experience? Are we

feeling the effect of some future event, or is there some
other purpose to this?''

"Or no purpose?''

"Don't say that, David. I can't believe that we've been
brought together like this for no reason at all.''

Any reply David might have made was cut off by the
sound of a door closing in the hall. They both started at the
noise, turning toward the open door of the stateroom, and
David walked to look down the hall.

"Hello? Connie?'' He stepped into the hall, his head
cocked to listen. Beyond him, Nicole saw a door open and
a dark-haired man emerge from one of the cabins.

"Just me," the man stated.

"Jerry.'' David's relief was evident in his voice, and he
walked toward the newcomer. "What are you doing back
here?''

"A sane person can only listen to so many reports before he has to take a break from the babble.'' Jerry spoke
with gruff humor, scowling around the unlit cigarette he'd
placed between his lips. "Who's this?'' He nodded past
David toward Nicole, who was standing in the doorway.

"Pardon me. Nicole, this is Jerry Brunsvold,'' he said,
stepping back to introduce them. "Jerry, I'd like you to
meet Nicole Ellis.''

"Oh, yes, your weekend guest.'' Jerry smiled tightly and
took Nicole's hand in his weak grasp. "How do you like
the tub?'' He lit his cigarette with a gold lighter, snapped
it shut and slipped it into the pocket of his slacks.

"It's a lovely boat," she replied. She couldn't read the
expression in Jerry's deep-set eyes but it didn't seem entirely friendly.

"Showed you the *Crab*, I assume. Our boy is quite an
ingenious fellow,'' Jerry said. "It's a damn nice little

gadget. You know, Dave, maybe you should rethink giving it away."

"Not you, too." David grimaced. "I've finally gotten Connie to let up on the subject and now you're starting?"

"No, just a thought. Well, I just wanted to pick up a couple of things and then I'll be out of your way." He walked back into his cabin with no more explanation.

"Let's go finish our coffee," David said, leading the way to the stairs.

"Is your partner always so abrupt?" Nicole watched David dump out their cold coffee and refill the cups. A wind had come up outside, rocking the ship slightly on the choppy water as thin clouds swept across the sky.

"Yes, he is." David was smiling as he sat beside her. "He takes some getting used to."

"I should say so." The coffee was hot and strong and strangely soothing despite its acid bite. "Have you said anything about your dream to him or Connie?"

"No. I thought it was only a dream till I met you. After that, I didn't know what to say about it." He sipped his coffee, wincing slightly at the heat. "It might not be a bad idea to tell Jerry. A fresh perspective could help."

"No, I don't think we should tell anybody. Besides, he'd only laugh at us."

"Jerry never laughs. But I suppose you're right. The paranormal isn't exactly his field."

"Right." But it wasn't a question of expertise that was bothering her. She didn't know what all of this was pointing to, but it involved gunfire. And the gunman she remembered was slight of build, much like David's partner. "Do you have a gun on board?" she asked impulsively.

"A gun? No, of course not. Unless you count the flare gun." David was looking at her more closely then, his features tightened with piercing inquiry. "Why do you want to know that?"

"Somebody has a gun," she said, tersely. Gunshots and rain, a man in dark glasses and silence, that's where everything ended. It ended with death, but whose and why? "What is going to happen on the sixth?"

"That's the date of my second appointment with Clint."

"Anything else?"

"Not so far. I suppose I'll hang out in the city for the day. Why?"

"Because I think I was right about that day being important. I don't know how literally we're supposed to take things like this, but I think we're being warned of something violent happening on the sixth."

"Okay, I'll buy precognition. But it doesn't account for the watches. How can a psychic phenomenon have a physical effect on an inanimate object?"

"I don't know, David. But the sixth is the day to watch out for. I'm certain of that." And the feeling that she was correct about that grew the more she thought of it, pushing back the confusion as it did. "All we need to do is find out why someone would want to harm us."

"But what if it's a warning against a chance act?" David raised one brow in doubt, feeling his ability to believe in such occult goings-on straining a bit at the volume of impossibilities she was presenting him with.

"No, a gunshot is too specific. It must be a premeditated act. Maybe not a gun, but definitely something with murderous intent."

"Do you really expect that someone may want to kill you?"

"No. I would think that the most likely target is you, David."

"Me? But I wasn't harmed in the dream."

"I'm doing the best I can to interpret this, but I can't explain it all." She laughed, encouraged to be able to have a direction to look now. "You're coming to the office on the sixth. So, what other business do you have with Clint?"

"None, really. He drew up the partnership agreement for me and Jerry, but that's all. But you can't expect Clint to be involved in this, can you?"

"We've got to be open-minded, David. Anybody could be involved." Even Jerry, she thought, though she wasn't about to voice the so far baseless suspicion.

"Well, I don't—" But David was cut off by Jerry's emergence from below deck.

"Off again," he called, barely pausing on his way to the aft door of the cabin. He was carrying a plastic suit bag over one shoulder.

"I thought you didn't like conferences," David said, smiling. "Taking your tux seems like an awfully big commitment."

"I don't like it," he shrugged at the door. "But there's no sense being antisocial, is there? Besides, somebody has got to do it, or they'll all forget who we are when it comes time to divvy up research grants."

"Right. Try to have a good time."

"You too." Then he stepped through the door and across to the gangplank.

"Why didn't he take his tuxedo to begin with?"

"I don't think he planned on having fun." Then, noticing the skeptical look on her face, he offered, "And don't start reading anything into it, either. Jerry is no more suspect than the man in the moon. And, for that matter, it isn't possible to be guilty of committing a crime that hasn't been committed yet."

"I know." Nicole scowled. It wouldn't help if she had to tiptoe around every person who might be responsible for the danger in her mind. "But we can't allow personal feelings to keep us from checking things through completely."

"But Jerry has no motive to want me harmed."

"Are you sure?"

"Of course." David didn't want to admit to even the possibility that his partner might be in any way involved with the chaos he'd envisioned. If he suspected Jerry now, he might never be able to trust him again.

"Say, do you have a last will?" That seemed like a solid lead into the heart of the matter, and Nicole leaned forward, eager to follow it.

"Of course." David smiled sourly, following the logic of the query but stubbornly refusing to volunteer any information. "But that doesn't give him any motive."

"Why not?"

"I'm not leaving him anything in the will. As my partner, he is contractually entitled to all of our research equipment in the event of my death, so there was no need to put him in the will. Besides, the will is out of date."

"How so?"

"Besides the charitable donations," he said slowly, "I left everything to Katharine." And he found himself thinking how foolish it seemed in retrospect that he had seen to her well-being in case he died but had never given a thought to the possibility of her dying first. But the pain that had dogged him since her death had changed perceptibly in the past couple of days. It had been dulled more by two days in Nicole's company than two years of self-exile working on the *Crab*. He looked at her, recognizing for the first time how much she had come to mean to him already.

"I was rather counting on the will to help us out," Nicole said, frustration roughening the edges of her normally fluid alto voice. "But in his case the contract amounts to the same thing."

"Sure, except that he already has access to everything he would get. No, it's not Jerry."

"Connie?" She was almost afraid to mention her, but it had to be said.

"No." David's voice held flat denial with no opening for argument. "She's not in the will and has no contract. She'd gain nothing."

"I didn't really suspect her, anyway," Nicole admitted. "After all, in my dream it was a man holding the gun."

"The only one I can think of wishing me ill is my cousin Bob," David said, smiling. "I don't suppose he'd do much crying at the funeral."

"Robert Philips? But, is he—"

"No. I wouldn't put that schmuck in my will for any reason. Of course, if I died, he'd have the strongest claim to my estate. But it'd be tied up in court for years . . . so what would be the point?" He sighed, then peered at her. "Have you even considered that the danger might actually concern you rather than me?"

"But I don't have enough money to move someone to kill me, much less a will leaving it to anyone."

"Which leads us back to the possibility that we're both suffering through some psychic practical joke."

"You don't really believe that, though, do you?"

"No, I don't. There has to be a reason that we've been brought together like this, and I don't think it's got anything to do with humor."

"I don't know what to think anymore," Nicole said tiredly. "I just don't know."

"Well I think that I'm hungry," David said, picking up their mood with his ebullient tone. "What kind of host am I, going this long without feeding you?"

"I hadn't noticed." Though she did feel empty now that the subject had come up. "But I am hungry."

"Good. Let me go rustle up something quick." He stood, walking past her to the hall that led to the galley. "Nothing fancy, I'm afraid. I'm too hungry to take much time."

"Let's go see what we can do," she agreed, standing.

"No way." David turned, holding out one hand to stop her. "Let me surprise you. I want a chance to impress you with my culinary abilities, limited though they may be."

"All right." She laughed, sitting down again. "But don't get carried away."

"Back in a minute." He hurried around the corner, and Nicole could hear a slight squeak as the door opened.

Reaching for her coffee cup, Nicole felt an unaccountable warmth pass over her face, like a blush or a whisper of an oven's heat. For a moment, she thought she saw a flash of light, too. Red-orange, like a light shining on closed eyelids, the light accompanied the heat and was gone as quickly, but she was left with a lingering feeling of unease. Something. What? Heat and light. She closed her eyes, seeing again the flash of light, feeling the heat, and hearing a faint roar. No!

"David!" Nicole sprang up from her chair, almost losing her footing as she turned awkwardly toward the galley. "David! Get out!"

But the blast threw her onto her back on the deck, sliding into a computer rack by the wall as a ball of flame shot out of the galley door with a loud whoosh. Heat and light, and then liquid running warm as blood against her legs.

The explosion had knocked the coffee pot off the counter, spilling its contents across the deck in a brown flood.

"David!" Scrambling to her feet, her ears still filled with the fierce sound of the blast and coughing from the harsh bite of smoke in the air, Nicole reached the galley door over a litter of debris thrown about by the explosion. "David! Are you all right?" Foolish question, but he had to be alive. Had to be all right. "David?"

There was no reply. Dense gray smoke curled up against the galley ceiling, rolling out the door and the broken window over the oven. There were no flames now, however, for the explosion had apparently blown the fire out in the same instant it was ignited. The pots that had been hanging on the wall lay scattered across the floor amid broken dishes, all on a gritty layer of sugar and flour and ground coffee. The room smelled strongly of smoke—and something else. Gas. It was still leaking!

Nicole ran around the prep table bolted to the floor in the center of the room and found David lying on his stomach on the other side. "My God!" Kneeling beside him, she was careful not to move him right away. He was breathing and didn't appear to have been hurt too badly, though his clothing was burned slightly and his hair was singed black at the ends.

"David!" She leaned down beside his ear and called his name firmly, fighting to restrain the trembling of her hands as she smoothed them over his back and face in an effort to rouse him without moving him. "David, can you hear me?"

He moaned quietly, his eyelids fluttering open.

"Can you hear me?" she called. Tears welled in her searching eyes as she clutched at his hand. "Can you feel your feet? Can you move?"

"I can, yes, I can." He groaned the words out, drawing one leg up beneath him as he pushed his other hand against the floor to prove himself. "Damn light," he moaned.

"Take it easy," Nicole cautioned him. "Where is the gas shutoff?"

"Cupboard. Beside oven." He'd managed to push himself up to his hands and knees, shaking his head slowly. "Right side."

"Take it slow."

"No, I'm all right." But he didn't feel all right. He felt as if a convoy of steamrollers had rumbled over him, and he wouldn't have minded lying there for a bit longer. But he, too, could smell the gas leaking from the blasted remains of the oven. Though the danger of a new blast was small, they had to shut it off and get out to fresh air. "Help me out," he said, trying to sound strong and alert.

"Just a moment." Nicole threw open the cupboard to the right of the blackened oven and found a silver knob on a pipe leading up from below. She turned it tightly off and then returned to David.

"Okay, David. Let me help you out of here." Nicole felt suddenly drained and unsteady. The shock of the blast was setting in, leaving her senses dulled by the sheer relief of hearing his voice and seeing him move again. But he needed her strength now and she had to steady herself to provide it.

Nicole helped him regain his feet and the two of them stumbled and slipped across the littered deck to the door and the fresh air outside where she laid him on the couch in the salon.

"Damn light," he said again, more strongly this time.

"What about the light?"

"It was broken." David tried to push himself up to sit but the throbbing in his head discouraged the move and he lowered himself back down. "The bulb over the sink was broken." He spoke slowly and carefully, listening to the strange echo his voice made in his head. "I was just switching on the light. Saw glass in the sink."

"The light was broken?" The meaning of his information didn't strike her at first. A broken light bulb seemed like a small worry after something like that. But then she knew what he meant, and the implication sent a chill through her. "Do you mean that the filament was bare?"

"Yes." He nodded but stopped, wincing.

"So the hot wire was exposed to the gas when you turned it on! That was the spark that set it off! My God, David! The explosion was intentional!"

They finally had their proof. Someone was trying to kill him!

Chapter Eight

Nicole's fear was no longer intangible. It had been pushed from the theoretical to the actual by a current of electricity surging through the exposed filament of a light bulb. Now she knew for certain that her fear was real. It was like a beast within her, threatening to devour her reason if she were to relax her grip on it. But if her fear was real then her antagonist was real as well, and an enemy of flesh and blood can be fought. So perhaps the chance of escape was more real now, too.

"You're very lucky," Nicole said, softly. Seated in an armchair beside David's bed, she was watching him eat a bowl of soup she'd heated in the microwave oven.

"I know." Swallowing a spoonful of broth, he smiled at her and nodded. "Gas explosions are tricky things. I'm lucky the light wasn't in line with the oven. That's where the blast was worst."

"What if the explosion hadn't blown itself out?"

"We probably would have had to abandon ship. You wouldn't have known where all the extinguishers are." He set the bowl aside on the bedside table and leaned back against the pillows behind him. Nicole had paid special attention to his comfort after the doctor left them, gathering pillows from storage until he was well padded. "How's the galley look?"

"A bit blackened, and the oven door is blown off. It's a mess, but mostly superficial."

"Good."

"But the condition of the galley isn't our real worry, is it?" She watched him seriously, wondering how he would deal with the idea of his friend trying to murder him. "Why would he have done it?"

"I don't believe it," he said stubbornly. "Not Jerry."

"Who else? Connie? Me, maybe?"

"No." David closed his eyes, imagining his friend slipping into the galley, blowing out the pilot on the oven and opening the gas, then carefully breaking the glass on the bulb. "He's got no reason to want to kill me."

"But he must have, and we'll have to find out what it is."

"I hope you don't mind if I find this hard to believe." He spoke more harshly than he'd intended, but it was so easy for her to suspect a man she didn't know while he had to deal with years of friendship before reaching the same conclusion. "I'm sorry, Nicole. I didn't mean to snap at you."

"I know. I really don't mean to rush you, but it can't be helped."

"I'm just glad I didn't let you come in to help me." David reached out to grasp her hand, holding it firmly in his as he marveled at the delicacy of her slender fingers and the wonderful softness of her skin. "I'd hate to see you harmed."

"I would too, I assure you." Nicole's heart raced at his touch. The warm pressure of his hand on hers produced a spark within her, less destructive but no less powerful than the spark that consumed the galley. David's being healthy and holding her hand felt more important than anything else right then, and she let the warm feeling overcome her as she gazed deeply into his eyes. Damn the world of trouble that surrounded them! All she wanted to do was sink into the heady, palpitating feeling that was growing between them now and let the world pass by.

"Why is this happening?" he asked, never slackening his grip or breaking the caressing contact of their eyes.

"I don't know. He might have money pressures you don't know about," she offered.

"No, I didn't mean that. I want to know why it's happening the way it is. And why were you thrust into the middle of it?"

"I've never believed in ESP, so I'm afraid I've never gone to the trouble of learning anything about it." Just sitting and talking with him like this was an exciting experience. But she had to maintain a minimal distance between her mind and her heart. "I . . . I've always preferred to have some proof of something like that before committing myself. I don't like to jump into things," she said, more to explain the confusion of her heart than her mind.

"Neither do I." His voice was soft and comforting, a gentle, reassuring purr, and he stroked his thumb across the back of her hand as he spoke. "But then it's been a long time since I've had such compelling evidence that it was time to commit. Nicole, I—" But he broke off then, fighting back a yawn behind clenched lips. "Oh, damn. I'm tired."

"The medicine is taking effect," she told him. "Lie back and relax."

"I don't want to sleep," he protested, yawning again. "I want—"

"Plenty of time for that in the morning." Nicole let go of his hand and removed a couple of pillows so that he could lie flat. "Rest now. Talk later."

"All right, Doctor Ellis." He smiled, catching her hand again briefly. "Will you be all right?"

"Yes, I'm fine. I don't think anything else will happen tonight."

"Good. You get some rest, too." Then he let his hand drop to the bed and lay smiling up at her as his eyes slid shut.

Nicole left the stateroom and went up to the galley. The darkened oven and the littered floor looked ominous in the darkening orange glow of the dying evening. *Someone planned this,* she thought. Someone wanted it to be far worse than it was. And the thought of how close she'd come to losing David chilled her momentarily.

Losing him? Yes, that was her exact thought. It had been a long time since she'd felt such a passionate need to keep someone by her. But that's how she felt about David Germaine. And it wasn't the fumbling need of a woman whose life was in turmoil but the well-considered feeling of a woman whose life had just been brought into dramatic focus. Now she realized that the sense of chaos she'd had before coming to the boat would be nothing compared to what she'd feel should she lose him now. She'd rather die herself than have him harmed.

How could she avoid his being harmed? What could she do? She knew what it was and knew that now was probably the only chance she'd have to take action. With that thought in mind she went below and entered Jerry Brunsvold's cabin, resolving that she would rather invade his privacy than stand by on some moral high ground and allow David to become a target again.

BRUNSVOLD'S CABIN was a disappointment. Though she wasn't sure what she expected to find in it, there seemed to be less than what might be normal. Every scrap of paper in his desk was of a scientific nature, every book on the shelves the same. The man seemed to have no interests beyond the sea and his work on it. And the only financial evidence she could find was hardly incriminating. The balance in his savings account was in excess of ten thousand dollars and he had over twenty thousand invested in tax-deferred annuities—neither a sign of someone desperate for money. So he wasn't a high-flyer, who might take a chance on something and be pushed to murder if it went sour. And the lack of personal correspondence suggested he was also someone without personal entanglements. Perhaps the most telling aspect of his room was the fact that though every desk drawer could be locked, none were. The man appeared to have nothing to hide.

Nicole returned to the salon in a sour mood. Jerry was the only one with an opportunity to rig the light bulb, so there had to be a motive hidden away someplace. But where?

The telephone rang, startling her. Then she ran to answer it before it woke David.

"Hello?"

"Hello. Who is this?" A gruff voice, sharp and impatient, barked over the phone. "Connie?"

"No, Connie is out." Nicole knew the voice. It was Robert Philips, David's entrepreneurial cousin. "May I ask who is calling?"

"Bob Philips," he said, tersely. "But who is this?"

"A friend of David's." She had the advantage of knowing him while he was in the dark about her, and felt instinctively that she should keep that advantage if possible.

"Where's Dave?" He apparently didn't have time for name games and dismissed her as being of no importance.

"He's asleep. He had an accident earlier." She didn't want to tip her hand by withholding more information than she should and so would give him that.

"Accident? What happened?" The concern seemed completely genuine, though knowing Robert Philips as slightly as she did she couldn't be sure.

"There was a gas leak and a small explosion in the galley. He's all right."

"My God! But did a doctor see him? Why isn't he in a hospital or something?"

"Yes, a doctor came. He said just to let him rest overnight. There was no concussion. No major burns."

"That's something, anyway." He sounded relieved. "How did you dig up a doctor who makes house calls on a Sunday?"

"It isn't hard to find a doctor in a yacht harbor," Nicole commented. "It was more a question of deciding which one."

"Is David asleep now? Can I speak to him?"

"He's sleeping. The doctor gave him something. May I take a message?"

"No, I have to talk to him in person. But I don't suppose it would be any use, no matter what condition he's in."

"How's that?"

"You may have noticed that my cousin is somewhat allergic to making money," the man said. "I have something very good going and...well, it doesn't matter. Where is Connie?"

"I don't know. She went out this morning."

"Jerry's gone, too?"

"He's at the conference." What was he fishing for?

"Oh, hell." He dismissed the whole subject sourly. "Tell David I'll call tomorrow. Goodbye."

"Goodbye," she replied as the connection was broken on the other end.

Was he involved in some way? It was something that hadn't occurred to her before, that it might be a business deal of Robert Philips's making that had drawn Jerry Brunsvold into the mess. The scientist needn't have any papers in his room if Philips was handling it. Jerry might have gone into a deal with him, putting future income up as part of some kind of buy-in. Philips had put together a deal like that before through Clint Forrester, and it had gone sour, forcing the partner to come up with additional cash in order to buy out of the arrangement. Could that have happened this time? Jerry had seemed to have such stable financial habits, but that was no true indication of what he might do if real riches were offered to him. If that were the case, there might not be incriminating evidence on the ship. There was no reason to count Brunsvold out yet.

Nicole went out to stand on the deck, looking up at the stars coming out overhead. Could there be an answer in their intermittent light? A week ago she'd have thought not, but tonight she was aware of a wide world of possibilities where nothing could be discounted simply because it appeared not to make sense. Appearances were deceptive, and reality was not as solid as it had once seemed.

A flash of light interrupted her thoughts and she could see a billowing cloud of flame rush out to engulf her as she felt the pressure and heat of the blast wash over her body. She had a clear image of the ceiling of the galley above her, flames licking across its surface. Then the vision was gone.

What was it? Perhaps an answer of sorts. What if she'd been in the galley during the blast? What if the flames had caught hold? But why imagine such a thing now? It hadn't happened like that. What was the vision trying to tell her?

Again a flash and heat, but this time from a vantage point in the salon, and this time the wall between the two rooms gave way with a violent burst of flame and debris. Again, why see such a thing? It hadn't happened like that.

Nicole shuddered. The night air seemed colder after the memory of such heat, the stars looked like the malevolent eyes of dishonored gods staring down at her. And fear rained down from the darkening sky; fear unreasoning and uncontrollable assailed her mind, sending her running for the fragile safety of the cabin with its own collection of physical dangers.

She threw the door shut against the night, switching on every light she could find in a frantic effort to keep the darkness out. Then she calmed herself and forced herself to sit, breathing deeply, willing away the fear.

What good was it to be endowed with precognition when she couldn't control it or interpret what she saw? And why variations of past events as well as future ones? *Why her?*

That thought was foremost in her mind as she clasped her hands in her lap and fought to calm the stammering pulse of her heart. Why had she been chosen? What had she done to deserve such confusion and pain? But then she wouldn't have gotten to know David Germaine. He'd have remained an intriguing face, a striking man, who passed through the office with no effort on her part to stop him or know him. Perhaps she had more to be thankful for than she thought.

But the lights seemed to dim then, replaced by the smoky interior of the galley as David leaned over her. He was saying something that she couldn't hear over the oppressive pounding of her heart. He looked so concerned—terrified, in fact. He was saying something to her, assuring her she'd be all right. But she wasn't all right, and the smoke turned to the gray of an overcast sky as rain began falling on her face. Rain, and wet concrete beneath her and a feeling of a great weight on her chest. She tried to talk, wanting to remove the worry from David's face and tell him she was all right, she'd just lost her footing. But she didn't know if he could hear her or not. The only sound was the staggering *ta-thump* of her heart. Staggering and slowing. Darkness. Very clearly she heard David cry out, "My God, don't die!"

Nicole screamed, flying up from the couch and staring around the brightly lit room, not knowing if she was there or just imagining it. And Connie Wright was approaching her from the door, a look of surprise wrinkling her brow.

"I didn't mean to scare you," she said. "Were you asleep?"

"What?" Nicole was trembling, breathing in shallow gasps. "No—yes, I must have been. Dreaming, I guess." She gathered her wits quickly to cover her distress.

"What happened here?" Connie spoke sharply, appraising Nicole closely. "You're a mess. And is that smoke I smell?"

"Yes. There was an explosion," Nicole said quickly. For the first time since the blast she was aware that she hadn't changed out of the white slacks that had been stained by the spilled coffee. "A gas leak."

"What?" Connie hurried toward the galley, seeing for the first time the broken window and what remained after Nicole's hurried cleaning job. "Where's David?"

"Sleeping. He's all right."

"What?" She paused a moment looking around in confusion, then piercing Nicole with her anxious eyes. "What happened to him?"

"He was in the galley when it blew up. He's fine, though. The doctor wants him to rest tonight."

"Oh," she said faintly, then suddenly shouted out in alarm. "The poor man! I have to check on him!"

"No." Nicole hurried after her as she turned down the hall towards the stairs. "Let him rest."

"I want to see him," Connie insisted, clattering down the steps to the sleeping quarters.

"Leave him alone, Connie." Nicole caught her just outside the door, grasping her arm firmly. "He's had a hard day and deserves to get some rest. Let's let him sleep."

"Hey, you're not in charge here, lady," Connie spat out. "You can't just come in and take over."

"I'm not trying to." The vehemence of the woman's angry words had taken Nicole aback. Connie's feelings for David must run more deeply than Nicole had imagined. "I just think it's best for him not to be interrupted," she said, cautiously.

"What you think isn't terribly important to me." Connie's eyes narrowed with anger as she stared Nicole down. "Now let go of my arm."

Nicole did as requested, unaware that she'd still been holding the other woman until it was brought to her attention. If she wanted to see him that badly, Nicole wasn't about to stand in her way.

Connie opened the door carefully and took a step inside. She stood without breathing for a long moment, staring at the man slumbering on the bed. Then she stepped back and closed the door behind her.

"He's all right," she said woodenly. Then she gave Nicole a withering look. "It's all your fault, you know. If you hadn't come here, everything would be all right."

"Please, Connie, I—"

"No, you came and confused everything, didn't you? Came and messed everything up," she proclaimed hotly. "Damn you!" She went to her own door, throwing it open.

"Wait!"

"Shut up," she said, without turning. "I'm going to bed."

Nicole was left to stare at the closed door. She had no idea how to bridge the gap that yawned between them. And now, with the clear possibility that David's friend and partner was trying to harm him, it was more important than ever that the two women be able to get along. But how could she break through the wall of jealousy between them? It would be especially hard now that her own involvement with David was heightening.

There was no answer, not now, and Nicole was more tired than she could ever remember being before. She retired to her own bed, seeking relief in sleep.

Some time later, she was awakened from a dream that lingered after waking. David was beside her in the bed, his hand smoothing the warm flesh of her shoulder and down over her hip as she leaned to kiss him. He seemed so warm and real beside her, his skin hot to her touch. But he evaporated in the moonlight, melting into motes of dust dancing mutely in the air. She lay back again, her heart racing as she blinked back threatening tears. Why was this happening to her?

DAVID WAS THINKING something similar when he awoke at three that morning and lay staring up at the ceiling. His head felt fine now, clear and coherent, though his body still ached all over. But it wasn't bodily aches that had awakened him tonight. He'd been brought up from sleep by a feeling that he'd overlooked something.

But what was it?

He sat up carefully, swinging his pajama-clad legs out of the bed and stepping onto the floor. The ship was swaying slowly in its berth, a lulling motion beneath his feet as he urged his tight muscles to take him to the door.

The hall was quiet, though he could hear Connie moving in her sleep when he paused to listen at her door. She had apparently gotten back while he was asleep. He was grateful to Nicole for keeping her from waking him, as he was sure she had. Connie was impulsive and would surely have shaken him awake to get the particulars of the incident if Nicole's more prudent nature hadn't interceded.

He couldn't hear anything from Nicole's room and felt embarrassed at listening, but he couldn't help but pause. She had managed to capture a firm position in his heart in the short time they'd known each other. He wanted to keep her safe and warm and free of any more bad dreams or visions. Nothing had prepared him for the feeling that surged through him as he stood outside her door. The eager shivering that assailed his stomach took him back to the uncertainties he'd suffered through in high school, making him thrill with anticipation even as it sickened him. Did she or didn't she feel the same as he did? Was her presence here prompted only by their strange situation, or was there more to it than that?

Chastened by the turn his thoughts had taken, David hurried up to the galley. Moonlight shone across the floor with an otherworldly glow that raised gooseflesh across the backs of his arms. There was a flashlight stowed in a utility cupboard by the door. He took it out and switched it on to find an answer to the question that had come out of his dream.

Actually, he'd been wondering about several things since the explosion but the hectic flow of events and his own in-

juries had kept him from acting on them. Now he could see
that the porthole over the sink had indeed been blown
open, the glass cracked. That was one thing he had remembered before the blast. The porthole had been unlatched and set ajar. Otherwise, the explosion would have
shattered the glass but left the frame of the window shut
tightly. It was a small point, but a nagging one. Why would
they have left the porthole unlatched? The gas had seeped
out through the slight opening and had never been allowed to reach a murderous proportion.

Still pondering that question, David knelt before the
stove and pulled off the access panel below the oven door.
By lowering his face to within inches of the floor, he was
able to shine the light beneath the oven and examine the
appliance's gas line. Yes, the nut connecting the line to the
oven had been unscrewed.

That's what had been nagging him. If the pilot light was
out, the oven would have automatically shut off the supply of gas. To ensure leakage, the line had to be interrupted before it reached the oven.

David replaced the access cover and stood up carefully,
his back protesting the strain of twisting it. If his would-be
murderer had planned things well enough to uncouple the
gas line and make sure the bulb's filament was exposed,
why didn't he or she secure the porthole? He couldn't
imagine a methodical man like Jerry making so obvious a
mistake.

Thinking about it now, David realized that, had the port
been closed, the blast would have blown the walls out,
killing both him and Nicole. There would surely have been
a fire, and the ship might have burned to the waterline
before anyone could have done a thing about it.

Only a small oversight had stood between them and
death.

Chapter Nine

"Surely you aren't letting a little explosion chase you away," David said, smiling wanly at Nicole as she snapped her bag shut. "We never did teach you how to run the *Crab*."

"Then I'll have to come back for the lessons, won't I?" She turned toward him, feeling a blush of happiness well up within her at the sight of him standing whole and well in the door of her cabin.

It had been an awkward morning with Connie there between them and their thoughts. She'd been full of questions for David, making a point of ignoring Nicole. Nicole and David had instinctively joined together in asserting that the incident had been accidental, keeping their fears and suspicions to themselves. After all, Connie knew nothing of Nicole's strange experiences or how they dovetailed with David's dream. It was a bit late in the game now to bring her in on it.

The only real acknowledgement Connie gave Nicole was when she announced her plan to leave that morning. Then she had smiled, saying it was too bad she couldn't stay and how much they'd miss her. But above the smile her green eyes held icy malice, accusing Nicole of complicity in everything that had happened. Nicole did feel guilty in a way—guilty of being unable to warn him in time.

And that was part of the reason she was leaving. She didn't want to be caught flat-footed again. Besides, the information that would armor them against a future attack was to be found in the city, not on the boat. And time was running out rapidly.

Now that she was actually packed, however, she found her resolve waning. What if she were wrong and there was nothing in Clint's office? What if a second attempt was made right here at the boat? But no, she had to cast those questions aside and follow her instincts, now more than ever. That's what her precognitive ability was for, she felt, to guide her to a happier conclusion. She had to learn how to work with the visions now.

"I think I know where to look for some answers, and I'm anxious to get to it," she told David, shoring up her determination with words. "I'll call if I find anything."

"What are you going to do?" A note of concern stole into his voice.

"I want to check something at Clint's office," she admitted.

"What? Now you think your boss is involved?"

"No, but I think Robert Philips may have a hand in it somewhere. He's the only one who seems to have any quarrel with you, so it isn't so farfetched to think he is connected."

"But how?" She'd lost him now. The man hadn't been anywhere near the boat, so how could he be involved?

"I'm just fumbling in the dark, really. But only some kind of money problem would have pushed your partner to the point where he'd do something this drastic." Nicole took her bag from the bed. "What if Jerry decided to take advantage of one of Robert's propositions, one that you'd turned down? I know about some of the arrangements Mr. Philips has put together in the past and you can believe me when I say that he doesn't allow his own assets to be placed in jeopardy. Jerry would have taken a beating if the deal went sour.''

''Jerry doesn't pay any attention to business matters,'' David said. ''He doesn't even have a checking account.''

''For your sake, I hope I'm wrong about your friend,'' she said. ''If I am, there won't be anything in Clint's files about it. But what if I'm right?''

''I don't want you to go,'' David said with sudden resolution. *Enough holding back, enough civility. Nicole may be walking into more trouble than she can handle. Stop her, or go along.* ''Not alone, anyway.''

''I've got to go today, David. Everyone will be back in the office tomorrow. We've got so little time.''

''Nicole.'' He grabbed her arms, stroking his hands tenderly upward to grasp her shoulders. ''I can't let you do anything dangerous. I can't take the chance that you'll be hurt.''

''Come on, David. I'm a full-grown woman.'' She smiled into his worried eyes, trying to coax away his fears.

''And I'm a full-grown man,'' he said, forcefully. ''Look what happened to me. They made one mistake, but we can't count on their making any more. If you're right about Jerry, then your only worry is here on the ship. But, if you're wrong, then you can't know where the threat lies.''

''But I won't know if I don't look.'' She let her case drop to the floor at her side and grasped his forearms gently, wanting to hold him but refusing to give her emotions a chance to embarrass her. ''I appreciate the concern, but I'll be all right.''

"This bravery stuff can only go so far, Nicole. If you'll wait until the police have been here to talk to me I can go with you."

"I'll be all right. Really." How could she argue with such heartfelt concern? How could she fight the power of those gentle blue eyes? But she had to fight, or be lost in a torrent of emotion that would pull her farther from her task.

"Don't go. At least wait for me to come with you," he urged, wishing he could find the proper words to say more.

"I've got to go now," she answered. He made it sound so easy. But he hadn't been surrounded by chaos as she'd been, and didn't know what it felt like to have control of his life stolen from him. She wasn't about to give in to either the jumbled visions or her own confused emotions. Still, she probably would have waited for him if he gave any indication of feeling more than simple friendship and concern for her. "There's no time to wait. Clint may be in later," she explained.

"Go at night. He won't be there after midnight, will he?"

"I can't get in then. They lock the building up after the restaurant on the main floor closes." Her heart contended with her resolve, fighting every move that took her away from him. "We've got to stay on course now if we want to find out what's going on."

"You're right," he said, bitterly disappointed in himself for not saying how he felt. But how he felt was confused and how she felt was unknown, so he dared not throw himself at her like a reckless teenager. He wasn't strong enough to take her rebuke.

"I'll be just fine."

"I'm coming to town as soon as the cops leave here," he declared.

"I'd like that, David."

"All right." He dropped his hands then, breaking the contact between them as if snapping a brittle stick. "Are you sure no one will question your being there on a holiday?"

"No. I'm quite a dedicated little assistant." She laughed. "It isn't the first holiday I've gone in to finish something up."

"Don't do anything to make this visit look suspicious, and don't stay any longer than you have to."

"I won't. Now I'd better go before it gets any later."

"Let me take your bag to the car," he said, and accepted it from her. Then he stood back to allow her to pass, wishing that he had the gall just to grab her and kiss her. But he did nothing but follow her down the hall with her bag.

"Drive carefully now, dear." Connie greeted her with manufactured warmth in the salon, taking her hand in both of hers and shaking it. "Traffic should be light now. You made a wise choice in leaving early."

"Yes," Nicole said, returning her smile with all the warmth she could muster. "I felt it was time I got going anyway."

"You are a rare person then, aren't you? Most people just don't know when to leave."

"I think maybe Nicole should ditch that job of hers and cruise to Australia with us," David said suddenly. He'd taken note of the tone of Connie's voice and the slant of her words and hadn't liked the none-too-subtle rudeness. It made him feel defensive about Nicole and want to do something to crack Connie's composure. "Would you like that, Nicole?"

"When do we leave?" she asked with a laugh.

"You'd be bored to tears," Connie said, missing the joking tone in David's voice. "Unless you can cook, of course."

"I'm sure you wouldn't like my cooking, dear," she replied, matching the other woman's tone. "I'll see you later, David," she added, turning away from the scowling blonde.

"As soon as the detective is finished," he promised. "I've got your address."

"Good. I won't be at the office long. I'll take that," she said, reaching for the bag. "You don't need to come out with me. 'Bye."

"Goodbye." David raised his hand in a halfhearted wave and stood watching as she strode resolutely to the door and out across the deck. *Why couldn't you open your mouth, fool? Don't be so afraid of being turned down or you'll never know how she feels about you.* And all he could do now was watch her walking out to her car with sour dissatisfaction knotting his stomach.

"Why are you going to town?" Connie spoke softly, though a hint of anxiety crept into her voice as she approached him.

"Some business with Clint," he explained. "And I'm going to take Nicole out to dinner." Then he turned toward her and asked firmly, "What did you think of her?"

"Her? I . . . well, I liked her, of course. She's not much like Katharine, though."

"Yes, but you mentioned that before," he snapped. "But then it would be pure foolishness for me to go looking for someone exactly like Katharine, wouldn't it?"

"I suppose so," she said, backing away from the fight inherent in his voice. "I had planned to go to the city myself. Is it wise to leave the boat unattended with those broken windows?"

"We've done it before." His head was aching, and he wasn't up to dealing with Connie's feelings about Nicole just then. "I'm going to lie down for awhile before the police come. Call me when they get here, won't you?"

He walked away, chiding himself for not seeing what had always been there before him. When Nicole had said Connie was jealous of her, he hadn't believed it. But she had no other reason for being so rude just then. No reason at all.

He had dated Connie once, long ago, but it had been more a case of mutual need for a companion at a scientific banquet than a date. They'd gotten along quite well, but there had been nothing romantic about the evening. He'd met Katharine, her older sister, when he dropped her off at her home and from then on he was at the house constantly. It had been very easy to carry on a friendship with Connie while dating Katharine, since they were in the same field, and he never imagined she might have grown to feel something more than friendship for him. Apparently, she had. Perhaps he should have wondered why she was so eager to help him with his work on the *Crab*, since it was more a question of mechanics than her field of biology, but he didn't. He'd merely been grateful for the help. He returned to his cabin wondering how long she had cared for him and feeling somewhat sad that he could not reciprocate. It was partly his own fault for keeping her so busy with their work, he could see that now. He'd have to find excuses to get her off the ship more often.

NICOLE HAD ALWAYS rather liked going in to the office on weekends when the rooms were all dark and filled with silence. It was much like the empty halls of the high school where her mother had taught English. Occasionally on weekends she would take her young daughter in to finish some work, and the long, silent corridors that echoed with only her footsteps always gave Nicole a calm and secure feeling. She didn't mind working late or on weekends because she was able to come full circle to that early comfort in the empty halls of Gilbert, Forrester and Dean.

This Labor Day Monday was different, however, and she felt it as soon as she boarded the elevator. The building felt like a mausoleum or a cave, growing ever darker as she moved up within it. The hall leading to the law offices held a malevolent hum of evil that seemed to emanate from the walls to fill Nicole's ears. Today, the office was a bad place, the scene of evil deeds, and she was walking into the center of it.

Her hand was trembling slightly when she slipped the key into the lock of the dark wood door to the reception office. Inside, it was the same paneled waiting room, perhaps a bit stodgy in its lawyerly look, but well in keeping with the nature of the small but well-recommended firm. For the first time, she realized that the reception office had no windows and was lit only by what daylight filtered down the corridor. Nicole switched on the lights and then walked slowly toward the dark-stained door of her own office, feeling that she was approaching oblivion.

It was immeasurably hard to turn the knob but she did it and stepped in to snap the lights on with an urgent jab of her hand. Nothing. The office was as she remembered it, her chair pushed back against the wall below the window, her plants in need of water and her nameplate in place. Everything was as it should be, but that didn't push back the dread she felt of being alone there. She wanted to turn and run.

Quickly, she moved first to the file cabinets in her outer office and found the folders beginning with P.

Philips. She laid the folder out on her desk and sat down to study the papers inside it. She had vague memories of the agreements, of which there were many. Robert Philips moved in and out of business arrangements as most men would change shirts, and while he didn't always show a profit, he never lost money for himself.

She couldn't see any mention of Jerry Brunsvold on any past or current deals, but that didn't mean he wasn't involved. She felt that it would have been something fairly recent or she would have known about his involvement by now. Clint Forrester wasn't a very methodical man, and he did at times forget to give her updated information on various contracts. And then there were Robert Philips's business habits to deal with. The man bought and sold companies as fast as the law would allow, sometimes signing ownership away the same day he'd accepted it. He might very well have hooked Jerry without advising Clint that he'd obtained another partner. That information would come in when it was time to dun the scientist for his share of accounts payable.

Still, there was nothing, and she put the file away feeling sick at the thought of staying there any longer. The next place to look was Clint's office, and Lord only knows where he might have the information squirreled away. On impulse, she removed the cover from her typewriter and fed a sheet of paper into it. It wouldn't look odd for her to be here if she appeared to be typing something. Then she stood and walked across to Clint's office door.

She touched the knob of the door.

Clint's desk chair was turned half away from the door, allowing only a profile view of the person seated there, very still and with his head cocked back, mouth gaping open. Flowing into the room, not walking but moving as though on a conveyor belt, Nicole's point of view was carried around to face the man, until she was staring in horror at the blood staining his shirt and at his glazed sightless eyes. Her breath caught in her throat, the air clotting as she tried to take it in. It was David Germaine in the chair, incongruously dressed in a dark suit and tie with a white shirt beneath it. He'd been shot once in the chest. Blood had come into his mouth. David, staring dumbly at the ceiling above Nicole's head, his hands clenched on the arms of Clint's desk chair, the knuckles taut and white.

And Nicole released the knob, gasping to breathe.

David is on the boat. David doesn't wear suits. David wouldn't be at Clint's desk. She gave herself a thousand reasons why the vision was wrong, but it still struck at her heart with immense power, as if he were actually dead. And David would die if she didn't find out who wanted to kill him. That was the point of everything, anyway. No matter why it was happening, from the first dream to this most recent vision, the message was to stop David from being killed.

And, if she imagined David being dead in Clint's office, she could draw the conclusion that she'd been right about there being important information there. That's the way things had worked so far. The dreams and visions didn't appear to be literally correct, but subject to interpretation.

But, to get at the information, she had to go into that office.

"Go on," she said, settling herself with the comforting sound of her own voice. "Its only a lawyer's office. He's not even a criminal lawyer."

Smiling, she grasped the knob and turned it.

And she stepped into yet another perfectly empty and normal office. The chair was empty and drawn up tightly to the desk. Everything was just as it should be. But the air still seemed thick and hot and filled with evil. And she still wanted to finish her business and get out as fast as possible.

Clint's files didn't have much to add to the Philips financial history. He was trying to put together a deal at the moment, however, and it looked interesting. In fact, the preliminary papers in Clint's file, which hadn't progressed to the point where they'd taken them out for her to put into their final form, indicated that his new venture was something far different from those in the past. This deal didn't appear to be another of his small-time buy-and-break-up ventures, but an honest attempt to build something out of several small companies. There wasn't much besides notes in Clint's long scrawl, but she couldn't see anything fishy in this deal so far.

It wasn't what she wanted at all. And Jerry Brunsvold wasn't mentioned anywhere.

She sat behind the desk and opened one of the drawers. Legal pads and papers and junk. The contents of the next drawer were of a similar nature. She was betraying the basic trust between her and her employer, but decided that she would just live with the guilt. He'd given her free access to everything with the implicit understanding that she wouldn't go into anything that didn't concern her. A legal assistant's integrity is every bit as important as that of the lawyer she works for, since she eventually comes to know every confidence he's been given, and she had been proud of never betraying the trust of her job. But now she'd shattered her own honor by digging through his desk and would gladly do it over and over again if it would protect David Germaine.

The bottom drawer on the right side held a box a bit larger than a cigar box, made of fine wood. She released the hook and lifted the lid, staring in shock at the contents. It was a gun case. Inside was a snub-nosed revolver with an ominous blue-black sheen. She hadn't realized that Clint had a gun. Hurriedly, she snapped the case shut and closed the drawer. Just looking at the weapon made her feel sick.

Perspiration was gathering on her brow as she opened the large drawer on the bottom left side of the desk. More file folders, as she'd known. Aaronson, Baker, Germaine, Morrison. Germaine? She lifted the file part way up to spread it open for a peek inside. It was the paperwork she'd prepared for the donation of the *Crab*. It looked as though all the copies were there.

Why on earth was that still in his desk drawer?

One click from the outer office sent her into motion, shoving the file back down and slamming the drawer even as she stood and returned the chair to its place at the desk. She was out of the office and behind her own desk before she'd even thought of what she was doing. She began to type a letter, randomly picking a client from memory and making it up as she kept a watchful eye on her office door.

When the knob turned, she stopped typing.

"Hello?" Her voice rasped tightly through her lips, and she cleared her throat, wishing she had agreed to wait for David.

"Are you alone?" It was David himself who pushed the door open cautiously and spoke in a low, careful voice.

"Oh, David!" Nicole jumped up and ran to throw her arms around him, trembling with relief. "I'm so glad you're here!"

"I am, too, now," he laughed, hugging her in return. "What's wrong?"

"The whole place feels wrong today! Can you feel it?" She let him go then, regaining her composure. But she left one hand resting gently on his arm, keeping contact with the special sensation of calm his touch gave her. "It's spooky."

"I always feel spooked when I'm some place where I'm not supposed to be," he said. "So I guess I don't know if it feels spooky here or not."

"And I had a nasty vision a few minutes ago, too," she continued. "I imagined you sitting dead in Clint's office. It was horrible."

"Me? Dead?" He glanced at the lawyer's door. "Okay, now I'm spooked."

"Let's get out of here," she said, beginning to walk around to turn off her typewriter. But another sound stopped her short. The outer door was opening! "Hurry, get under my desk!" she commanded.

"I won't fit under there!" he whispered frantically as he circled the desk and knelt down.

"Just get in! I don't have a closet! And keep your feet on my side so they don't show."

He made a ridiculous sight as he doubled over and slipped backward into the knee well with his head jammed between the bottom of the drawer and his knees. Nicole didn't take time to laugh at the sight, but shushed him when he tried to protest again.

Clint Forrester came down the hall toward the door David had left open just as Nicole sat down again, sliding her knees in beside David and leaning forward slightly to look as though she was in all the way.

"Another holiday shot to hell, huh?" Clint called out as he walked through the door. "Both of us wasting this beautiful day in a stuffy office."

"It looks like it," she said cheerfully. David's head was pressed against her left thigh, and she could tell from his small movements that he was struggling to keep from laughing. "Why are you here?"

"I did my best to avoid it by taking a briefcase full of work home with me, but of course I had to forget something."

"Isn't that always the way it goes?"

David slipped beside her, slid his left arm around her knees and clutched at her leg to hold his position.

"I thought you were on the *Katharine* this weekend." Clint stood two feet in front of the desk, shaking his key ring casually in one hand and staring at her as if she were a witness on the stand. "What'd Germaine do, throw you overboard?"

"No, I wanted to beat the traffic, so I came in early."

"That was a practical idea." He nodded. "So you figured you'd get a jump on the week."

"I'm almost done."

"Good." He paused, pursing his lips as if experiencing a new and somewhat sour taste. "About Germaine..." he said.

"Yes?"

"Well, I don't presume to tell you your business. But, well, he is a client, after all." One eyebrow rose. "Not a major client, so I suppose it's no problem. But you never know."

"I'll be careful not to compromise the firm," she said, thinking of how she was already compromising it in the name of David Germaine.

"Oh, don't worry about it," he said. "I'm just being an old worrywart. He's probably a pretty good match for you, for that matter. Both of you are such practical, level-headed people. But I hope you two don't hit it off *too* well."

"Why not?" David was clutching her legs with both hands now as his feet fought to maintain a grip on the smooth office carpet without making any noise. The pressure of his hands on her thighs sent electric tingles through Nicole's body, and she felt certain she must be blushing.

"Because if you get serious about him, he'll steal you away to go sailing around the world or some damn thing. I'll have to hire a new assistant. That's why." He smiled then, starting toward his office. "Hard to find people who'll work on holidays."

"Clint?" As much as she wanted to extricate them from their predicament, she had to ask her question while he was there and in a good mood. "Is Robert Philips putting together some new deal?"

David jerked one foot up beneath him, rattling his back against the drawer slightly, and Nicole adjusted herself quickly to account for the sound.

"Philips?" Clint regarded her cautiously. "He might be. Why?"

"Jerry Brunsvold asked yesterday."

"Brunsvold? What did he want to know?" He walked back toward her desk, coming toward the side this time.

"It sounded like he was thinking of investing," she said quickly. Nicole turned to keep facing him, pressing her knees against David's ribs. "He just asked what Philips was putting together."

"Robert may have approached him, I suppose," the lawyer mused. "But I doubt Brunsvold has any money to invest. Probably some dinky IRA somewhere but no real money."

"It sounded like he'd done business with him before." *Don't come any closer,* she prayed, taking note of the foot protruding from beneath the desk beside her chair.

"No, not him. Robert has been trying to get his cousin to invest for years but David is too smart for that."

"Why do you say that?" She'd never seen him in such a talkative mood about business matters before and had to take advantage of it.

"Come now, Nicole," the lawyer said, like a patient teacher. "What Robert Philips generally does with a company may be legal but it's hardly going to generate good publicity. David Germaine needs to maintain a good all-around reputation and stay away from corporate sharks. Mr. Philips, on the other hand, has been moving steadily up the food chain, and he hasn't continued to grow by worrying about what people think of him."

"That's not a very kind thing to say about a client, is it?" She hooked her foot around to tap at David's exposed foot. He took the hint and hopped it under the desk, increasing the warm pressure of his body against her hip and thigh.

"I'll let you in on a secret, Nicole," Clint said. "I have quite a few clients I don't care for personally. But Philips may be reforming on us. What he's trying to do now should have some good results. As far as Brunsvold is concerned, however," he continued, turning back to his office, "he should leave what little money he has in his mattress, or wherever he keeps it. Philips needs major cash to pull the deal off and can't mess with small money."

"He needs David's investment?"

"Yes, I'd say he's desperate for it. Money is tight right now." He opened his door. "Run out and have some fun now, all right? You're making me feel like a slave driver." Then he entered the office and closed the door behind him.

"Let me out!" David whispered urgently from beneath the desk.

Nicole wheeled her chair back quickly and stood up. "Sorry," she whispered. "Let's go."

He crawled out from under the desk and rose painfully. But Nicole didn't give him time to stretch, turning off her typewriter and shooing him out of the office ahead of her. Only when they were safely in the hall and waiting for the elevator did she allow either one of them to stop for breath.

"Not that I didn't enjoy my visit to your office," he said, smiling impishly, "but was it really necessary for me to hide? And, having hidden, did you two have to spend all that time gossiping?"

"Yes, it was. I didn't know who it was," she said. "And he wouldn't have spoken so freely if he'd known you were there, would he?"

"No, I suppose not." He laughed as they stepped into the elevator. "I hope you forgive my hands, but those tight jeans don't give a guy much to grab on to."

"I didn't mind the hands at all," she said, allowing a bit of her honest feelings to slip into her words. "I should get you under a desk again sometime."

The elevator doors closed slowly, sealing them away from discovery as the car carried them down to safety.

After the elevator began its descent, a figure emerged from the shadowed end of the hall. The person moved quietly, hands hidden in the pockets of his brown raincoat. Without pause he opened the door to Gilbert, Forrester and Dean and stepped inside, pulling the door shut quietly behind him. There was a small click as the lock slid home.

It was several moments before another sound could be heard in the hallway. It was a single muffled burst like a balloon popping, or perhaps a firecracker. Moments later, the figure emerged from the office carrying a manila file folder. He switched off the lights behind him and hurried back to the shadows near the stairwell.

The hall would remain quiet and empty until morning.

Chapter Ten

"I'm not sure about Jerry Brunsvold's involvement anymore," Nicole told him as they walked down the avenue away from the office building. "There's no mention of him anywhere in the files."

"I never could believe Jerry was out to get me," David said. Emboldened by their recent adventure and her words at the elevator, he slipped his arm around her shoulder. "But that leaves us with no suspect at all, doesn't it?"

"Maybe I was entirely wrong about Robert Philips being involved." Nicole was discouraged by the visit to the office. It had seemed like a simple matter to tie Jerry Brunsvold to one of Philips's quick-sale deals and obtain a motive. Now Jerry was all but ruled out and they were no closer to knowing what was going on than they had been before. "It wasn't his face I remembered from the dream, anyway," she admitted.

"But that doesn't necessarily mean anything," David advised, hoping to buoy her obviously flagging spirits. "It was probably a kind of generic dream-face."

"I saw your face pretty clearly, though," she said. "I would think that the other man's face was just as specific."

"I don't know what to say, Nicole." They stopped at the corner, his arm still comfortably around her shoulder as they spoke. "The fact is, it still all seems like little more than a bad dream. People don't really see the future, do they?"

"I thought you believed me."

"I do. We had the same dream, after all. At least, it seems that way. And we both have wristwatches that chose the same day and time to stop. I don't have any explanation for that phenomenon," he said, laughing in wonder. "But does it mean anything?"

"Yes," she replied, turning within his arm to grasp his shoulder and look up into his patient eyes. "I can feel that it means something. Time is slipping away and every second that passes makes the feelings stronger. If we don't find out what is happening and put a stop to it, something very bad will happen at noon on Wednesday."

"Damn," he said simply. Looking at the people walking around them on the street, he felt as if they were prisoners within the busy movement of humanity. Every plan, every simple joy was on hold until they could come to grips with the strange events tearing at their lives. In any normal life he would take this fine woman to dinner and perhaps a show. He would be spending his time getting to know her. But now his priority was to chase a dream. And he was living this strange life in fear of the time on a watch face.

But in any normal life, the galley on his boat wouldn't be a blackened mess. And in light of that his trepidation about the wristwatch seemed quite prudent.

"Are you hungry?" There were still some normal human activities to attend to, and he was suddenly aware that he hadn't eaten anything since a light breakfast before Nicole left. "I could really use a pastrami on rye. Yes, I think that's exactly what I need right now. What about you?''

"Oh, that sounds like heaven," she agreed. "I know a great place just a couple blocks over. Come on."

Stepping away, she slipped her hand into his and led him to the corner and across the intersection in the direction of Hoffman's Deli.

"It's a great place," she was telling him as they walked hand in hand along the street. "Hoffman's. I'd go there every noon if I could stand the calories."

"Not another dieter!" he lamented.

"My mother always told me, 'You've got to watch what you eat so that it doesn't eat you.'" She was laughing now, happy to be holding his hand and sharing something other than fear with him. Happy to be alive on such a beautiful day.

"That doesn't make much sense," he said, grinning.

"Not if you're going to insist on being logical, it doesn't. You've got to allow for some poetic license."

"I guess I can give your mom some leeway. Where does she live?" They'd reached the corner across from the deli and were waiting for the light to change.

"A small town near Boston. My dad was a lawyer. Mom taught English."

"Retired?"

"Yes. A year now."

The light changed and they crossed, still hand in hand.

"And you have a sister in college?"

"Yes, studying communications upstate. You don't have any brothers or sisters?" She spoke easily, though a dark feeling welled within her as they stepped onto the sidewalk in front of the deli.

"No, I'm the only one. I gave up wishing for a brother long ago." He stopped then, noticing that Nicole had slowed her pace just as they were approaching the door. The peculiar look of shock and confusion growing on her clear, intelligent features alarmed him. "What's wrong?"

"Here." She whispered it, her eyes moving quickly to take in the ordinary doorway and the people moving by. "Right here."

"Here what?" He didn't see anything abnormal about the place. "What do you mean?"

"This is it." She stepped forward then, a couple of feet in front of the door to Hoffman's. Suddenly she dropped to one knee on the sidewalk, feeling the pavement with her hand. She could remember it being wet, hard, and cold. She could remember the door against her back just before she fell. Falling. Yes, with a tightening feeling in her chest like a band of steel being drawn in to shorten her breathing.

Kneeling here now, she felt the same constriction and had to fight for breath. It was here! This was the dream place! This was where— Where what?

She looked up at David in alarm, her face twisted with fear. "This is the place," she said. He was above her, his face shadowed against the strip of sky between the buildings. Above her just as he would be on Wednesday at twelve-forty-one. And the look on his face right now was a fainter image of the horrified concern that she would see in his eyes on Wednesday. This Wednesday, the day she would be killed! "My God!"

"What is it?"

But she'd stood up abruptly, staggering away from him along the avenue and gaining momentum until she was running headlong through the holiday shoppers.

"Wait!" David ran after her, sprinting to close the distance she'd put between them during his surprised immobility. "Nicole!"

She didn't hear him calling. All she could hear was the
gun firing again and again. That was the place. She had to
get away from it, run as far and as fast as she could from
everything associated with that place, that horrible section of pavement.

"Hold on." David caught her just before the next street
corner, grasping her shoulder and spinning her to contain
her within his arms. "Calm down, Nicole. You're all right.
Nothing is happening. What was it?"

"That's the place in the dream!" Her voice sounded
strident and harsh as she heard herself blurting out the
words. It was the voice of a crazy woman. It couldn't be
hers. And only then did she become fully aware that she'd
run away from the deli, away from David.

"The deli?" He didn't know how to alleviate the fear in
her eyes. He didn't know what she was seeing, only that it
frightened her horribly. He only knew that he wanted to
smother that fright and keep her feeling safe in any way
possible. "That's where the gunman was?"

"Yes." Nicole swallowed hard, coming to herself once
more.

She felt nearly as foolish now as she had been frightened then. To have run like a chicken with its head cut off
was inexcusable. It was pointless to give in to fear. But the
realization had struck so suddenly that she'd been unable
to keep herself from running from danger. But the danger
was lurking in time, not in a place, and she wouldn't avoid
it by running.

"Oh, David, it was so strange." She let him gather her
close against his chest as he had the other night on the ship.
Let the passersby think what they will, she needed the
comfort of his arms just then, for she'd just received a
clear and certain confirmation of her own death. "I saw
blood on the sidewalk. *My* blood! And you were standing

over me just as you will be on Wednesday. You were right, David. I'm the one who will be shot. Blood on my lips, you said. Yes, and blood on the sidewalk. So much blood!''

"Quiet now, Nicole. You're safe, and you are going to stay that way. I won't let anything happen to you, dear Nicole. I'm here for you.''

Yes, he was there for her, but she couldn't help feeling that there was an element of fate in this that couldn't be held back by his strong determined arms. As with the spilled wine at the gallery opening, they might be able to alter events but they couldn't avoid them. She would never avoid her fate.

Central Park seemed worlds away from the city surrounding it. The trees swayed in the late afternoon breeze, sighing out their soothing song in the warm air as Nicole and David sat on a bench and dined on hot dogs and sodas. She felt much better here, away from all the buildings and sidewalks that reminded her of the deli and its horrible piece of sidewalk. Happy endings seemed possible here, amid nature.

"What did you say about some letters in Forrester's desk?" David leaned back on the bench and rested his arm behind Nicole's shoulders.

"The papers he dictated to send to Woods Hole," she told him. She finished the last of her soda and placed the can beside her on the bench, leaning comfortably against David's arm. So what was the point caring for this man, if she was about to lose her life? "I made three copies and there are still three copies in the file I found in the drawer."

"He just hasn't sent them out yet," David said.

"Apparently not. But why not? I was so wrapped up in my strange situation that I didn't notice at the time that he never mailed anything. He's usually more efficient than that. Could he be trying to delay the deal for some reason?''

"Why bother? He can't gain anything by that.'' He found himself focusing on her face with rapt attention, watching the way her eyes crinkled at the corners when she pondered new ideas and how her smile produced a delicate dimple at the corner of her mouth. Hers was a beautiful profile.

"Are you listening?'' She turned to catch him watching her, and a pink flush of embarrassment tinted her cheeks.

"I'm sorry,'' he said. "I'm afraid I was staring.'' And he wasn't at all abashed about admitting it to her. The feelings that he'd been fighting to hide didn't seem so surprising anymore. It felt natural to be enthralled by her lovely face. "You were saying that Clint may be in on one of the deals?''

"Yes, though I don't know what he would put up to get in.''

"Doesn't he have money?''

"Yes, in stocks and annuities. But not as much as he did before the crash. He's still leery about eighty-seven. The stock market may have recovered, but a lot of small investors haven't.''

"And he might be buying his way into one of Robert's ventures by offering to secure the *Crab* as his buy-in.'' David nodded, seeing the logic in that idea.

"I suppose so.'' Now she was staring, coyly enjoying the thoughtful expression that graced his strong face with such gentle concentration. "Unfortunately, that doesn't account for the explosion in the galley. Clint is no murderer, nor would he cooperate in murder. I wouldn't go so far as to say that he wouldn't do something to steal the robot away from you, however. But I can't see how any of it would make any difference. I mean, he can't actually take it away or give it to Robert."

"It makes sense, though." *Yes,* he thought, *perfect sense.* But not enough sense to justify what was happening.

"How? If he stops your donation, all that happens is that you retain ownership of the device."

"No, Albany Manufacturing retains ownership," he told her. "Remember? Robert has been drooling over Albany Manufacturing for the past month. They built the *Crab* to my specifications, and they hold the patents to all the new hardware that we devised for it."

"So if Robert Philips buys the company, he would be buying the *Crab* as well!" Now there was a piece of information that fit all the facts quite nicely. Maybe they'd made some progress today after all.

"That's right."

"Can Robert be so sure of convincing you not to give it to the Institute that he'd have Clint delay the donation?"

"He doesn't have to buy the company if I'm dead," David said, seriously. "The company would revert to family ownership in that case."

"Right over to cousin Robert."

"You got it."

"But would he rig a gas line to ensure inheriting the company? Just how bloodthirsty is your cousin?"

"I wouldn't have thought he was that bloodthirsty," David admitted. "But I've changed my thinking about a lot of things lately."

"So maybe we still have a suspect after all."

"I hope so. But I wish we could come up with a suspect who wasn't either a friend or relative of mine. We've never been very close, but I still don't want to see Robert guilty of anything like murder." David smiled ruefully, thinking how normal all of his interpersonal relationships had seemed before he'd been forced to examine them. "But," he added, tightening his arm around her shoulders protectively, "I'll be more than happy to throw the bunch of them in jail if it will get us through Wednesday intact."

"Well, thank you very much," she said with a laugh. Then she stated more seriously, "But it wasn't Robert Philips that I remember from the dream. It was a small man with a thin face."

"And Robert is a bit stout and all of six feet tall. But then he wouldn't do it in person, anyway. He'd hire someone." David pursed his lips thoughtfully, trying to figure out some way to find the gunman. Proving his cousin was behind something like this might take too long. "How much do you remember of the dream? Anything more about the man?"

"Just pieces. More now, though." And she shuddered at the memory of the feeling that had stabbed through her outside Hoffman's. "You were opening the door. We were talking. A guy in a raincoat and dark glasses came up to us and, and . . ." And what? How do events progress between his arrival and her lying on the pavement? *Come on, Nicole, remember!* "And he was pointing his gun and firing. I reflexively reached for you. The bullets got me," she said with growing conviction. "I fall back against the open door and slide to sit on the pavement. He—he runs then. Yes, and you reach for me and help me to the sidewalk. That's the part I most remember, the part where I'm lying on my back looking up at you."

"That's enough." David placed one hand softly against her cheek, tilting her face to look at him. God, how that look of terror in her eyes frightened him. "It's still just a dream, no matter what. And you aren't the actual target."

"But he's going to kill me. No matter who he wants to kill, I'm the one who will get shot!" Nicole felt as though every event happening in the world right then was occurring simply to put everything in order for her murder. It was fate, inevitable and compelling. Things happen because they are ordained to happen, not because we will them, and it was only some kind of cosmic joke that was allowing her to glimpse her own end in this way.

"But it's not going to happen," David said, pulling her head in against his chest and smoothing his hand down over her hair. He wasn't sure that anything could be done, but the least he could do was try to alleviate her fears a bit. "We're going to stop it from happening," he told her, praying that there was some way he could be sure.

"I don't want to die." She blinked against the tears welling in her eyes. Surely she was stronger than this, but the tension had been so great for so long that it finally demanded release in the small trickle that she allowed to escape.

"You aren't going to die," he said, with as much conviction as he could muster. "You're not going to die."

But the lowering sun didn't seem quite as warm as it had been, the sky not so blue. And Nicole could see only one outcome unless they made some progress fast.

Of course, she could run. Her best defense might be to put some distance between herself and David Germaine. But that wasn't a solution that she could allow herself to seek. Who was to say that the same outcome would not happen in another city? Maybe it would be another gunman for another reason. Perhaps she was simply fated to die, and that was the most horrible of the horrible thoughts assailing her. At least until she knew for certain, she should try to piece together the puzzle, identify the gunman, and stop that nightmarish finale from happening.

She raised her head to look into David's eyes, wondering how much of the compassion there was pity and male protectiveness. Would that feeling be there if circumstances were different?

"Nicole, I don't want you to worry about anything," David said, before she could find a voice for her feelings. He spoke carefully, trying to find the proper way to relate his suspicions without causing her any more anxiety. "But there are some facts we'll have to face. We understand the nature of what you've been going through now. And I think I understand why the warning you were given showed you in the victim's role rather than me."

"Why? I'd think that my getting shot would be more a case of being in the wrong place at the wrong time than the result of any actual desire to harm me." And now that she'd calmed down, letting her fear be blanketed in the warmth she felt for David, she realized that was exactly the case. No one wanted her to die. He was right in saying that she would be safe.

"No, I don't think so," he said, solemnly. "I think the visions you had were meant to allow you to save me. I don't know how ESP works or how your mind picked up on a threat to a stranger's life, but I do know now why you saw your own death so specifically. I've been alerted to the threat, but in alerting me you put yourself on the scene when their first attempt went awry. Now you're a witness. If I am killed—no matter how accidental the death might look—you are there to discredit the accident. You are a witness who must be taken care of in order for the plan to work. You're a target, too. Your mind would quite reasonably warn you of danger to your own life before warning about mine. And it was that danger that compelled you to get yourself into this mess by unwittingly joining yourself to my fate."

"But I saw the shooting before I ever met you. I wasn't in danger then," she pointed out. There was something missing in that explanation, a vital point that should clear everything up. "The dream isn't a gift of prophecy except in that it would seem to be a self-fulfilling one. I felt that there might be something on your ship or in your life that would explain the dream and visions. I wouldn't have spoken to you in the office or accepted your invitation except for the urgency of that dream."

"But are you sure I wouldn't have invited you anyway?" He smiled, thinking how odd this conversation might seem to anyone eavesdropping. "Perhaps the dream was never meant to warn me, but you. Perhaps I would have invited you and you would have accepted without any prompting, and the dream was a vision to alert you to the danger you would be putting yourself in."

"I suppose it doesn't matter whether we put the cart before or after the horse, does it? You're obviously right about my being included in it now, so we've got to get to the bottom of it for both our sakes. God, how I wish we could tell the police about it!"

"So do I." He smiled. "I can just imagine the greeting we'd get if we tried to tell your story to the police."

"What did the detective say this morning when you told him about the explosion? Did they come to collect evidence?"

"I didn't tell them," he said, hesitantly. "I don't know why, either. But I felt that I had to stick to the explanation that it was an accidental blast and not say anything about the light bulb or the line being unscrewed."

"But that is concrete evidence, David!" she cried out in alarm. "That's the only thing you could have told them to get it on record that someone is trying to kill you."

"I know. But they would have wanted to search the whole boat and get my full statement and all that other cop stuff. I couldn't sit still for it. Not today. I had to come here to find you, Nicole. It wasn't right for you to be risking your life alone."

"I told you I'd be fine," she said, equally warmed and angered by his manly concern for her. "There was nothing for me to worry about at the office."

"There's no way you can be sure of that," he pointed out. "Besides, whoever rigged the galley must have sneaked on board in the middle of the night to set it up. And my cousin wouldn't hire anyone sloppy enough to leave clues. No, the afternoon would have been wasted. I'd rather leave it as it is. We can always present our evidence later."

"You should have told them now." But she was pleased at the choice he'd made. And, despite her assurances to the contrary, she had been deathly afraid when she went into the office. Seeing him at the door was exactly what she needed right then.

"It's done, anyway. And now we'd better think of what comes next. Time is running out."

David stood then, a light breeze ruffling his sandy hair. He extended one hand to Nicole, bringing her up and back into the protection of his circling arm as they walked out of the park and back toward their cars.

As they walked along the avenue one careful block over from the deli, Nicole couldn't help being encouraged by his closeness. He did harbor some feeling for her, and no matter how closely he might guard it the affection was obvious in little things like the arm around her shoulder. He must feel something to be so unwilling to allow space between them.

It was several blocks from Central Park to Nicole's office building, and they walked slowly as they searched for a way to get proof of the plot that could be presented to the authorities. But, as they walked, Nicole noticed a car double-parked midway along the block. It was a red Dodge, an Omni. It seemed strangely familiar, but she hadn't quite decided where she'd seen it before when they passed it and she let it slip her mind.

The car, however, wasn't so easily forgotten, for it was back parked at the curb on the next block after they crossed the intersection. And then she remembered that she'd seen that red car waiting two blocks back. That couldn't be coincidental. The driver of the car was keeping track of their movements!

It wasn't until they'd reached the next intersection that the driver tired of watching them and moved to confirm her suspicions. He was at the corner waiting to make a right turn as the signal changed to allow pedestrians to cross. Nicole and David entered the crosswalk alone.

Just as they reached the center of the street, the red Dodge roared into action and squealed around the corner directly at the two people standing in its path!

Chapter Eleven

"Look out!" Nicole had been watching the car from the corner of her eye, or she might not have seen the movement in time. But the driver jerked the wheel sharply to the right and the car responded a split second later, giving her enough warning to push David ahead as she ran.

The car passed inches behind them, the breath of its passing fanning their backs as they leaped for the safety of the far corner. They stood gasping for breath and straining for a glimpse of the offending vehicle's license plate.

"ZPT-946," David said, grasping Nicole's shoulders as much for support as to be sure of her safety. "Is that what you got?"

"Yes. A New Jersey plate." That was all she could say at the moment with excitement surging through her as she fought for breath.

"Damn, that was close." David turned, looking thankfully into her eyes. "You're very observant."

"I thought he might be following us," she said. "But I wasn't sure."

"Following?" A small, thoughtful smile spread across his lips, and his gaze sharpened.

"Yes, except that he seemed to be always in front of us. Not behind. Always double-parked about midblock as we walked."

"That's it, then. He was watching for a street when we were crossing alone to make a try for us." He grasped both her shoulders in his hands and pulled her close in an exuberant embrace. "But he missed us, and now we've got his license number. Let's go find a cop."

"Wait a second," she cautioned. "What are we supposed to tell them? We can't prove that he was following us."

"We don't have to. We report him as a reckless driver," he laughed. "He did almost run us down. And whether it was intentional or not doesn't matter."

"And they'll find out who the car belongs to."

"Right."

"Good plan, Sherlock," she said, happily. "Where's the nearest police station?"

"THAT SHOULD COVER IT," the young officer told them as he took the carbon pack form out of the typewriter. "Reckless endangerment. Jersey plates. We should be able to get a handle on this soon enough."

"How soon?" Nicole asked impatiently.

"We'll have New Jersey DMV run the plates and issue a warrant. It depends on how easy it is to find the guy."

"But how soon?" David echoed Nicole's impatient tone, tapping one finger on the edge of the worn old desk the officer sat behind.

"I don't know." He shrugged. "A couple days, I suppose."

"Is there any way we can find out who was driving sooner than that?" Nicole's heart sank at the thought of so much time passing before the authorities could find the man behind the wheel.

"It isn't customary to contact you with the driver's name until it goes to court." The officer wetted his lips, looking at them with renewed interest. "Is there some reason you need that information? Do you think you might know who was driving?"

"No, not at all," David said, quickly. "But he came damn close to cutting us off at the knees, and we're more than a little bit interested in him."

"I understand that." He stood up. "But it isn't a good idea to dwell on things like this. The city is filled with bad drivers—most of them in cabs." He laughed, walking around to escort them from the precinct house.

"I suppose you're right," Nicole said conversationally. "He probably didn't even see us. But that doesn't mean he should get off scot-free, either."

"He won't. You two take care now," he told them as he stopped at the booking desk. "Look both ways before crossing."

"Right," David said, sourly. He took Nicole by the elbow and led her onto the street. The muted orange of the sunset seemed such a malicious color now, the streets filled with unseen enemies. "That did us no good," he said. "A couple of days may seem like quick work to them, but it won't get us information in time to help."

"Let's not get discouraged," Nicole advised, slipping her arm around his waist. "I have a friend who might be able to help us faster than that. We'll go to my place and call her."

"Great! Say, I've got a rental car parked by your building. Did you drive?"

"Yes, straight from the boat. You follow me and park it in the garage near my apartment. You don't want to risk leaving it on the street."

"No, I guess not." They reached the crosswalk, both of them pausing for one extra look before stepping out with the other pedestrians. "Why do you have a car in the city?" he asked, as they walked along the street to her building.

"I'm not a native New Yorker," she said, explaining it succinctly. "It's foolish, really, since I don't use it in the city at all. Mostly I pay for garage space. But it does allow a certain amount of freedom when I want to get out of town. I'm not tied to the train schedules."

"That makes sense. I can never remember the schedule when we dock at Long Island, so I'm always stuck renting a car to get in and then paying to park it. I don't like being at the mercy of other people's schedules."

"Impatient fellow?"

"Maybe," he said, smiling. "I don't mind waiting for some things, but I can't abide standing on a platform waiting on a train."

"Here's my car." Nicole stopped at the Skylark parked at the curb. The meter had long expired, but there was no ticket adorning her windshield. Perhaps the generally lessened traffic of the holiday had slowed down the normally punctual traffic police as well.

"I'm at the end," he said, pointing down the block. "I'll be along in a second." He walked quickly along the street while Nicole went around to unlock her door, then he turned and called out, "Drive carefully, Nicole. Watch out for little red cars."

"I will." And she got behind the wheel smiling, warmed by his gentle concern and their ease together. This man was special, someone to hold on to if she could. But was there anything to hold on to? She felt there was, but could sense a certain reserve holding him back, something that kept him from opening up as she'd hoped he would. But it was all hoping at this point. The feelings she saw might be nothing more than concern for her in their strange predicament. She might be misreading everything and building her emotions on a foundation of sand. She just couldn't be sure of anything yet.

David followed her to her apartment, rerunning images of their near miss through his mind. Reckless drivers. Drunken drivers. Whether the incident was deliberate or not, the thought of Nicole crushed by a ton of steel sickened him, bringing back thoughts of another automobile that had shattered his life and stopped him from planning on the future. Death is so easy and so unexpected. Any mindless fool with a driver's license has the ability to alter countless lives with one unthinking act, and to entrust one's future happiness to the odds of chance destruction seemed utterly foolish to him.

So he drove on, cursing himself for a fool who could see the proper course to take but was unable to force himself to follow it. The feelings that had begun to thaw over the past couple of days had been chilled by the speeding car at the crosswalk. And no matter what he might know or feel, the memory of Katharine killed by random chance held his actions in check. Don't commit yourself to anything that can't be locked up safe and sound, don't trust your heart to anything as tenuous as life. Never claim as your own something that can be taken away so easily.

"HOME SWEET HOME." Nicole switched on the light and stepped in, motioning broadly for David to enter. "I think the place might even be fairly tidy, too."

Neither she nor Sara were compulsive housekeepers, but neither were they habitually messy, so she hadn't been worried about bringing David home on short notice. Then Nicole was suddenly shocked to realize that she hadn't had a man up in the two years Sara had roomed with her.

She did notice a musty odor on entering, however, but the rooms had been closed up a couple of days so that probably wasn't out of the ordinary.

"Nice place," David commented, stepping into the living room and looking around at the artwork adorning the walls, the simple furnishings and personal items placed about the room. "Homey."

"Sara provides the art," Nicole said. She walked past to the kitchen, switching on the light. "She works in a gallery, so I left that part of the decor to her good taste."

"Works in a gallery? What does she do, steal the paintings?" He joined her in the kitchen, feeling better now that they were off the street and in the relative safety of stone and steel.

"I don't ask," Nicole laughed. "Would you like coffee?"

"Yes. If you're going to have some, I will."

"I live on coffee." She rinsed out the carafe of the coffee maker and used it to fill the machine. Then she took the old grounds out and dumped them, wrinkling her nose at the dusty odor of the damp grounds.

"Where is your roommate?" David felt rather silly after he'd asked. It wasn't any of his concern where the other woman was or when she would be coming back, but he felt compelled to know.

"Home for the weekend," Nicole said, measuring out new coffee. "They just opened a new exhibit last Friday, and she's got a couple of days off. Back tomorrow sometime," she added, wondering if he might take that information as a hint. And wondering, also, if he should.

"Yes, you told me about the opening." He leaned against the counter and watched her prepare the coffee with sure movements of her lithe body. He wanted to touch her, to stroke his hand along her arm and twine his fingers into hers, wanted to feel her leaning back against his chest as her dark tresses tickled his cheek. But he merely stood there unable to find the words that might break his own reserve and allow him to discover if she might want the same. And to make the move without words was unthinkable, a breach of trust between them that he couldn't commit.

"Okay, as soon as I find my phone book, I'll call that friend." Nicole turned, catching the serious look in his eyes before he could cover it with a smile. "Is there something wrong?"

"No. I'm just concerned that your friend won't be any faster than the police. What does she do?"

"She works for Mr. Gilbert, another lawyer at the firm. He handles the criminal cases and presents the majority of the court cases. He's got contacts in the police department that she can get to without too many questions. I don't think it would be too out of line for her to run a license plate through the DMV."

"No, it shouldn't be," he agreed, watching her sorting through the phone books and papers stacked neatly in the corner of the counter by the refrigerator. "She won't be able to do it until morning, though, will she?"

"No, but she should have a name and address for us before noon." She found her spiral notebook of personal numbers and took it out. "Here we are."

"Good."

"I hope she's home." Nicole found the number and dialed quickly, aware of his eyes on her and the unaccustomed feeling of a man's presence in the apartment. It was a good feeling. The phone rang four times before it was answered.

"Hello?"

"Hi, Jane, it's Nicole."

"Oh, Nicole," the other woman cooed happily. "How was your big weekend? I heard about your invitation to visit Mr. Germaine on his ship. You did go, didn't you?"

"Yes, I went." Nicole smiled. Jane Lee was glad to see any sign of social activity on Nicole's part. "And that's why I'm calling now, in a way."

"About the visit? You know I'm always interested in getting the lowdown before it's been through the gossip mill. What's up?"

"It's more a professional matter than personal," Nicole said. She glanced at him and reddened, quickly repressing the feelings that poured over her. "David and I were in town this afternoon when we had a near miss in traffic. A red Dodge nearly ran us down in the crosswalk."

"Really, dear. My goodness, are you all right?" The motherly concern in the older woman's voice was a comfortable hedge against the memory of the event as Nicole related the story.

"Yes, we're fine," she assured her, glancing at David seated at the kitchen table. "But David thought he recognized the car. I said that you could check out the license plate for us and tell me who it belongs to. Can you do that?"

"Yes, I should say so. But why on earth does he need to know? If he knows the person, he should confront him in person."

"It's a bit complicated, I'm afraid." Nicole thought of improvising a reason for their interest, but realized that the truth was her best bet for plausibility. The truth as they believed it, that was. "It has to do with the robot submarine David is donating to the Woods Hole Oceanographic Institute. We're not sure, but it may be possible that someone is trying to stop him from giving the machine away."

"I hadn't heard about the donation," Jane said. "Is it one of Clint's matters?"

"Yes, that's why David was in the office last week. But there've been some threats issued since then, and it's just possible that someone is trying to take over the company that holds the patents on the robot. They might want to nudge David out of the way so they could finish their arrangements before the patents are signed over to Woods Hole."

"Gracious, do you really think so?"

"David does, and I don't doubt him. The car seemed to be quite intentionally aimed at us, Jane, and I can't see any other reason."

"Certainly I can check on it then, dear. Did you go to the police?"

"Yes, to report the incident, but we don't have any proof of it being deliberate. They won't tell us who the driver is until he's been found, and David would like to find out what's going on as soon as possible. How long would it take you to find out?"

"Not long at all. We have fairly constant contact with the Department of Motor Vehicles. You give me the plate number now and I'll call first thing in the morning."

"Thank you, Jane. You're a life saver." Nicole sighed in honest relief that they might have a conclusion in sight.

"It's a New Jersey license plate. That doesn't matter, does it?"

"Not at all," Jane assured her. "What's the number?"

"The number is ZPT-946," she said. "Did you get that?"

"ZPT-946. I got it. Is there anything else I can do?"

"No this is plenty. Thanks."

"You take care of yourself now, dear," Jane cautioned. "But don't let one bad driver spoil your feelings for David Germaine. You're not getting any younger," she admonished with motherly confidence.

"I know," Nicole said, laughing. "And don't worry, I won't. Good night."

She hung up the phone still smiling. Jane was right, after all. She shouldn't let anything turn her away from admitting her feelings. Nobody was getting any younger. Yet her life might be cut short. She couldn't give in. It would be too cruel for them both.

"How long will it take?" David stood, looking down at her with careful hope in his eyes.

"Not long, she says. Tomorrow morning, I'm sure." But, having disposed of their business at the apartment, Nicole felt suddenly awkward and shy. It might be foolish to feel that way at twenty-seven, but she did and covered the feeling by getting cups for their coffee. "We should eat something," she said, aware of the emptiness within her own stomach. "I'm sure there must be something frozen that we can pop into the microwave."

"Sounds good. I should really take you out to dinner, though."

"Thank you for offering, but I think I'll stay inside for the moment."

"I understand the feeling." *Don't chatter on aimlessly making small talk! Have you forgotten entirely how to talk to a woman whom you desire?* But he felt as though he had, and accepted the coffee cup silently.

"Smells kind of closed-in here, doesn't it?" Nicole caught the musty odor again near the kitchen door. It resembled the smell of old coffee grounds.

"Slightly damp, yes," he said. "Not bad, though. I didn't really notice until you brought it up."

"I'll open some windows."

David helped by throwing open the windows in the living room while she went to the two bedrooms. City air drifted in to cleanse the air of stuffiness, bringing with it the sound of cars and people on the street. It was a sound that David was no longer accustomed to, the sound of lives being pursued, hopes being realized, or shattered. Even with six other people on board, the predominating sound on the *Katharine* had been that of the vast silence of the sea. The vast, lonely silence.

"That's better," Nicole proclaimed, rejoining him. Seeing him at the window, it struck her that he looked strangely tired. There seemed to be a weight on his broad shoulders just then, something dark and heavy. He'd said on the boat that he was enjoying himself, though he hadn't for a long time. It was clear now that the man in the red Dodge had sapped some of that enjoyment, and she wished she had the power to bring it back.

"Not quite the same view as at sea, is it?" She joined him at the window, standing close enough to feel the warmth of his body and hear his measured breathing. "People, people, everywhere."

"I'll admit it's a bit strange." She smelled so good to him that he couldn't help but smile. No matter what happened, he would always cherish these hours of conversation. Even if they couldn't hold back the tide of fate, he'd be thankful for this time. "But I like it. I think I spend too much time at sea. For one thing, new fashions always amaze me."

"You're not the only one there. I envy the chance you have to get away from everything," she said with heartfelt sincerity. "I've got a couple of million people around me every day, and it gets a bit trying at times."

"And I've got only six. Maybe I envy you your millions."

"Shall we trade lives?" She looked up at him and tried to gauge the emotion behind their thoughtful appraisal. "Providing I can get a doctorate in ocean sciences before the boat sails, of course."

"I'm afraid trading is impossible. We are what we are, whether we like it or not." Then he paused, pursing his lips before saying, "But that doesn't mean we can't make a change of course from time to time. We must have that much control over destiny."

"I hope so," she said, her heart beating so loudly that she feared he might hear it. "But it doesn't seem that way sometimes. It seems we're locked into a groove in the system and forced to continue going around and around within the same limited area. It doesn't look like there's any way out."

"But there must be," he said, urgency animating his features as he placed one hand against her arm as softly as he might handle a kitten. "We have to overcome inertia, that's all. We have to get past the fear of giving up familiar surroundings in favour of the unknown. We have to try, don't we?" He sounded anxious for confirmation, as though his words held more meaning than they could express.

"Yes, we have to try."

Nicole let her gaze linger within the world in his eyes, eyes that seemed to hold so much feeling while refusing to let it go. His hand felt hot on her arm, a soul-warming heat that was comforting and frightening at the same time. She wanted to be enclosed in his arms and bound securely by that heat until the strangeness and fear of it could give way to the pleasure. She couldn't remember ever wanting a man so badly. But she couldn't find the strength needed to break through her instinct that it wasn't right. She felt that she shouldn't allow her emotions to be twisted by circumstances, even as she wished they would be.

To be rid of the pressure of time and fate would be bliss, but, until they were out from under the cloud of uncertainty, she couldn't be sure enough of her own feelings to trust herself to his. Until Wednesday at noon, the world would be an uncertain place where nothing could be trusted. Until they caught the gunman from her dream, Nicole couldn't be certain that either one of them had a future they could count on.

"I've got a couple of those gourmet things in the freezer," she said, her disappointment in herself almost choking off the words. "Shall we eat?"

"I'd love to have dinner with you, Nicole," he replied. "Anything would be just fine." And he let her go to the kitchen, watching her walk away with sadness clouding his eyes.

I don't know how to save her, he thought. *I can't conquer destiny.*

"I'M SO GLAD to have found you home, dear. I know you weren't expecting me to call tonight, but I couldn't wait." Jane Lee called shortly after nine, sounding well-pleased.

"Wait for what, Jane?" Nicole slid her plate across the counter toward the sink as she held the receiver expectantly to her ear. They'd just finished their meal when the phone rang, and she'd grabbed it in the midst of the cleanup. "What's up?"

"I made that call for you, dear. I remembered a man on the New Jersey force who works the night shift. They're usually quite willing to help out on a civil suit. I could think of no reason to wait, since I knew this fellow, so I went ahead and called."

"Didn't he wonder why you were calling at night? Especially on a holiday?" A swell of eagerness rose in Nicole's chest, and she motioned for David to join her by the phone.

"I told him I'd forgotten to request the information before the long weekend and that I'd be in dutch if I didn't have it for Mr. Gilbert to take into court with him in the morning. I feel like a spy, Nicole. It's so exciting!"

Her voice was shrill with it.

"This is great, Jane. What did you find out?" She clicked a pen into readiness and waited, poised over her message pad.

"He just called back with it a minute ago," the other woman said. "And the car is a 1988 Dodge Omni. It's registered to a Mrs. Paul Antonelli at 423 Ocean Avenue, Jersey City. Cheryl Antonelli. Did you get all of that?"

"423 Ocean Avenue," Nicole repeated. "Yes, I got it."

"Do you think that will help Mr. Germaine?"

"I don't know, Jane, but I appreciate your ingenuity."

"Glad to have helped. You be sure and tell me about it tomorrow."

"I will. Good night." Nicole hung up the phone and handed the notepad to David. "Do you know a Paul Antonelli?"

"No, but that doesn't mean anything." A frown pleated his brow as he gazed at the notepad. "You sure know the right people, don't you?"

"I had no idea I had such wide-ranging contacts, myself," she said with a laugh. "Are we going to check on Mr. Antonelli?"

"There's nothing else to do," he said. "It might be better to wait until morning, though."

"Why? So I'll be at work and you can go without me? Not on your life! Let's get over there right now."

"Wait a second," he said quickly, stepping into the doorway to block her movement from the kitchen. "We can't go bursting into someone's home at night without warning."

"Why not? He certainly did his best to run you over without warning." David's immobility puzzled her. Surely he couldn't expect to protect her by dragging his feet at this point. Time was against them, and information was their only weapon.

"But the car is registered to his wife. Would a man take his wife's car out to commit murder?"

"Well, I suppose not," she admitted, her eagerness tempered somewhat by the thought. "But that's all the more reason to get out there right away. We want to know if the car is even there."

"But we have to be sure we know what we're going after. Maybe the car was stolen," he said patiently. All he wanted to do was to keep as much distance between Nicole and danger as possible. But he was hard-pressed to find a reason to hold off driving to New Jersey. "Or, worse yet, maybe they are part of this mess. Maybe we'll show up at their door only to fulfill your dream a couple of days early."

"But we won't know unless we try, will we?" *Yes,* she thought, *he's trying to protect me. And he knows full well I'll never go along with that.*

"I've got a better idea." He stepped around her then and found the proper phone book by the fridge. "We'll call them up."

"Call them? But what can you say to find out anything?"

"I'll tell them I'm a cop." He shrugged, paging through the book until he found the right section of the alphabet. "They do it all the time on TV."

"That's illegal," she pointed out.

"Oh, don't mind that. I'm just doing what the police will be doing in a couple of days, anyway. Yes, here they are." He pressed his index finger beneath the number in the book and held it as he picked up the receiver. "Antonelli, Paul and Cheryl."

David punched out the phone number quickly, grasping his lower lip nervously between his teeth. The phone rang on the other end of the line. He let it ring ten times before he hung up. Nobody home.

"No answer?" Nicole asked.

"Not at the moment, no." David frowned. Something about the name nagged at him. He didn't know anyone named Paul Antonelli, but it felt as though he might know Cheryl. At least it seemed that he should.

"Then we'll drive out and take a look." Nicole strode out of the room, grabbing her purse from the secretary by the door. "Come on."

"All right." He followed her then. There was no point in foolish chivalry, and no time like the present to keep acting. If they stopped now, events would overcome them. "You'd better take a jacket. It'll be cool tonight."

"Right. But you don't have anything," she said, stepping over to the closet.

"I'll be all right."

Nicole threw open one of the folding doors of the closet and reached inside for the short windbreaker hanging amid the other jackets and sweaters inside. A musty odor, damp and cloying, billowed out with the movement of air. She leaned in to look over the items inside, but there didn't seem to be anything out of order in the closet. She took the windbreaker from its hanger and closed the door.

"There's your musty smell," David commented. He was standing by the front door waiting for her, his nose wrinkling with slight disgust. "Someone left a wet coat in there."

"Sara, I imagine," Nicole said, slinging the coat over her arm. "I haven't been anywhere to get wet lately." But something wasn't right about that odor. It had a tangy, iron smell to it, an ominous smell that didn't belong in her apartment at all. And she couldn't think of any clothing inside that would allow mildew growth.

"Smelled pretty strong." David opened the door. "You don't suppose there's plumbing in the wall back there that might be leaking?"

"It might be." Nicole spoke absently, hardly paying attention to her words. It wasn't right. Something wasn't right. And the feeling of doom that had shadowed the past week filled her heart with trepidation as she stopped walking toward the man waiting at the door. "It could be plumbing, couldn't it?" she asked.

"What's wrong?" David saw the frightened confusion in her eyes, and he was suddenly as afraid as she was, though he didn't know what caused the feeling. "Nicole? Is something wrong?"

"I don't know." He sounded so far away, his voice faint against the sound of—of what? Rain? Yes, she could hear rain falling as she stood there, perfectly dry in her apartment on a cloudless summer night. Rain. And she thought

f wet garments left in the summer heat, rain-soaked and
discarded in a pile to let bacteria grow in the warm, moist
material.

*She was opening the closet and dropping a bundle of
clothing inside. It made a clunking sound when it hit the
floor amid the shoes and boots there. The room was dark,
the draperies drawn, but she closed the closet door and
walked through the apartment without turning on any
lights. She knew her way well enough by now. In her room,
she took off her wristwatch and laid it on the dresser. Then
she turned back the covers and got in dressed only in her
panties. And then it was raining.*

"Nicole!" David closed the door and shouted out
frantically at the woman standing immobile before him.
She'd begun to say something but had suddenly stopped,
her eyes darting about randomly as she cocked her head as
though listening to something. He'd already called her
name twice with no response, and now he moved to grab
her. "Nicole!"

David was calling her. It wasn't raining, wasn't dark.
She wasn't lying in bed but standing in the entry with the
scientist shaking her gently by the shoulders. "Nicole?" he
called again. And she could see relief in his eyes as he came
into focus before her. Where had she been?

"Can you hear me now, Nicole?" David was asking her.

"Yes." She sounded so feeble, like a frightened child.
"Oh, David, I just had a strange image. So strange."

"What was it?" He kept his grip on her shoulders,
afraid to break contact for fear she might go away entirely.

"The closet." And, as though the word worked some
dark magic, she was suddenly afraid of the closet. She
snapped her head toward the innocuous double doors, her

eyes widening as if to see through them to the danger inside.

"What about it?"

"It's— I don't know. Something about the closet. Oh,
David, I'm afraid."

"I'm here, Nicole." He slipped one arm around her
shoulder, watching her in concern. "Don't be afraid." But
he was all too aware of his inability to defend her against
what was scaring her. He couldn't understand it, couldn't
see the danger, but could only believe it was real because
she felt it.

She reached up to grasp the hand clasping her shoulder,
finding a measure of strength in his strength. Then she
stepped out from under the security of his arm and reached
for the knob of the right-hand door. Taking a deep breath,
she slid the door open.

There were coats on hangers, and above them a shelf
holding boxes of scarves and hats for the winter. Everything was as it should be. On the floor lay shoes in a dis-
ordered tangle, just as they'd been left to await their call
to use. Nothing new there.

But there was something. The shaft of light illuminating the interior of the closet caught the edge of something
else on the floor. A splash of blue, printed material—a
paisley print. Shocked into action, Nicole dropped to her
knees to stare in at the spot of color. Yes, and the material was wrapped up in a heavy tan material.

"What is it?" David was standing over her, trying to
keep his body from cutting off her light while he peered
inside.

"Oh, God." She sighed. Her body blocked out the light
as she began to reach in toward the cloth, making the closet
floor seem as dark as a cave. Fighting the fear that coursed
through her heart and strained to pull her hands away, she

grasped the crude bundle of material and pulled it out into the light.

It was her raincoat. The sleeves were tied around the folded bundle, holding it safe and tight against discovery. Compelled onward now by the fear that had tried to keep her away, she struggled with the fat knot, pulling the sleeves apart and lifting the collar to shake the contents free.

Her new gray shoes fell onto the floor tangled up in the challis dress she'd bought for the opening.

Don't touch anything! Don't! But she lifted one shoe with horrified curiosity, noting the way the leather was puckered slightly above the sole. And it was dirty, as though she'd been wearing it on wet streets. She dropped the shoe, grabbing the dress and lifting it. The material was damp. Impossible. It couldn't still be wet after— *Gunshots! No!*

"Oh no, oh no," she head herself saying as she stared in shock at the crimson stain that discolored the front of the dress. Deep red, blood red, and crusted to a powdery residue. And in the center of the stain two ragged holes marred the bodice. "Oh no, oh no," but that couldn't be her voice from so very far away. She'd never been that frightened in her life.

Gunshots! No!

It was raining, washing down over her face as she screamed up at the overcast sky. She didn't think she'd ever stop screaming.

Chapter Twelve

The rain would fall forever, it seemed, pelting the concrete with musical pattering sounds. The rain would fall to drown her screams and muffle the sounds of an exploding gun. The rain of fate, unrelenting and sure, would march across time to find her and bring her dark oblivion.

She was aware of David beside her and could feel his capable arms surrounding her in a futile attempt to shield her from fear. Futile, because the fear was already embedded deep inside and the danger was time itself. She heard him gently call her name as he held her to him, rocking her within the cradle of his arms. But she couldn't respond because her attention was held rapt by the memories within her—memories unleashed by the sight of blood.

Crossing the street. The rain was falling in a misty drizzle, occasionally condensing into actual drops. Her shoes were wet, and she would have to wipe them once she'd gotten into the deli. The traffic stopped and she crossed the street in an awkward trot along with only three other people. A man was approaching the door of the deli in sync with her—tall, in a dark topcoat.

"*Hello again,*" *he said, smiling. David Germaine, with a streak of rain running down one side of his face. He pulled the door open.*

"*Goodness, I didn't expect to run into you here.*"

The first time they met, she'd felt uplifted by the chance meeting. This time, in memory, she watched from within herself with a certain awe at the meeting, at the miracle of chance.

"*I've been sightseeing,*" *he said.* "*Well, now that we've found each other, we needn't have a lonely lunch.*"

But that was exactly what he had said before, of course. There was no change, could be no change. It was merely memory, and the interest, the affection she saw in his eyes was just hope on her part.

"*I guess not.*"

Don't stop here and chatter. Go inside! In! But she could only watch as they made small talk at the end of time and another man rushed up to them before they could go inside. Impatient little man. Sunglasses. The collar of his brown raincoat pulled up and fedora hat pulled down. He bumped into Nicole, knocking her away from David.

And the gun rose again, its short black barrel aligning itself with David. In the clear light of memory she saw the blotch of scar tissue on the back of the man's left hand, his gun hand. And then she jumped between the two men, her gut reaction. The gun went off, the report echoing in her ears as she slipped to the ground. Scuffing the heels of her shoes on wet concrete. Staring as the gunman ran away and David knelt beside her.

And the rain fell around them as David fought to help her stretch out. Falling heavier now, the rain splattered her face like tears as she watched the gray sky and David's frantic face. His features grew dim above her. She watched everything fade into blackness and the sound of rain.

*And then the machine gun clatter of the alarm clock
started her screaming again.*

"It's all right. I'm here. I'm with you, Nicole. Don't
worry. I'm here." Rocking her and holding her to him and
wanting so badly to make everything right that he could
feel his heart pumping frustration like fire through his
veins.

When she first saw the clothing she'd just stared, picking up first a shoe, then the dress. "Oh no, oh no," she'd
said, as though the garment posed a physical threat. Before he could ask about the clothing she'd dropped it
stiffly, staring blankly ahead as her mouth dropped open
and a cry of pure anguish poured out.

He had held her then, rocking her on the floor of her
apartment while she sat limp and unresponsive in his arms.
He held her close and safe, stroking her hair the way he
might comfort a frightened child. "I'm here. You're safe,"
he said. And he'd kissed her cheek, the salt of her tears
bitter on his lips as her cry faded to a moan and then to silence.

David carried her to the couch, laying her down carefully and removing her shoes. Then he'd gone in search of
something to bring her around, finding a bottle of house-
hold ammonia beneath the sink but opting instead for
liquor as a less jarring way to bring her back to him. If that
didn't work, he could always try ammonia later. And now
her startled cry had brought him running again.

"Nicole? Can you hear me?"

Her eyes shifted toward him, seeming to see but not fully
focus on her surroundings.

"I found some wine. I suppose whiskey is what's called
for in situations like this, but you and Sara don't seem to
be hard-core drinkers." He kept talking, hoping the sound
of his voice would help reassure her somehow as he let go

long enough to fill the glass. "Here. I'm pouring a glass for you. I could do this like in the movies and just pinch your nose and pour it down your throat, but I don't want to drown you."

Drown? Water? What was he remembering about water? He could almost hear the rain falling, almost see a picture of her jerking away from him against the door of Hoffman's Deli. But the image was fuzzy, mostly a blur of movement in uncertain memory. Was he remembering his dream?

"You are safe, you know." But it didn't seem like the truth when he said it out loud. Even he didn't feel safe, though he didn't know why not. "Safe as houses, right? Here, have a drink."

She remained sitting rigidly upright, but her eyes were blinking, mouth working uncertainly as a look of concentration came over her face. "A scar," she said. "Left-handed."

"Oh, thank God!" David put the glass down quickly and threw his arms around her, hugging his face to her neck. "You'll be all right. Really, Nicole, I promise."

But he didn't feel any hope until her arm rose to return his embrace. Only then did the clouds of doom admit even a ray of hope.

The alarm clock had gone off in darkness. In darkness, she felt David hold her to him. He sounded so worried. She wanted to reassure him that she was all right. She'd just slipped, was all. But no, that was—was? No, that hadn't happened yet.

And when the light came back, she was in her own apartment holding tightly to the man whose life she'd given her own for. By a quirk of fate. An accident.

"David," she sighed. "God, David, I remember it." But seeing him look up at her then took her words away, and she let a swell of emotion speak for her as she found his lips with hers.

The kiss was hard and desperate, an affirmation of life she so urgently needed just then. But neither one of them drew back from that first contact. They let the kiss swell into a passionate expression of heartfelt union, a release for all the feelings they'd withheld from each other. His lips were soft and warm and eagerly moving on hers, her tongue moving on the fringe of their union. And every vibrant touch of his mouth as he kissed her cheek and neck and nuzzled against her throat sent a shiver through her that made her feel more alive than she had ever hoped to be. Alive! Alive with love and passionate need. Alive with the heat of longing pressing against her stomach. She was alive!

The initial kiss had caught David off guard. The iron wall around his heart had already been opened by his concern for her, and the feeling of Nicole in his arms and her lips on his threw that barrier down without resistance. He'd yearned for a chance to show his feelings for her, and now he gave in to his desires without thought of loss or gain. His only concern was to express his love.

Now they were held together by a bond of mutual desire that tightened with every caressing movement of hand and lips, and Nicole arched herself urgently against him in an emphatic celebration of life. His taut muscles danced beneath her hands as she rumpled his shirt up to slip her hands eagerly over the hot flesh of his back. David returned his lips to hers and lifted her to him, his strong arms locking her to him as he massaged the soft fabric of her blouse across her back, as she clutched his back with the full urgency of her desire.

But the touch of David's lips, his hands, were only a teasing taste of what Nicole longed for, and her hands moved without command to work at the buttons on his shirt as she let her lips roam over his throat.

Fear and worry gave way to the urgency in their hearts, and they hurried to free each other from the restraint of clothing. They rolled to the floor, laughing as David pushed the coffee table aside and tasted her silken skin, caressing the soft contours of her body. Nicole's eager hands explored him, and before long gave in to the urgency goading her. Never before had she felt so loved, so possessed.

For moments she clung to him, refusing to release him and give up the lingering heat of their passion. They both felt as though they'd passed through a barrier that would never have been broken if they'd tried to assail it with mere words. The commitment they each felt gave them a new sense of shared destiny.

"I'm alive," Nicole whispered, kissing his cheek tenderly. "You made me alive."

"I don't know about that," he answered in a husky whisper. "But I'm sure going to do my best to keep you that way."

"YOU WENT AWAY, and I didn't think you were coming back." David was seated beside her on the couch, his arm protectively around her shoulders. "I was scared," he admitted. "What happened when you saw those clothes?"

"I remembered it, David," she said, incredulously. "I remember what happened." Nicole was dressed in her pajamas and dressing gown, and was seated comfortably beside him with her feet drawn up beneath her.

"Remembered what? Your dream?" *And what was I remembering?* he thought now. *A man with a gun.*

"It wasn't a dream." She spoke slowly, wanting to be absolutely understood, and, more importantly, believed. "It happened."

"What?" He instinctively knew what she meant but couldn't yet believe it. Though he knew in his heart that it was more than a dream and that he'd seen that ruined blue dress before, he didn't want to believe it.

"It wasn't a dream." She swung her legs off the couch and leaned forward to look earnestly into his eyes. "Neither one of us was dreaming, David. I don't know how to explain it, but I know it's true. I got shot in front of Hoffman's. Will get shot. He was trying to shoot you, but I got in the way. That's why I was lying on the sidewalk in the rain. That's why I got so freaked out when we walked to the deli today. Because it really happened. I just didn't remember it clearly."

"You realize what you're saying, don't you?" He rose to sit on the couch beside her, taking her hands in his and holding them tightly. "In order for it to have really happened, we must have—"

"Yes, slipped back a week in time somehow." It sounded so unreal when she said it but absolutely real when she felt it. "I know it sounds crazy, but that's what happened." Nodding solemnly, she knew she was right. "I was wearing the clothing in the closet when it happened. That's why I reacted so horribly when I saw it. See? Everything makes sense this way."

She shifted to slip one leg beneath her and sit facing him, her growing excitement compelling her to move. The more she thought about it, the more real it was. That's why the dream had always felt like a memory. That's why she remembered Sara's opening and the wine stain.

"I wondered why I felt so utterly compelled to buy that challis dress and those shoes," she said, smiling in awe. "I had to because I did the first time. See? And now I'll bet you that there is a perfectly good dress hanging in my bedroom closet and a pair of shiny gray shoes on the shoe rack."

"But why would there be?" He was remembering the rain even as he tried to find an explanation. Remembering the rain and her startled gasp as the gun went off. The rain had been cold on his neck when he leaned over her.

"Just because there is," she said. "That's the only reason I have."

"This is incredible." He rubbed his fingers over his brow, raking them back through his hair. "But even theoretically, it would take a massive amount of energy to move through time. Einstein postulated that—"

"That's just science," she cried out. "It doesn't matter. This is real, and it really happened. That's why our watches stopped at the same time! 12:41 is the time when we went back! But the watches can't run backward, and it seems that they can't or won't count time they've already counted, so they're waiting for that moment to come around again!" Everything could be explained simply by believing the impossible.

"It seems to be right," David said, hesitantly, "but I'll be damned if I can understand how it might work."

"It doesn't matter how! Get those clothes. I'll show you." She ran to her bedroom closet, finding the dress in place on the hanger and the shoes on the rack as she'd expected, and then hurried back to the living room with them.

"My God." David was seated on the couch, the rumpled clothing from the closet on the coffee table before him, and he stared in shock at the dress Nicole brought out with her. "I remember seeing the dress now," he said. "And it wasn't from the dream—well, I mean, from the street. It was in the office. I was in the office sometime before we met in front of the deli. I remember that!'' Every piece of physical evidence brought back fresh memories, and he was awash in images confirming what had apparently happened. ''This is nuts.''

''I know. But just look at this, David. I bought the dress and shoes for Sara's gallery opening. I got wine spilled on it there. The first time, the spill was on the right side of the skirt just below waist level,'' she said, concentrating on the now dim memory. ''It was a big stain. A full glass.''

David picked up the dress from the pile, lifting it to orient himself and looking for the stain. Sure enough, there was still a faint discoloration right where she'd said it was and showing where the stain had been mostly removed. Then he looked at the dark and ominous stain above it, noting the two holes that would have been directly over her heart.

''See?'' The sight of the bloodied dress still shocked Nicole, but she was over the major scare now. Once she had an explanation, however crazy it was, she could find a way to deal with it. She had to. ''And because we were back a week, the dress was still at the store waiting for me to buy it. Now, there are two of them.''

''Why aren't there two of you and me, then?''

''Don't be silly,'' she scoffed.

''But how could it work that we just jumped back into our lives a week earlier? How did your clothes come back with you?''

''I don't know.'' Nicole frowned then, unable to remember what happened after the shots. ''I have a vague memory of coming in the door and taking my wet clothing off. The apartment was dark, and I just tied everything up and dumped it in the closet like we found it. I walked into the bedroom, took off my watch, went to sleep and didn't wake up until the alarm went off and I remembered what I thought was a dream. I don't know why the clothing came back with me, but I seem to remember wanting to keep it out of sight."

"No doubt you didn't want to remember the shooting," he said, grasping her hand again. "I didn't."

"I hid the evidence and pushed the memory away, but it kept coming back." Then she smiled, regarding him tenderly. "The only thing I wanted to remember was you, David. The only good memory."

"And all I remembered was you." Returning her gaze, he knew that nothing could have made him forget someone like her. "But why didn't I remember more?"

"Because you weren't shot, I guess," she said. *But you might still be,* she thought. *As I will be.*

"What's wrong?" he asked, seeing the worry clouding her hazel eyes.

"We keep talking about this in the past tense, David. But it isn't. It's future." Nicole felt her resolve cracking under the renewed weight of time and fear, crumbling under the certainty of destiny. "It hasn't happened yet."

"It won't happen," he said urgently. "We won't let it happen."

"But I couldn't avoid getting that wine stain," she said, fear creeping into her voice. "Couldn't stop you from being in the galley when the gas exploded. I couldn't stop anything!"

"No, but you changed it," he pointed out, slipping his arm around her shoulder. "For that matter, you weren't even on the ship the first time the galley blew up. If it even did blow up before. That's a major change."

"How do you know I wasn't there?" She remembered the variety of images she'd had of the explosion that evening on the ship and wondered which version had happened before. "I must have been."

"No, I would have remembered that. Remembered you," he said, with certainty. "But I don't remember any of it."

"Nor do I. And I surely would have remembered if—" But she stopped demurely, remembering the image she'd had of them kissing and the vision of him in bed with her. She knew she'd have remembered if that happened.

"If what?"

"Nothing. But I had visions of the explosion that were different from what happened. One where I was there with you, and one where the whole wall blew out."

David seemed about to say something but stopped, his expressive lips tightening pensively. "You've always been more in tune with this time thing, Nicole," he said, slowly working the thought over in his mind. "Maybe what you were seeing were other possibilities. Events as they might have happened. Other choices that weren't taken."

Which would explain the images she'd had of them together on the boat. In truth, under different circumstances she might have made love with him much earlier. Those visions might very well have been alternate avenues of reality.

"Why are you smiling?" David asked, smiling himself.

"I had a vision of the two of us together on the ship," she admitted now. "I didn't believe it at the time, didn't understand it."

"Other possibilities," he said, and he leaned to kiss her lightly, then again more firmly. "And it's one hell of a case of déjà vu you've got going here. But it gives us a real advantage now, doesn't it?"

"Sure, we know where the threat is," she said. "But we haven't exactly found out who the gunman is, have we?"

"We will. Remember Cheryl Antonelli. And what was that you said about a scar?"

"Yes!" The memory had almost slipped away again, but it rushed back with vivid clarity when he mentioned it. "He had a scar on the back of his hand."

"What kind of scar?"

"It looked like a burn. A straight slash of scar tissue across the back of his left hand. He was left-handed," she added.

"Left-handed, with a burn across the back of it." Maybe they did stand a chance of catching the man. Maybe. "And he is connected in some way to Cheryl Antonelli."

"Or he stole her car, and she doesn't know him at all."

"Don't be negative," he said soothingly. "He doesn't know that we have any knowledge about him, so we've got a head start. It's still two days away."

"Yes, two days. Only two days." Nicole shivered in the sudden chill of that thought. *Actually less than two days till Wednesday noon.* "It might be worse to know, David. What if we can't really change anything?"

"We *will* change it. Inviting you to the ship was a massive change, Nicole. It's made a world of difference to me."

"And to me," she said with a laugh. She snuggled tightly against him, using his warmth to fight off the chill.

"It might be that the explosion, as well as our near miss in traffic, happened because you came to the ship."

"Oh, I can't bear the thought that I caused that!" she cried. "You could have been killed."

"But we wouldn't have had any proof if someone hadn't rigged the oven," he said, stroking his hand down over her shoulder. "And we wouldn't have a license number."

"I suppose not." Though she still didn't relish the idea that her visit had caused him harm. "But why would my presence force their hand?"

"Because without you there were no witnesses, I suppose. But there would still be Connie, though. Maybe it's because you're Clint's assistant. If he is in on it, they might have thought you came to tell me what he was up to." That made sense, and David felt more optimistic having a theory to work from.

"But I don't know anything. We've just been guessing."

"They wouldn't know what you know. And you said yourself that it was odd he didn't mail the letter to Woods Hole. Robert Philips doesn't leave anything to chance. He wants Albany Manufacturing for some reason and I won't give it to him. Not alive, I won't."

"Why would he be so vicious?"

"I've never gotten along with the cousins," David said. "Grandfather left me the yacht along with my pile of money, and that got their goat to begin with. Nobody on the Philips side could stand the sea, but they surely loved having a yacht to show off. When I got it, they got mad. But when I refitted it for research, they were furious. Tried to take it from me. I wouldn't put it past Robert to want Albany Manufacturing simply because I own it. And, to get the *Crab* in the deal would be icing on the cake for him. Boy, could he rub my nose in it then."

"He couldn't actually make something like that stick, could he?"

"He could try. And we'd be in court for years."

"You have rather tangled family relationships," Nicole pointed out.

"Yes, and to think that it all started because my father and his mother didn't get along as children. Lydia Philips is a spiteful old crone, Nicole. Not someone who stops short of getting what she wants. That's where Robert gets his mean streak.''

"How can we prove any of this?" She wanted to hide, simply hide away till Wednesday was safely past.

"The first thing to do is to talk to your boss, I should think. Then we'll follow his lead.''

"Okay. And we'll visit Mrs. Antonelli.''

"First thing in the morning," he said. "But I don't think we should make any move tonight.''

"No. I don't feel like going out in the dark. In fact, I feel sleepy." Her eyelids felt heavy, suddenly drooping in response to the full day they'd put in. She couldn't solve everything in one day.

"And I should go," he said. "You'll be safe here, won't you?''

"Yes, I will." Though she didn't want him to leave. The lingering desire within her swelled at the thought of his going. "It's Wednesday I'm worried about.''

"Don't worry. We'll find the man and find out who hired him. That's all it will take. And then it will be over.''

"God, I hope so." She let him remove his arm and stand, grudgingly watching him walk around the coffee table to look down at her. "I just wonder why this happened to us. People get killed every day and don't get a second chance. Why me?''

"Maybe you have a guardian angel," he said. "And maybe it doesn't matter why. We just have to make the best of the opportunity. Good night, Nicole.''

"Good night." She got up and walked with him to the door. "Watch out for red cars," she told him.

"I will. I'll be at your office first thing in the morning." He opened the door and stepped partway into the hall. Then he stopped and leaned in to kiss her on the cheek. "Pleasant dreams," he murmured, stepping out quickly and closing the door softly behind him.

"Pleasant dreams," she whispered to the door.

But, though she'd been brave at parting, the pile of clothing on the table didn't serve to create hope. She looked at it one last time. The dress and coat were both bloodstained, as was the brassiere, and the shoes were water-damaged and scuffed from concrete. The musty smell of mildew clung to them, bringing images of death and decay.

You can't stop the hand of fate, she thought. *And you can't rewrite history.*

No, Nicole didn't expect to have pleasant dreams that night.

THE KATHARINE WAS DARK and silent, rocking gently at her mooring on the Sound. David hurried up the gangplank and unlocked the door to the salon. Stepping in, he noticed the smell of Connie's perfume in the air. She must have come back aboard not long before him.

David felt chilled and uncertain as he locked the door again and prepared to go below. Time travel? How?

But the time for questioning was long past. As Nicole pointed out, there were too many things with no other explanation. He'd become convinced that they were sharing some kind of extrasensory event, so why not accept time travel? Why not, indeed?

He hadn't wanted to leave Nicole alone tonight. Quite the opposite, in fact, which was one very good reason for leaving. He had wanted to stay and gorge himself on the sweetness of her lips and revel in holding her willowy body in his arms. He wanted merely to continue to experience the sight, sound and feel of her, and if it went no further than their eager kisses, he'd have been perfectly happy. But that was out of the question, and he knew it. She was vulnerable now and didn't need to be pressed into a sweet relationship. Regardless of that, however, he knew that what he should have done was to stay there on her couch where he could stand guard overnight.

But he hadn't done that because he'd begun to have an idea of where he'd heard the name Cheryl Antonelli before. An idea, but no proof yet. That's why he'd felt compelled to return to the ship—to get the proof without drawing Nicole into it. With luck, he would be able to confront his suspect alone.

"Is that you, David?" Connie called out from the hall.

"Yes, I'm home." He could hear her padding along toward the salon, and a moment later she emerged with her white robe pulled tightly around her. "You just get in?"

"A while ago. Why?" Connie scowled at him, seemingly annoyed that he'd come in.

"Just curious. What's up?"

"Why should something be up? Christ, David, I can lead my own life without reporting in, can't I?"

"Of course." He decided that he must have awakened her. She always was a crabby riser. "You just seemed a bit put out, is all."

"Did you have fun with your little friend?" Connie regarded him sourly, hugging her arms to her chest as though she was cold.

"Sure," he said, noncommittally. "Went to the park. You know, New York stuff."

"I don't like her, David," she said abruptly, dropping into one of the canvas chairs. "She's not your type."

"Wait a second, Connie. I don't need your approval for my friends, you know." A surge of protective anger flowed through him.

"She's not at all like Katharine."

"That's fine. I'm not trying to replace Katharine."

"You couldn't replace her," the woman said. "Never. Especially not with that fortune hunter."

"Are you jealous?" he asked, point-blank. There could be no other reason for this behavior.

"Jealous?" Connie exploded with surprise and anger. "You've sure got some nerve, thinking I should be jealous. What kind of stud do you suddenly think you are?" Then she smiled, losing some of her edge. "Besides, I know you too well to be interested."

"Good. Because I'd hate to think my reliance on you has led you to believe anything beyond that."

"No way, Dave. That's just your idiot friend talking to make you think that."

"You did give her a rather cold reception," he said. "And I can't think of any reason for you to dislike her so."

"It's your life." Connie stood with a shrug, walking back toward the hall. "I just think that you should be old enough to control it pretty soon. First Kate and now this city girl."

"What about Katharine?" He followed her to the hall, confused by her reference to his late wife.

"Nothing." She continued walking.

"What about her?" He spoke quite forcefully then, feeling himself on the verge of grabbing the woman.

"You couldn't make a move without her, either," Connie said, stopping and looking back at him. "And then you had me holding your hand while you wallowed in grief. Now you've picked up that tramp and you're already letting her tell you what to think. You've got to think for yourself, David. If you did, you'd know when some little schemer is just trying to get a leg up in the world."

"You assume too much, Connie," he said, his voice hard with congealed anger. "I'm not necessarily planning anything permanent with Nicole."

"No, you're not planning anything at all, are you?" Connie smiled, with a knowing look. "But maybe *she* is. Good night."

David couldn't allow himself to carry the discussion any further. The subject was making him far too angry. So he let her go without a word. After a moment, he walked down the hall to the library, which they used as the business office. He went to the file cabinet and opened the drawer containing the personnel files.

Somewhere in there, Cheryl Antonelli's name was written as a reference of some kind. He didn't know who she belonged to, however, and they'd gone through a fair number of college interns and part-timers over the years. It took nearly ten minutes to find the name, but there she was.

Next of kin: Cheryl Decker-Antonelli, 423 Ocean Avenue, Jersey City, New Jersey.

She was Lance Decker's sister!

Chapter Thirteen

Instead of cold cereal, Nicole breakfasted on a soft-boiled egg and toast and orange juice. She didn't even glance at the morning news, which she had watched the first time she'd lived this day. She replaced her conservative tan suit with a white cotton blouse and blue skirt. In short, she did what she could to alter this Tuesday morning from the one she dimly remembered upon waking. She didn't expect that it would make any difference in the long run, but it did enhance her confidence a bit to prove that some things could be affected by her actions, even if they were very small changes.

She called the boat just before leaving for the office, getting Connie on the line. "Is David there?"

"Nicole?" Connie sounded happy that morning. "No, David went out quite early."

"Really?" The news worried her. He hadn't mentioned any intention of doing anything before talking to her. "Did he say where he was going?"

"No. I'm sorry, but he didn't say." Then she paused a moment and continued in a tightened tone. "Nicole, I'm sorry about the way I acted the other day. I wasn't very hospitable, and David mentioned that you were upset. I'm very sorry."

"Oh, he shouldn't have said anything, Connie." Nicole was somewhat abashed by the unexpected apology, and confused about why David would have brought up the subject at all. She hadn't wanted to make an issue of it.

"I shouldn't have been so brusque with you. And, after what nearly happened to you guys yesterday, I thought I should tell you. I really am sorry," she said, adding, "You have enough on your mind these days."

"Yes, well, I hope we can be friends, Connie," Nicole said, awkwardly.

"I'm sure we can, Nicole. And, if there's anything I can do to help, just tell me."

"Thank you. I just have to get in touch with David. Did he say anything about going to Antonelli's?"

"Antonelli?" She spoke slowly, meditatively. "No. He was gone when I got up."

"Thanks. Tell him I called, won't you? 'Bye."

"Goodbye, Nicole."

Nicole hung up with fear creeping in again. David had left early without telling either one of them about it, and that didn't seem to be in character. Surely, he would have called her if something came up. Wouldn't he?

She left for the office concerned by the thought that he might have followed that lead without her. After all, he'd tried to stall her out of it the night before with no reason beyond misplaced chivalry, so it wasn't out of the question that he would have simply followed through on that intention this morning.

It was good to have a man who felt compelled to shield her, but it was also quite annoying, and she had yet to decide which reaction was strongest.

DAVID PARKED HIS RENTAL CAR down the block from the small brick house on Ocean Avenue in Jersey City. The red

Omni was parked in the driveway. He sat behind the wheel for a moment, holding the keys loosely in his hand and watching the driveway two houses down and across the street from him.

He wasn't very eager to go to the house just at the moment. If this was the wrong move, it could conceivably hasten Nicole's fate rather than avert it. But, if he didn't make the move, he had no chance at all of stopping the bullets due to arrive tomorrow noon. He wasn't an indecisive man by nature, but he wasn't accustomed to making life-and-death decisions for other people, either.

You know Nicole would be out of the car by now, he thought. She'd be leading the charge. *The only reason you're here without her is because you know you wouldn't be able to hold her back.*

Thinking of Nicole and the head-on approach she took to her problems steeled his resolve. Even if he did alert Lance Decker that they were on to him, it couldn't make matters any worse than they would be tomorrow.

David threw the car door open and got out, walking quickly across the street. Lance probably wasn't staying at his sister's house, but she might have an address for him. Then he would confront him and find out what he was involved in. He knew that Lance would be no trouble when confronted face-to-face. But, if he was allowed to sneak up behind them, he might be lethal.

David rapped on the frame of the metal screen door and waited. It was 8:50, late enough to call on a workday. Knocking again, he was rewarded with the muffled sound of footsteps from within the house. A moment later, a round-faced woman with short red hair answered the door.

"Yes?" she said, smiling.

"Cheryl Antonelli?" he asked, wondering how to put his questions to avoid raising suspicion.

"Yes, that's me."

"I'm David Germaine," he said, holding his hand out to her. "Lance's boss. Ex-boss, I guess I should say."

"Oh, Mr. Germaine." She took his hand and shook it lightly as a perplexed look formed on her face. "Sure, but isn't Lance working for you any more?"

"No, he's not." David tried to sound sorry to have lost the man but wasn't sure if he'd pulled it off or not. "And that's why I'm here, Ms. Antonelli."

"I thought he was still working on your boat," the woman said. "He didn't say anything about quitting. When did he quit?"

"About a month ago, I guess," he replied. "Haven't you seen him since then?"

"Sure, I saw him this weekend, but he said he was working on a marine survey of some kind with you."

"No, he left us when we got back to the States," David said. "But he told you he was still on the crew? Then you don't have a local address for him?"

"No, I don't believe so. He didn't quit, did he? Did he get fired?" The look on the woman's face had already answered the question, telling a lot about the young man's past performance as well as his status in his family.

"Yes, I'm afraid things didn't work out and we had to let him go."

"I should have known," she said. "My brother has had trouble with holding a job. He was the baby in the family. You understand."

"Yes, I think I do. He's a nice young man, but he's—"

"Lazy," she finished for him. "Yes, I know. He's probably embarrassed about losing such a nice job. That's why he didn't say anything. But what did you need? An address?"

"Yes, I don't have a forwarding address for him."

"You could have just called to get that, couldn't you?" A touch of suspicion stole into her eyes. "Why do you need his address?"

"It's a little embarrassing, Ms. Antonelli." David shrugged his shoulders. "Your brother came to the boat on Saturday asking for a week's pay he said I owed him. I had thought I'd settled up on his pay, and I told him as much. I've spoken to my partner since then and we found that he was right about the money. I owe him for a week."

"I'm sure he'll be glad to hear that, but to come in person?"

"Well, when we spoke on Saturday I pretty much implied that he was trying to get something for nothing. All but called the poor boy a liar. Now it turns out that he was right. I wanted to apologize for my behavior as well as pay him."

"That's very kind of you," she said, her suspicions seemingly appeased. "We're all quick to judge, aren't we? But not many of us are as quick to admit an error."

"I'm not applying for sainthood, Ms. Antonelli," David said with a laugh. "I just wanted to make it right if I could."

"I'd sure like to help, but all I have is the mailing address he had before he went overseas with you. I'm sure it's been rented by now."

"Most likely it has." This news put a crimp in his plan, but maybe something could be gotten from the old address. "Do you have the address handy, though? If I can't find him, I'll mail his check to you."

"Yes, I've got the address. I'll get it." She scurried back into the house, letting the screen bang behind her, and returned in a moment with a slip of paper, which she handed to David. "This is it. I don't think it'll help now, though."

"I'll see. And, if you see your brother soon, please tell him that I need his address for my unemployment records. Do you see him often?"

"He was here this weekend," she said. "Needed my car to move some things. I'll pass your message along when I see him next time."

"Thank you," David said, moving down one step from the door. "And tell him that if he needs a recommendation, I might be able to work something out."

"I'm sure he'll need it. Goodbye."

David hurried back to his car. He probably wouldn't be able to find Lance with an eight-month-old address, but at least he'd confirmed that the boy had been driving the car over the weekend. Now, if he could only get his hands on him before tomorrow noon!

He started the car and left the quiet neighborhood of brick houses and tree-lined streets and headed back toward the Holland Tunnel. He wasn't eager to make the drive clear across the city to the Brooklyn address the woman had given him, but there didn't seem to be any alternative.

Concentrating on his driving while his thoughts wandered over the many questions presented by the situation, he wasn't paying much attention to the vehicles around him. So he didn't notice the motorcycle that moved with the traffic a couple of cars behind him. He probably wouldn't have recognized the helmeted rider, anyway.

CLINT FORRESTER was normally a very punctual man, but not that morning. Nicole had arrived at a quarter to nine, ready to confront her employer with their suspicions as soon as he arrived, but her questions had to wait. At ten o'clock, after she'd finished checking the correspondence he'd left, she called his home. His machine answered,

providing no information except that he wasn't there. Mrs.
Forrester was in California for two weeks. There was apparently nothing she could do but wait.

She'd been unsure about coming to work at all today,
and now she wondered again if her time wouldn't have
been better spent searching for an answer with David. But,
it was apparent that events could be altered by what they
did this time around, and she hadn't wanted to risk the
possibility that not going to work might alter events un-
predictably. She knew too little about everything to move
in more than small steps away from the original day. And
she had hoped to talk to Clint that morning, as well.

Nicole scoured her mind for information on the original Tuesday. From what little she remembered it had been
a dull day, though she remembered Clint coming in by
nine-fifteen. She was clear on that point. Yet, now it was
after ten and he hadn't appeared. Where was he?

There was nothing to do but cancel his morning appointments, and she set about that task efficiently and then
tidied up the office a bit. Amusingly, she'd found that the
letter she had begun to type to camouflage her presence
there on Monday was the same letter he'd dictated and left
for her. So she'd had a head start on her work and was
faced with a morning of waiting.

She didn't know what could have caused Clint Forrester to step out of character so drastically unless there was
some truth to their supposition that he was involved in the
mess in some way. Perhaps he'd found out about the attempts on their lives and had decided to get away from the
scene of the crime. With that thought in mind, she began
to put through a call to California to see if he was with his
wife. The call was interrupted, however, by a visitor.

"Clint in?" Robert Philips was half way to the lawyer's
office door before Nicole stopped him.

"No," she called, replacing the phone in its cradle. "He hasn't come in yet. May I help you, Mr. Philips?"

"No." Robert Philips was a stocky man with a habitual scowl, which he was wearing now as he thrust his hands deep within his trouser pockets and turned to look at Nicole. "I have to talk to him right away," he said, urgently. "Where can I reach him?"

"I don't know." Nicole shrugged. She was accustomed to the urgency with which Philips treated everything, but there was an extra edge to his voice today. This visit might be truly important.

"Come now, you must know." A look of smug disbelief asserted itself on his fleshy features and he narrowed his gray eyes to look at her with suspicion. "I don't care if he wants to grab a longer holiday, but this can't wait."

"I really don't know," she asserted. "I've just cancelled his morning appointments and I was about to call his wife in California to see if he might be there."

"You really don't know?"

"No, I don't." She responded to the look of panic that flickered across his normally confident visage with concern. She knew that look. It was a look she'd felt herself wearing many times over the past week, the look of a person whose world was about to collapse. "I wish I could help you. Can you tell me what you need?"

"I don't think so." He rubbed his fingers across his forehead, smoothing the panicked look away.

"If it's paperwork of some kind, I'm sure it's all right if I go through the file and get it for you."

"No, it's personal. Clint doesn't handle my personal business. I just had to talk to him."

"Family business?" Nicole ventured. Clint's disappearance and Robert Philips's worry about family business seemed to confirm their hunch.

"Yes," he said. Then he looked at her more openly, his eyes widening as if to make sure he saw all of her. "Don't I know you? I mean, of course I know you. But haven't we met elsewhere or something?" He laughed nervously at the apparent contradiction in his remark.

"I can't think of anywhere outside the office," Nicole said.

"But I— Sure, you were at the boat!" His smile wasn't entirely happy. "I spoke to you on the phone the other day when I called the boat. You wouldn't tell me your name."

"I didn't know how proper it would look for me to be with a client," she explained with a shy smile, improvising as she went along. "You know."

"Sure, I know. So you were there when the gas blew." Now he walked up to stand directly before the desk, clasping his hands loosely in front of him. "What happened?"

"The pilot light blew out, I guess," she said. Didn't he know what happened?

"The pilot?" His eyes wandered upward slightly, as if he were thinking, then returned to her face. "No, couldn't be. Even if they sold such unsafe appliances these days, David wouldn't buy one. There'd be a thermocouple on the valve to close it if the pilot went out."

"I didn't look at it," she said. If Clint had avoided suspicion by leaving town, perhaps this one would do it by publicly disbelieving the easy explanation. "What do you mean?"

"Just that it couldn't be the pilot. The line might have been cracked, though. I suppose that's possible," he said, speaking like a man trying to convince himself of his own statement. "Was David seriously hurt?"

"Winded, mostly. The window was open slightly, so the gas hadn't built up too drastically."

"Good." He seemed genuinely relieved to hear that. "And the boat wasn't too badly damaged?" Now he was beginning to sound like himself.

"No. A new paint job should do it. And a new oven, of course."

"Good. Not my boat, anyway, so I don't suppose it's my worry."

"Is your business about David?" At this point, she felt it was important to ask right out rather than try to finesse it out of him. Time was too short for finessing. "Maybe I can still help you."

"No, not at all," he said, quickly. "I'm probably all too worried about it, anyway. When he does get in, have him call me, won't you?" Now the professional smile returned and he stepped back toward the door. "I'll be at my office."

"I'll do that."

Pausing in the open door, the businessman looked back at her with a smile, saying, "Tell my cousin he'd better keep the boat in better shape than he is. No, say *my* boat. That'll get him."

"Why would you want to annoy him?"

"Family tradition," he explained, then spoke more seriously. "And my offer is still open for Albany Manufacturing. Tell him I'll guarantee continued operation of the facility. And I'll put it in writing. He doesn't have to worry about the jobs."

"I'll tell him."

Philips hurried away without further words, leaving Nicole to wonder if anything had been confirmed after all. He didn't sound like a man plotting murder, or even a hostile business deal, for that matter. No, he'd sounded like a concerned relative, albeit a rather combative one.

The phone rang, taking her away from her speculation once more. "Mr. Forrester's office."

"Nicole Ellis?" The voice sounded familiar, but she couldn't place it.

"Yes, this is she."

"Jerry Brunsvold," he said, quickly. "Is David there?"

"No, he's not, Mr. Brunsvold."

"What the hell is going on?" he asked abruptly.

"What do you mean?" Nicole felt off balance for a moment. Even though she might want rapid action at this point, events were moving much more quickly than she'd anticipated. Had her coming to the office today helped to keep things on track, or had she unknowingly altered time beyond repair?

"The boat," the man said. "I'm here now. You people blew up the galley and didn't tell me about it! Why not?"

"It wasn't serious, Mr. Brunsvold. We didn't think it necessary to disturb you at the convention."

"What a load of crap!" he exclaimed. "My partner damn near gets blown away and you people don't want to disturb some stupid convention? And what's up with David?"

"I'm afraid I don't follow you at all."

"He left this morning without even talking to Connie," the man explained, sounding as though he expected her to have gleaned the information from what little he'd said. "That's not normal. And now some woman from Jersey City just called, claiming to be Lance Decker's sister and leaving a message to call her about her brother. Why is he trying to get hold of that deadbeat?"

"I didn't know about that. Who did you say called?"

"Someone named Antonelli," the man said. "I don't know her."

Nicole started. David had discovered the woman's connection to him and had gone without her to speak to Mrs. Antonelli. "Did she leave a number?" Nicole asked excitedly.

"I don't know, I'm not an answering service." He sighed audibly. "And what about the *Crab*? Are we giving it away or what?"

"Yes, you are giving it away."

"Then your boss better get on the ball. The Woods Hole people are wondering what's going on."

"What do you mean?"

"They haven't heard anything from Forrester. The last they had was when David called them nearly a month ago. I thought the deal was set, but they told me they hadn't received any paperwork yet."

"It's only been since last week," Nicole said. "The holiday weekend might have delayed the mail."

"He should have called them," Jerry pointed out. "I don't understand any of this."

"Do you want to give the machine away?"

"Of course I do," he insisted. "David is the mechanic, not me. And we don't run an equipment supply house. Give it away so we can get back to real work."

"I'll check with Mr. Forrester," Nicole said.

"Yes, please," the man said, calmer now. "How is David?"

"He's fine. There was much less flame than I'd have expected," she told him.

"With the window open the gas just leaked right out," he said, thoughtfully. "The gas bottle below is empty now, so it must have been leaking all day."

"I'm sorry we didn't call you, Mr. Brunsvold, but neither one of us wanted to put a damper on the holiday."

"Believe me, a convention is no holiday." He laughed. "And call me Jerry. To cop a cheap phrase, Mr. Brunsvold is my father."

"Right, Jerry," Nicole answered. "I'll remember that, should I ever meet your father."

"You'd better. He likes being called Mister. Well, I'll get out of your hair. Tell David to call me if you see him."

"I'll pass your message along."

Brunsvold hung up.

Without further delay, Nicole found the phone book for Jersey City and looked up Mr. and Mrs. Paul Antonelli. If the woman had any news that might help, Nicole wanted to know before events got moving so swiftly that she wouldn't be able to hang on. Right now, she was hanging on for dear life.

DAVID HAD FOUGHT THE TRAFFIC through Manhattan, jockeying for position with a succession of taxis and fellow out-of-towners through the bumper-to-bumper swirl that formed between the canyon walls of the buildings. It took an hour and a half to travel the distance a crow might fly in ten minutes, and he arrived in a sour mood. Never again would he take a car into the city. No appointment was so urgent that he couldn't wait for the train.

The address was a second floor walk-up in a squat, ugly building with a stoop crowded by teenagers with nothing better to do than scrutinize his movements at the door. As he expected, Decker's name wasn't on any of the mail boxes.

"You kids live here?" He turned to stare back at them.

"Yeah, why you asking?" A lanky young man in gang colors spoke up.

"I'm looking for a guy named Decker," he explained, stepping down to speak to him. "Lance Decker. You know him?"

"Yeah, but he moved out last winter." The kid smiled. "You a cop?"

"No, I'm not." And David was struck by the incongruous thought that maybe he should change his wardrobe if he was being mistaken for a policeman. "I'm looking for Decker."

"Friend of his?"

"He worked for me once."

"Yeah, you don't look like no friend of his. But that junkie is gone."

"Junkie? What do you mean?"

"Clean out your ears, man," a second boy said, laughing. "The guy was snow-blind all the time. Or, maybe you're the guy who was selling it to him."

"You kids better make up your minds." David laughed. "I either look like a cop or a pusher, but I can't look like both."

"Yeah, Carl," the first boy said. "No self-respecting dealer would wear those pants." He motioned to the creased tan twill trousers David was wearing.

"So, do you fashion experts know where Decker went?"

"Didn't leave no forwarding address," the boy said. "My old man is the super, so I know. We threw all his mail out months ago."

"Is there any new mail?"

"Junk mail. Stuff from Ed McMahon. We just toss it."

"Thanks, guys." David returned to the sidewalk, pulling the keys out of his pocket. "Aren't you supposed to be in school or something?"

"I don't know," the boy named Carl spoke up. "What month is it, anyway?" And they laughed in unison.

"Say, is that a rental?" The first boy nodded toward David's car. "'Cause I know a guy who could take it off your hands. You might make a couple bucks."

"No thanks, guys. If I lose one, I might not be able to rent another one." David got into the car and pulled away from the curb. It looked as if he'd be showing up at Nicole's office with nothing to offer her by way of encouragement. The morning had been a total waste.

Moments after he drove away from the building, a motorcycle passed in pursuit.

"MRS. ANTONELLI?" Nicole held the phone loosely in her hand, forcing herself to relax as she spoke and looked out her office window at the buildings beyond it. "I'm Nicole Ellis calling for Mr. Germaine," she said in a crisp, businesslike tone.

"Hello." The woman on the other end of the line sounded friendly, though she spoke haltingly. "Isn't Mr. Germaine available?"

"Not at the moment, but he asked me to return your call. Did you have some information for him?"

"Lance called me and I passed on Mr. Germaine's message. He said that he doesn't have a mailing address just yet."

"I'll tell him that." It appeared that the woman's relationship to the ex-crewman was the most important information to be gotten here, and she wasn't going to learn any more on the phone. "Was there anything else?"

"No, I just thought I should give Mr. Germaine Lance's message." She spoke slowly, as though making a decision about something. Then she said, quickly, "Well, there is something else. I'm worried about Lance. I wouldn't say anything, but Mr. Germaine must already know about it or he wouldn't have fired him. You see, I think Lance is off the wagon. He said some terrible things."

"He did? About whom?"

"About Mr. Germaine. He's not rational when he's like this, and I don't think he'd actually be dangerous, but he might end up hurting himself. I just wanted to let Mr. Germaine know about Lance so he could keep his eyes open."

"I'm afraid I don't follow you exactly, Mrs. Antonelli. What about Lance?"

"He sounded high when he called," the woman said, letting the worry she'd been holding back flood her voice. "He said he didn't want the money anymore. He threatened Mr. Germaine, too. As I say, he's never followed through on anything when he's been like this, but that doesn't mean I should just forget about it, either. Lance has been clean for over a year, but they say that once you start in again you go right back down to where you were when you quit. We had him hospitalized the last time, and he sounds every bit as bad now. So you tell Mr. Germaine that it might not be wise for him to continue looking for Lance. In his state, he might try something foolish and get both of them hurt."

"I'll pass that on," Nicole promised. "And don't worry about your brother. We'll watch out for him."

"Good. I'm really torn about it, but I just couldn't live with myself if something happened to either of them because I didn't speak up."

"Of course. Thank you."

"Goodbye." The woman hung up quickly, and Nicole replaced her receiver thoughtfully.

Nicole smiled at the thought of David trying to spare her from danger by looking for Lance Decker himself. She'd been right about his unannounced activity this morning.

But it seemed that he'd run into a brick wall so far. Would this new knowledge help in any way?

Lance Decker was an addict—to what, she didn't know—and he had made threats against David. Would a junkie be able to fulfill such threats? Lance Decker might know his way around the ship, but would he have settled for so subtle an attack as a rigged gas oven? She couldn't be sure. But, if the whole thing boiled down to the threats of one disgruntled employee, why hadn't Clint Forrester contacted Woods Hole?

No, knowing about Lance's addiction didn't help at all. It was entirely possible that he was acting on his own. But, he'd be the perfect fall-guy for a conspiracy as well. Having a paranoid junkie kill the man who fired him and accidentally kill a bystander in the attack—probably resisting arrest and being shot by the police in the end—would be a very neat way to take over David's assets without suspicion.

No matter what the cause, the deadly motion of events in time seemed unstoppable. Nicole shivered at the memory of the attack at Hoffman's Deli, wondering again how they could possibly stop it from happening.

Stop it! You'll be killed for certain if you allow yourself to be petrified with fear! But she couldn't shake the icy shiver on the back of her neck or lose the feeling that there was nothing they could do to hold back the hands of time.

But why did Robert Philips appear so nervous? Were his attempts to get David's company at the root of everything? No, he was a relative, after all. He couldn't be part of it, could he? She didn't know enough of their family history to say. But, if he was involved in some way, she might be able to prove it right here and now.

Clint must have something on paper to provide them with evidence of the plan behind the gun that would be in

Decker's hand tomorrow. Philips had wanted to talk to Clint in person, so if there was a connection Clint must be the one who can tie them all together. And, if he wasn't going to show up, she'd have to go through his office and find the evidence for herself.

Nicole pushed her chair back and stood up resolutely. She wasn't about to wait to become a target. Her search last night had been hampered by lack of time and the feeling that she was violating Clint's trust. But Robert Philips's visit confirmed Clint's involvement, and she didn't owe any loyalty to a man who would conspire to commit murder.

Hurrying to the door of Clint Forrester's private office, she only paused a moment before grasping the knob to listen for anyone approaching the outer door. She didn't relish the thought of being caught searching Clint's private files. Then she grabbed the knob and began to turn it.

A dark feeling of violent death swept over her as she touched the door knob. There were no images, only a certain awareness of death that clamped around her lungs as she pushed the door open. The sensation was so strong that she wanted to turn and run, but she held firm and pressed in on the door to step into the sunlit office.

Inside, the air seemed thicker than normal—jellylike and cloying to breathe. The first thing she noticed was that the ashtray was on the corner of the desk with a water glass beside it. There was a cigarette crushed out in the ashtray, and the glass held about an inch of liquid. Then she looked across the desk toward the chair.

Clint Forrester was staring straight into her eyes!

Chapter Fourteen

David gave the keys to his car to the parking attendant and stood looking over the street for a moment as the man hit the gas and squealed up the ramp into the parking garage. With nothing to show for his quest, David wasn't eager to bring it up at all when he went to see Nicole. She'd want to mix into it, and he couldn't bear the thought of placing her in any danger. Lance Decker wouldn't be dangerous if he could catch him off guard, of course. But David felt that Murphy's Law applied explicitly to their situation. What can go wrong will go wrong.

It was amazing how quickly and completely Nicole had come to shape his thoughts. No matter how he tried, he couldn't help the path his thoughts took into the uncertain future. And he had to admit that he desperately wanted them to have a future together. If they could only avoid what seemed an almost certain fate, there might be a chance for them. Then, maybe, he would be able to admit his feelings. And he might learn how to experience optimism again.

He walked along the street wondering what move would be prudent to make next. Time for indecision was running out fast and he couldn't bear to lose her through the wrong choice.

The next move was obviously to go to Robert Philips with their questions. The man was more of a shark than he'd ever thought if he would go to the extreme of murder to get what he wanted. He was more vicious than the boy he remembered fighting with in summers long past.

David smiled slightly at the memory of their youthful battles. They'd sparred constantly when the families would get together, which was often when their grandfather was alive. They were never very violent fights, but they were quite serious. Robert always had to prove something, it seemed. He wasn't satisfied unless he came out on top.

The last time they'd actually come to blows, however, Robert Philips had not been the victor. David remembered that conflict clearly, especially the way his aunt shouted from the porch for David to leave her little boy alone. And the reproachful tone she'd used on her son when they were separated was unnerving. It was the losing, not the fighting that she'd minded, and hearing her reprimand Robert had almost made David wish he had lost. He'd almost felt sorry for the boy. They had never come close enough to a fight again after that summer.

It was funny, but he now realized that he couldn't remember why any of their fights started. They just happened, like a cloudburst out of a clear blue sky.

The light had changed, allowing the mass of pedestrians to start across, leaving David standing at the corner thinking his faraway thoughts. But then he stepped out, grinning at his woolgathering as he hurried to catch up before traffic resumed its normal deadly pace.

A blur of motion, and the sound of a motorcycle separated itself from the traffic sounds as something slammed into his ribs and knocked him to his knees. The pavement rose up before his eyes, darkening and then returning to

clarity as he supported himself with one hand and shook
his head.

"Hey, buddy, you all right?" A man leaned down be
side him, grasping his arm. "Idiot on the cycle could have
killed you."

"Damn kids," someone behind him said. "He kicked
him. You saw that, didn't you? Kicked him on the way
past."

"What?" David pushed himself up, wincing at the pain
in his left side. "He did what?"

"Kicked you. I saw it clear as day." A middle-aged man
in shirtsleeves nodded seriously as he spoke. "Some kid
out for excitement."

"I didn't see no kick," the first man said. He was gray
haired and wearing an Islanders jacket over the blue crew
neck that strained across his gut. "But it coulda hap
pened that way. Knocked you down like a sack of pota
toes."

"Sure feels like he kicked me," David admitted, rub
bing the sore rib tenderly. "I'm all right, though."

"Damn kids," the second man repeated. "They have no
moral guidance these days. Anything for a thrill. The lit
tle bastards."

"I know what you mean," David said. The light
changed for a second time, and he started across care
fully. "Thanks," he called to the men remaining on the
curb.

"Sure, and keep your eyes peeled for those kids," he
admonished.

I'll keep my eyes open for Lance Decker, David thought.
He just hadn't anticipated that the man would be so dull
as try the same mode of attack twice. How much damage
did he think he could inflict with his foot? Why would he
even bother?

HIS EYES WERE OPEN in an accusing stare, his mouth gaping and encrusted with dried blood. Staring from the grave in mute accusation, his shirt bloodied in a large irregular stain, a small hole at the top of it. Staring at her as she stood in the door. Staring just as she had imagined David doing only the day before and in almost the same position in the room. Around him the office was in perfect order, as if waiting for him to come to life and begin his day's work.

The cold hand of death gripped Nicole by the throat as she stood in the door and stared back into those dead eyes. It gripped her and held her there to absorb the finality of Clint Forrester's condition until she knew with absolute certainty that it was just a preview of *her* fate and, probably, David's. *You can't stop fate, can't hold back time.*

I should get help. But the thought wasn't enough to move her leaden limbs. *Call the police. Call David.* But she couldn't move and couldn't slow her gasping breath as she fought to get air past the grip death had on her throat. Couldn't prevent anything. Couldn't avoid death. *Oh, God, help me.* And she stood trembling in the cold grasp of death as she felt the tears washing down her cheeks with no hope of ever stopping.

"My God!" Jane Lee's horrified cry beside her startled her into motion, and she spun toward the woman and tried to say something. But nothing came out, and Jane's face darkened before her as she hyperventilated from her ragged, gasping breath. She was suddenly light-headed, and the floor was tilting up at her until it pulled her down to sit, trying to stop breathing, stop thinking.

"Nicole! Oh, here, let me find a paper bag." Jane was scurrying around the office somewhere, but all Nicole could see was a dim view of the office carpet as she leaned on her hands, panting against the shock. "Help!" Jane

called out. "Somebody call the police! Here, Nicole, take
this." And she knelt beside her opening a small paper bag
and pushing it toward Nicole's face. "Breathe into it.
have to get help." And then her hurried footsteps moved
away as Nicole took the bag and held it feebly over her
mouth and nose with one trembling hand.

Then there were other footsteps and other voices. She
was helped to her feet and led down the corridor to a conference room where someone helped her to lie down on the
long couch. Nicole could barely see any of this and
couldn't understand what they were saying. All she could
see was Clint Forrester's dead eyes and all she could hear
was her own heartbeat.

You can't avoid fate. Everybody dies sometime.

And she couldn't avoid the memory of what her heart
would sound like as it stopped beating.

DAVID TURNED THE CORNER as the sirens grew behind him.
A police car threaded its way through traffic and moved
past in the same direction he was walking. And it stopped
before Nicole's office building!

He was running before he could think. In, and to the
elevators, but the cops had just taken one up, stranding
him in the lobby. He couldn't wait for another car, so he
ran to the stairs and up, his sore ribs throbbing from his
desperate movement. Throwing himself out of the stairwell door, he stumbled into the reception room of the law
office only to be stopped by a crowd of people standing
irresolutely around the desk.

"Nicole!" He shouted her name, not caring how he
looked or sounded as he searched the faces around him for
hers. "Nicole!"

"She's lying down." An older woman came toward him,
a worried smile on her face. "You must be David."

"Yes, I am. Where is Nicole? Is she all right?"

"She's fine," the woman assured him. "A bit frightened, but fine, otherwise."

"Where is she?" He couldn't concentrate on the woman's face and the voices around him seemed to be little more than a cacophonous babble. He had to find Nicole.

"Here, I'll take you." She grabbed his hand, leading him past the other people. "I'm Jane Lee," she explained.

"Oh, yes," he said absently. "What happened?"

"It's Clint," Jane said, but a young police officer cut her off when he stopped them in the hall.

"Please, wait in the other room," he said, sounding unsure of himself. "We don't want to mess anything up."

"Where's Nicole?" David asked him.

"This man is a friend of Mr. Forrester's secretary," Jane explained to the officer. "He doesn't want to go to the office, just to the conference room right there." And she pointed to the next door in the hall.

"Well, I suppose—"

But David had already bolted past him and through the partially open door of the conference room to kneel at Nicole's side where she lay on the couch with her eyes closed.

"Nicole," he said softly, placing his hand on her shoulder. He wanted to pull her into his arms and hold her until he could be reassured by her heartbeat but he was afraid to startle her. She looked so young and frail lying there, a little girl trapped in an adult abomination. "Nicole? Nicole?"

"Nicole, are you all right?" And David held her shoulder, leaning over her on the wet pavement as she stared up into his worried eyes. She wanted to tell him that she was all right. She'd just slipped, was all. But no words

*came out. She wasn't even sure that she was moving her
lips, and all she could hear was her heartbeat continuing
its steady pace. It wasn't faltering to a stop but continuing
to pump life through her veins. Wasn't stopping, as she
knew it would.* "Nicole!" David shook her. "Come on,
darling. Please say something." *And that didn't fit the
dream, didn't belong on the wet street that faded into the
paneled walls and book-filled shelves of a conference room
in the office. What was happening now?*

"What happened, Nicole?"

And then she realized that she wasn't lost in the dream
but alive with David beside her, and she let her arms fly
around his neck to hold him close and warm to her. For a
moment at least, she could be safe in his strong arms.

"He killed Clint," she gasped. "He was dead in the office the whole morning and I didn't know it. I walked in
and found him sitting there in his chair staring, staring
at—" She broke off in tears, unable to continue.

"That's all right. You've had a shock," David con-
soled her. "But you'll be all right. Don't worry now."

David's arms almost had the power to make it seem like
a dream, and she allowed herself to experience the love and
security that she had feared she would never feel again.

"We'll get whoever did this," David said, rocking
slightly as he knelt and held her tightly in his arms. He
could feel her heartbeat against his chest, matching its
rhythm to his. She was safe, and for that moment in time
David really believed that they could succeed. Anything
was possible while he was holding her.

"Just hold me," she said. "Don't even talk. If I talk I
have to think, and I don't want to think. Hold me." The
small movements of his muscles as he held her and stroked
her hair aroused a passion that she let wash through her
unabated. That passion was an elixir against pain and Da-

vid was her shield against death and she needed the positive force of life to reassure her just then. Anything was
possible when she was in his arms, and she had a future as
long as it was with him. He was her future. Love was her
only hope.

"WHEN DID YOU ARRIVE at work this morning?" Detective-Lieutenant Sam Potter sat easily in an armchair across
from Nicole and David on the couch. He held a notebook
loosely in his right hand, a pen in the other.

"Shortly before nine," she answered. Rest, and David's
arm around her shoulder, had strengthened her for the
questions that had to be answered.

"And you just went about your business?" He looked
at her impersonally, his pen poised for a reply.

"Of course I did. I finished some letters." The man's
official manner and questioning stare made her feel guilty
of something.

"Was it normal for Mr. Forrester to be so late?"

"No, he was normally quite punctual," she said coldly.

"What does that have to do with his death?" David
glared at the officer. "I told you about Lance Decker. Go
find him!"

"You said that you thought he tried to run you down on
the street," the policeman pointed out. "But, true or not,
you can't prove it has any bearing on Mr. Forrester's
murder."

"But at least it's a lead! What Nicole did or did not do
this morning doesn't mean anything. The man has been
dead for hours, for crying out loud!"

"Calm down, Mr. Germaine. We're looking into your
information."

"Good. Is Nicole a suspect in the murder?"

"No, not at the moment," the detective admitted, scratching his pen through his thinning thatch of gray hair. Then he said to Nicole, "Do you smoke?"

"No, I don't."

"Which puts her a bit farther down the list of suspects," the man said, making a note in his book. "Does your Lance Decker smoke?" he asked David.

"Yes."

"Do you happen to know what brand he smokes?"

"Marlboro. The long ones," David told him.

"Light or regular?"

"Light." It was amazing what small things a person remembered about another person though they might take little notice of it at the time. "What does that prove?"

"Maybe nothing. But the cigarette butt in the ashtray was from a Marlboro Light."

"There," David proclaimed. "That should help tie Decker into this."

"Maybe." The officer finished writing in his book and looked at the two people on the couch. "We'll know better when they've run a check on the fingerprints on the water glass. I noticed that the glass didn't quite match the rest in his set. Why is that?" he asked Nicole.

"I don't really know." Something about her memory of the scene was nagging at her but she couldn't think what it was. "He had a different set before but broke most of the glasses over time. It may be from that one."

"Makes sense."

Another notation was made on the pad, and Nicole watched the deliberate movements of the pen in agony. Wouldn't he ever be finished with questions?

"But why would this Decker fellow want to kill Clint Forrester? From what you told me, Mr. Germaine, he was mad at you, not Forrester."

"I think they were working together," David said. He hadn't mentioned the incident in the galley of his boat before and explained it now, with Nicole confirming the fact that the lawyer had neglected to contact Woods Hole about his donation.

She also told the detective about her discovery of the gun in her employer's desk and learned that a search of the office had failed to turn it up.

"So you think Forrester and Decker were together in a conspiracy to steal your invention?"

"That's the best explanation we've been able to come up with."

"Did you have any reason to think Decker was prone to violence? I mean, is he the type of man who would agree to commit murder for such dubious benefit?"

"I wouldn't have thought so," David admitted.

"Yes, he would." Nicole sat forward then, remembering the conversation with Lance's sister. "I spoke to his sister on the phone this morning."

"You knew about her?" David regarded her in surprise. They hadn't had time to talk about anything but the fact of Clint's death before now. "How?"

"Jerry called looking for you. She had called the boat for you and he told me who she was."

"She told you something that has bearing on the case?" the detective prompted.

"Yes, she said that Lance had fallen off the wagon. She suspects that he's on drugs."

"Yes, the boys at his old apartment said he was a coke addict," David said. "I didn't really believe them."

"Why not?" Detective Potter spoke while writing in his book. "You say he worked for you? Didn't you know?"

"No. He didn't appear to be using anything while he was on board ship with us. I fired him because he was lazy. He certainly didn't exhibit any nervousness or other signs of cocaine use.''

''That's because he was off of it then,'' Nicole said. ''His sister said that he'd been in the hospital to kick his habit. Apparently, he'd gotten violent and they had to have him committed.''

''Violent?'' Now the officer was smiling as he wrote.

''See?'' David said, eagerly. ''Now we've got some reasons to suspect Lance. I don't see how he got together with Forrester, but he sure wasn't happy about being canned. And, if he is using again, it wouldn't be too hard to conceive of his trying to kill me.''

''Okay, we'll put him at the top of the list,'' Potter said. ''And I hope you're right, because I enjoy being able to call a case closed every now and again.''

''Believe me,'' Nicole said, taking David's hand. ''You aren't any more eager to close this case than we are.''

''And maybe with police help, we finally will be finished with it.'' David looked into her hopeful brown eyes. There was a gallant battle being fought behind those eyes, a fight to push away the fear and despair that assailed her.

''I assume you told the Long Island authorities about your suspicions,'' the policeman said, standing up tiredly.

''No, we didn't,'' Nicole admitted. ''But we didn't know about Lance then. We didn't know who loosened the fitting on the gas line.''

''I'll fax my report to them,'' he said. ''Can you give me a description of Decker?''

''He's pretty normal-looking,'' David replied. ''Blond hair.''

''He has a narrow face with thin eyebrows. I think,'' Nicole said, quickly. ''Looks young. And, there is a burn on his left hand. Isn't there, David?''

"I don't—yes, he did have some scar tissue on the back of his hand."

"Color of eyes?" Potter looked at Nicole for a reply, but she only shrugged. The man at the deli had worn sunglasses.

"Blue, I think," David said. "Set close together."

"He's left-handed," Nicole added. "Rather short, too."

"Okay, that's enough for now. We'll visit his sister. She'll most likely have a photograph. Do you have her address?"

"423 Ocean Avenue, Jersey City," David said.

"All right then. I'm finished with you. You had better report in with the police on Long Island so they can route a patrol past your boat tonight."

"Do you think he'll still try something after this?" Nicole had been on the verge of optimism, but Lance hadn't been caught yet, and she was still very much in danger. "He's ruined any profit that might be gained from killing David by shooting his own partner."

"He's obviously not thinking rationally if he thought that kicking a man from a motorbike would cause any permanent damage," the detective pointed out. "He's a junkie, Miss Ellis. Don't plan on any logic from him."

"What do you suggest that we do?" David stood, too, still holding Nicole's hand.

"If you want to be safe, take your boat out to sea for the night," Potter suggested. "He can't get you out there."

BUT BEFORE THEY COULD DO anything to see to their safety, there was one more stop to be taken.

"The only way Clint Forrester might have profited by holding back on my donation was if Robert expects to get Albany Manufacturing away from me in the very near future," David said, as he and Nicole hurried along the busy street. "They couldn't market it without the patents, and only Robert would be in a position to get them."

"Maybe," Nicole agreed. "Clint was his lawyer, after all, so there is a connection. But you might be wrong about him, too."

"I don't mind being wrong," he insisted. "What I mind at this point is not knowing." They entered the building where Robert Philips had his office.

"How do we handle this?" she asked, as the elevator doors closed before them. "He'll never admit to anything."

"The trick with Robert is to get him off guard, angry. He can't concentrate when he's mad." David smiled, giving her hand a squeeze as the doors opened on his cousin's floor. "Don't worry, the best way to handle it is to go in swinging."

Nicole followed David into Robert Philips's plush office, lacking his sureness in the situation. David had become increasingly agitated as they approached the building. He'd mentioned bad blood between them, and it was obvious that lack of contact over the years hadn't diminished it.

They barreled past the protesting secretary and into the man's office without knocking. "I'm sorry, Mr. Philips," the secretary started to say, but he motioned that it was all right as he continued talking into the telephone.

"I'll call you back later," he said, hanging up and regarding David in surprise. "Hello, David," he said simply, a serious expression on his broad features. "Hello again, Ms. Ellis."

"Your partner is dead, cousin, so you might as well call it off now," David said, angrily.

"What?"

"Forrester is dead."

"Yes, I heard. But when did he become my partner?" His eyes shifted focus past David, indicating something amiss in the denial.

"I don't know when, but you've got to be the greedy pig who put him up to sitting on my donation!"

"I didn't put your lawyer up to anything," Philips said, his own anger rising suddenly. "I didn't even know about that thing of yours until he called me."

"So you do admit trying to steal it." David crossed his arms, glaring across the large desk at his cousin.

"No, I don't." But then he smiled lightly, relaxing. "But I knew you'd be pissed if I got it and your company. That's why I went along with it when Forrester called."

"What did he say?" Nicole cut in. Whatever had driven the two men apart as boys was impeding their progress toward an answer now, and they needed an outsider to mediate before they came to blows.

"He said that he would be able to talk David out of giving it away. He wanted stock in my new company in exchange for keeping such a valuable asset in the family, so to speak."

"So you decided you would just kill me and get the company the easy way," David said, sounding somewhat defeated. No matter what, he didn't want to think such a thing about his relative. He hadn't realized how badly he wanted to be wrong until now.

Philips paused for a moment, smoothing anger from his face and calming himself before he spoke. "No," he said. "I didn't. That's why I was in such a rush to see Clint this morning. I didn't think a gas explosion in the galley could have been accidental. And I never really believed that Forrester could deliver on the *Crab* deal. Not until I heard about the explosion, that is. Then I knew that he must have arranged the blast to uphold his end of the bargain."

"And you came to make him stop?" Nicole prompted.

"Of course."

"Why would Clint do something like this?" Nicole sat in one of the chairs before the desk.

"He was broke," Robert said. "That's why. He held a great deal of stock on option when the market crashed in '87 and he hadn't made a right move since. His wife has money, of course, but they were barely speaking. He had to get some cash quick if he wanted to hold on to his sanity."

"I knew he lost money," Nicole said, "but he never let on it was that bad."

"Appearances were very important to Clint," Robert said.

"Didn't you think it was a bit strange for him to be offering another man's property to you like that?" David sat, too, his anger and frustration leaving him now. "How could you agree to his deal?"

"It didn't cost me anything," Robert said lightly. "And if he did get it from you, you'd be mad as hell. I kind of liked that idea. The guy was crazy for money, so it didn't seem like it would hurt to humor him."

"But they tried to kill us!" David said. "They're still trying."

"Hey, I didn't have anything to do with that." The heavyset businessman leaned on his desk to stare at his cousin across from him. "I only agreed to give him stock in exchange for the *Crab*. It was simply good business to hang on to anything that might make money for me."

"But how on earth did you expect to get Albany Manufacturing without putting a gun to my head?"

"By begging, if I had to," he answered, earnestly. "I need that company. And the company needs me. You're not an idiot, David, and I knew you'd see it my way if you ever actually listened to me. I just had to get through the family bullshit first."

"You don't need it," David sneered. "You just want to gut it and sell it for a fast profit."

"I'm willing to admit I've done that in the past." Philips glowered at his cousin. "Business isn't always polite or fair, David. But I need Albany Manufacturing for something far different. I've succeeded in acquiring a string of small manufacturers and transportation companies and I'm putting them together under one management so I can get a bid in on some juicy government contracts that are coming up. Albany Manufacturing is a key piece for me. I have to keep it all in New York State to avoid the hassles of interstate trade laws, and because I can move faster that way. Without Albany, I can't guarantee being able to meet the deadlines."

"I don't see why you expected me to agree that making you richer was in the best interests of my company."

"Maybe you are an idiot, Dave," the man said. "Albany Manufacturing is just a piddly little company with thirty employees that happens to turn out a very good product. But good work isn't enough when it costs them as much as it does. They're too small and the big boys will eat them for lunch once they notice them. Then where are those jobs, David? Where's the security you think you're giving them by keeping them small? They'll be forced out of the market because they aren't able to shift gears fast enough to keep up. They were working half shifts for a month last winter because they didn't have anything to do. If Albany comes in with me they'll have a broader base to work from. And, if we get that contract, they'll be in business for years on that job alone. Big fish eat little fish, David, the same as in the ocean."

"So why are you suddenly so interested in building up a business? You've always been content to take your profit and run before."

"Maybe I'm finally growing up, Dave," he said. "Maybe I want to build something."

"But you just couldn't resist a chance to take a poke at me in passing, could you?"

"No, I guess not. It seems to me that the last time we got into it I came out on the short end of the fight." Philips rested his elbows on the desk, bridging his fingers before his face. "And when Grandfather left you the boat, my mother raised holy hell about it. She lost that fight and made sure I didn't forget it. And I always knew I'd do a better job with your company than you have. It's family tradition, boy, and I wanted to rub your nose in it if I could."

"That's a dumb way to run a business." David smiled.

"You always manage to piss me off. And I don't like to lose," the other man said. "Forrester seemed to be offering me a way to go out a winner. It's funny though, but when I heard about the explosion it all seemed kind of dumb to me, too."

"We really are cut from the same cloth, aren't we?" David regarded Robert differently then, wondering how he'd missed the intelligence behind the man's swaggering manner. "I guess our problem is that we're both poor losers. Our parents gave us a fine example with their bickering over the years."

"Definitely genetic," Robert said. "Tell me something. Knowing me as you do, what satisfaction did you expect I would get out of killing you? I could hardly laugh in your face then, could I?"

David chuckled, leaning back in his chair comfortably. "No, I guess you couldn't. I didn't want you to be the bad guy. I just expected you to be in it somehow. And I was right about that.''

"I don't want your damn submarine thing. I only want the company.''

"I'll think about it,'' David promised. "Maybe we can both end up as winners and let it go at that.''

They left the office no wiser than before. Family harmony was a long-term investment, and they had their sights set on the short term. But knowing that it was Lance Decker behind things didn't help. He could still achieve his goal at any time. And it was obvious from his behavior that he was set to complete his mission regardless of whether he profited by it or not.

Lance Decker had to be captured before either one of them would be safe.

Chapter Fifteen

The sun was already scraping the tops of the World Trade Center towers when Nicole and David drove out of the city, and it had begun to fill the sky with fiery orange light by the time they reached the *Katharine*'s mooring. They spent most of the drive in silence, broken by intermittent attempts at conversation. Mostly, however, they each had their own thoughts to preoccupy their minds.

"Time doesn't seem to have changed," Nicole said, consulting the frozen watch she'd put on after Clint's death. She wasn't sure if she was hoping for good luck in wearing it or if she just wanted it handy in case it began to move again. She only knew that it made her feel better to wear it. "It must have, though."

"Clint's death is a big change, that's for certain," David said thoughtfully. "I wish I knew if it was a change for the better or worse."

"It's horribly frustrating." Nicole fought back the fear within her, taking reassurance from his nearness and his quiet strength. "Maybe only the sequence of events is changed. Maybe he died after me the first time around, or would have if we hadn't taken this strange jump backward. Maybe the killer has stepped up his timetable. He could come for me at any time."

"No," David said quickly, reaching to take her hand. "This has to be an improvement for us. Whatever plan is in motion, it has to have been severely screwed up by Forrester's death. That gives us an advantage. We'll solve this thing."

"I know we will, David." Nicole tightened her grip on his hand, hoping her words would help to reassure him. "It's just frightening to know he's coming for me, even to know who he is, but to have no way of protecting myself."

"What I should do is buy you a plane ticket out of here," David said. "You'd be safe in another town."

"No," she answered. "I have a feeling that if I don't face it here where I know what to look for, my fate will just catch up with me somewhere else where I won't be able to see it coming."

"That's a pessimistic attitude," he commented, though he didn't try to persuade her otherwise.

"I just feel that way." She spoke quietly and watched the traffic, feeling the weight of events planned by time on her shoulders. "Ever since I found Clint in his office I have known for certain that I'm meant to stay right here. Only by facing it here do I have any chance of beating the odds."

"I thought I should mention it, anyway," he said. "Though I think I'm feeling the same way. A little voice in the back of my mind says that we've got to stick together. Besides, if Lance Decker is the worst we have to fear we'll do all right."

But neither one of them believed it was that easy. A person can stay lost in the city for a long time if he wants to. The flow of events didn't seem to dictate a set timetable, for, as Clint's death had proved, they could veer dramatically away from their original course. So there was no reason to suppose he couldn't strike earlier or later than 12:41 tomorrow.

Nicole watched David behind the wheel. The sunlight was golden orange on his face, lighting his firm features with a radiant glow. He looked to be made of stone in that light, indestructible and unworried. He was a man who could be counted on to keep his calm and think things through in a serious situation. But she'd seen beyond the solid exterior to the warm and caring man who could hold her tenderly and soothe away her fears. He was a man with a deep sense of family who, despite his bluster, badly wanted to make peace with his childhood rival and had finally fought against his own stubborn competitiveness to do so today. This was the man she'd grown to love. But he was someone who, she'd begun to feel, could never feel the same way about her.

The *Katharine* lay quietly tied to the pier, a dark and forbidding hulk against the flaming backdrop of sunset on the Sound. David parked the car as close as possible in the lot and then took Nicole's suitcase from the back seat and led the way along the dock toward the boat. Nicole scanned the vessels parked in the slips on either side as they walked, waiting for the messenger of death to rise from the shadows. But no one rose, and they reached the boat unimpeded.

"Wait a moment," David said quietly, as they stepped onto the deck. "I'll take a quick look."

"Be careful." Nicole crouched down, peering into the dark cabin. She could see nothing until he returned and switched on the lights in the main room.

"We're all clear," he said, opening the door. "Connie isn't here. She must be in town with friends again tonight."

"Then we have the boat to ourselves?"

"Yes," he said, watching her with carefully appraising eyes, "we do."

"WHY DID THIS HAPPEN TO US?" Nicole asked the question with little hope of ever receiving an answer. "I have never done anything I know of to deserve a second chance. Why me?"

They were sitting on the couch in the salon with the lamps low and the deck lights illuminated to catch anyone who might try to board. If fate was to come for them, it would have to come through the light and they had resolved to stay awake through the night to watch for it.

"I don't think we're supposed to question it," he answered. *Why indeed,* he wondered. *Why put me so close to this wonderful woman? Why must I fight with the foolish idea that we might have a chance together?*

"Maybe not, but I can't leave it alone. Are we only postponing the inevitable?" The question started a tremor of fear in her stomach, but she swallowed her anxiety. "Let's face it. In the real world, they'd have had the funeral by now."

"Don't think about it," David said quickly. He slipped his arm around her shoulders, needing to feel her warmth as much as he wanted to calm her. "Because it isn't going to happen that way. Lance Decker is our only worry now, and he'll be caught."

"But if he isn't, there's every chance that my funeral will take place right on schedule, David. There's no guarantee—" She couldn't continue. A knot of sorrow choked the words off in her throat as tears welled in her eyes. "I'm so scared," she whispered, turning her face against his shoulder.

"Don't be scared. There never were any guarantees, were there? None of us has any assurance of living to a ripe old age.'' David spoke as though he'd only just realized that simple fact and was somewhat in awe of it. ''But I'm going to do my best to be certain that you do.'' He reached up to push her silken hair back from her cheek, wiping the tear away with his thumb. ''Look, the police will patrol the marina every hour. Our alarms are all switched on and everything is lit up as bright as day out there. He can't get to us without warning.''

Nicole clung to him, wanting to believe the optimism in his words. Life couldn't be so cruel as to put them together like this only to snatch happiness away again, could it? A life that would allow a second chance must also allow them to make use of it, and she felt then that the only good use for this opportunity was to find love. So she held him tightly, letting the steady sound of his heartbeat drown out the fearful staccato of hers.

Nicole felt that being with David was the sole purpose of everything at that moment. He was the reason for this twist of time and fate, the reason for living she'd never known she'd lacked. If she could have him, even for a moment, then all the fear and confusion was worth it. And to keep him forever would be heaven. Blinking back the remaining tears, she looked up into his tender eyes as he held her. How could he not feel anything? There must be some feeling there, locked behind the grief he felt for his late wife. He couldn't be so concerned without caring.

''David,'' she began, but the words weren't there. Words weren't important, only actions and emotions. And, as if they shared the same thought, they moved in tandem to join their lips in a kiss.

His touch melted away the oppressive darkness that assailed her thoughts, replacing it with sparkling hope and endless desire. The muscles in his back danced eloquently beneath her hands as he tightened his embrace. She responded with joyousness, smoothing her hands over his warm back as his lips trailed along the line of her jaw to her throat. His tender hands slipped across to one breast, waiting to be rebuked. And, when she responded by moving her own hand up to his cheek and drawing his lips back to hers, he let his hand work wonders that took her breath away.

"Nicole," he sighed, kissing her cheek and the tip of her nose. "I don't—"

"Yes, you do." And she cut him off with a kiss, stifling the negative in his words and approving the positive in his hands and lips. "We both do," she sighed, smiling into his eyes.

"I've tried to be your friend," he said, carefully. Her eyes were mysterious orbs of passion before him, killing his resolve with their merest glance. No matter what he felt was right, he couldn't stop touching her. Couldn't stop loving her.

"You are my friend," she said, breathlessly. "The only friend I need."

"But this is more than that, Nicole. Friends don't—" *Don't what?* he wondered. *You try to be a friend when you want to be a lover, and you can't be one without the other.*

"I need a friend who will hold me and make me feel as alive as you are making me feel right now," she insisted, her own restraint only a memory after his kiss. "And I think we both know it's gone beyond friendship."

"But what if this is only the circumstances talking? What if it's just, just . . ."

"Pity?" she asked. Then she laughed, stroking his cheek and loving the concern he felt about his motives. "Then pity me, David. Pity me some more."

She punctuated her demand with a kiss, affirming her own passion for him. But David tensed in her arms then, lifting his head quickly and slipping his hand away from her heated body.

"What is it?" Nicole shrank back at his listening pose, her heightened emotions giving way to an even stronger sense of foreboding.

"I heard something." Looking around the room, he saw nothing unusual. The lighted wharf beyond the ship was empty, the alarm buzzer had not gone off. But still, there had been something, a clicking sound that didn't belong, hovering there.

"What?" *No, no, don't freeze now.* But she felt herself falling into the grip of the same mindless immobility that had captured her at Clint's door.

"Wait a second." David stood and moved quietly to the hall. "I'll check below," he whispered, smiling reassuringly.

Nicole tried to calm herself as she waited on the couch, but a fearful darkness stole into her mind like ink soaking into a paper towel. But there couldn't be anyone on board. It was just a sound.

The bore of the gun was pressed against her forehead and beyond it, at the end of his extended arm, she could see the little man from the deli. But it wasn't raining and he wasn't wearing his sunglasses now.

Nicole leaped up from the couch, accepting the warning of her vision without thought and taking a step toward the door to the deck. The police should be around again soon, and if she opened that door the alarm would go off to summon them.

But the warning had come too late. An arm came out of the dim light and circled her throat, throwing her back onto the couch as the man jumped up before her. Now the gun was pointed at the center of her forehead, as in the vision.

"The party is over." The voice was a harsh and tight whisper, hissing past teeth, bared in a smile. "You shouldn't have stuck your nose into this," he said, just as he'd said in the vision she'd had on the boat last Saturday.

Nicole couldn't force any response through her constricted throat. Her limbs were leaden weights, unable to take any action to save herself or warn David.

"Shouldn't have come out here," Lance added, tightening his finger on the trigger slightly. "All I want is Germaine, honey. But we can't have any witnesses left." His eyes kept darting toward the hall entrance as he spoke, waiting for the scientist to enter.

"The police," Nicole whispered hoarsely. "They know."

"They know shit," he snapped. "I've got my route out of the country all mapped out. They'll never know where I've gone."

"But how did you..." She couldn't breathe well enough to talk; her lungs pumped wildly as she stared at the waiting killer's face.

"Get on board ship?" He smiled. "I hid in Connie's closet. Lover boy didn't search so good as he thought. And now you'll both pay for it."

"It's not too late," she said then, forcing the words out. She'd seen a movement behind him. Someone was on deck moving stealthily just below the windows toward the door. "You can go back into the hospital, Lance. They can help."

"I'm not crazy, honey," he stated. "I'm going to be rich."

"Rich?" she said, repressing a gasp as she realized that David was standing outside the door, holding a fire extinguisher in his hands and motioning for her to do something. "You won't get any money now." What did he want her to do? Yes, the door. He wanted her to cover the sound of the door opening!

"Of course I will," Lance snorted. "Everything is on track, babe."

"You idiot!" she said, raising her voice as much in fear as necessity. "You won't get—"

"Shut up!" he hissed at her, snapping his free hand out to grasp her throat again. He couldn't shoot her until he'd taken care of David. "Shut up," he repeated, pressing the gun to her temple.

David had taken advantage of his angry movement to open the door and slip into the room. Twenty feet of cabin with a long conference table in the center impeded his movement, however, and he had to move carefully now. He placed his foot on the canvas seat of a chair at the table, watching Lance's hunched back as he put weight on it and used the unstable surface to step up to the table top. The man's whispered threats against Nicole inflamed him, and he wanted to take immediate action, but his scientifically trained mind forced him to ease his weight onto the table and avoid making noise until he could get as close as possible. Lance had a gun, and one wrong move could end it all very quickly.

"Why should I shut up?" Nicole's spirit came back to her at the cold touch of his hand. She hadn't been given this chance only to sit like a stone and let it happen. "You're going to kill me anyway."

"Just shut up!" Tightening his grip on her throat, Lance glowered at her. The gun moved away from her head as he leaned closer to her. "I don't have to wait for him," he said. "There are no guns on this boat, so I'll get him any way."

"Lance!" David shouted, lifting the extinguisher up as the startled man spun toward the voice and spraying him full in the face before he could bring his gun around.

The icy breath of the CO_2 extinguisher spilled over Nicole's face as she jumped at their staggering assailant and threw her arms around his chest. "Damn it!" Lance screamed out, choking on the gas that blinded him as he turned the gun toward David. But Nicole pushed his arm up just as he fired, sending the bullet through the ceiling of the cabin as David ducked away. Lance twisted, spinning Nicole off him to the floor.

David swung the extinguisher bottle against his shoulder as he jumped down from the table and turned on the man. But Lance staggered around the table, kicking a chair at the scientist's legs. Then he pointed the gun toward them and fired without aim, the bullet shattering a window behind them. David fired another blast from his makeshift weapon, stunning Lance again and forcing him to retreat toward the door. He couldn't clear his vision enough to aim and fired blindly to slow their pursuit, putting a bullet into the wall.

"Get down!" David commanded, running at Lance. Swinging the extinguisher like a baseball bat, he knocked the man back again and ducked away from the weapon that swung back at him.

Nicole circled the other side of the table in a crouch. She wasn't going to let the killer get away!

But Lance, blinking his eyes clear, bolted for the door, realizing that he had the advantage of distance in his weapon. Just outside the doorway, he turned and aimed squarely at David who was lunging through the door at him. "Die, sucker!" he snarled.

"Drop the gun!" A new voice, coming from the darkness on the dock, said.

Lance jumped back and turned toward the new threat, his gun rising as four shots rang out in the still night. He snapped back from the impact of the bullets, blood blooming red on his chest. His hands flew up and the gun clattered uselessly across the deck. He landed on his back like a stuffed doll, and then fell still. He didn't move again.

"Are you people all right?" Two uniformed officers clattered up the gangway, their guns up and ready as they approached the dead man. "We heard the shots."

"Thank you." Nicole sighed. It might have been bright sunshine on deck, the way she felt right then. It was as if a storm had passed over and the light beyond it was brighter than any she'd ever felt.

"That's the man," David said. "Lance Decker." Then he turned to gather Nicole into his arms gratefully and hug her with unbounded joy. "It's over," he said. "Finally over."

Chapter Sixteen

The boat swarmed with police for hours after the officers called in the shooting. Mostly, it was bookkeeping, gathering facts about the shooting to establish that the policemen had fired out of necessity. Nobody seemed especially saddened by the form under the plastic sheet. But then Lance Decker hadn't been particularly sad about his plan to put them in a similar position.

"That was a short investigation." Detective-Lieutenant Potter from Manhattan entered the salon where Nicole and David sat drinking coffee and waiting for the police to finish. "Just the kind I like."

"No more than we liked it, Lieutenant," David said. "It's after midnight. Why did you come all this way?"

"I live in Queens," he answered. "It's not that long a drive. Besides, he was our suspect so it looks good if we put in an appearance. It was lucky you had them patrol the neighborhood." He looked around at the shattered window and the telltale holes in the wall and ceiling, which the police had circled in red chalk.

"I'll never grumble about a parking ticket again," Nicole said, smiling up at the officer.

"Must have been quite a scuffle," he said. "You hur any?"

"Not at all," she assured him, grasping David's hand in hers. "I feel wonderful."

"Good." The detective smiled, looking from her to David. Then he took the notebook from his suit pocke and flipped it open. "Figured I'd update you on your boss while I was here, though I don't suppose it matters any more."

"Were you able to find something out this soon?" David asked.

"I cheated," Potter said, sagging into one of the can vas chairs as he found the correct page. "I had them con centrate on Lance Decker. He was fingerprinted shortly before he went into the hospital last year. Felonious as sault. First-time offender, so they bargained down to hos pitalization. You ought to check your employees out bette if you let a man like that get past you," he chided David.

"I'll install a polygraph next week," David said.

"Well, his prints were on the glass, as clear as day. An the saliva on the cigarette butt matches his blood type. I'm sure we'll find that the gun he had with him tonight wil prove to be the one that killed Forrester."

"Are they about done yet?" David asked impatiently "I don't have enough room for all of them to stay over."

"Should be done," the detective said, standing "They'll have a week of paperwork to do, of course."

Out on deck, two policemen had lifted Lance Decker body onto a stretcher and were carrying it off as the oth ers began gathering their gear. Nicole and David walke out with Lieutenant Potter. "When do we sign our state ments?" David asked the officer in charge.

"Tomorrow afternoon. Anytime." The policeman spoke grimly, his task at the scene being much more involved than Potter's. "Don't change anything for now. We might need more pictures."

"Don't worry, I'll leave it." Though as David looked at the crimson stain with the body outline chalked around it he couldn't help but shudder at the thought of not washing it away. They'd traded one life for another that night; time had claimed its victim after all.

THE POLICE LEFT Nicole and David stranded in an awkward silence. Relief wasn't a large enough word to describe how they felt, but then neither was emptiness. They stood in the salon like strangers, each wondering what the next word should be and hoping the other would say it.

"That's the end of it," David finally said, his voice sounding small and far away. "All over."

"I guess so." *Why am I so unable to say what I think?* Nicole wondered. *And why can't he just come here and hold me?* "I'm unemployed now, too," she said, smiling to realize that it hadn't occurred to her before.

"You're going to law school anyway," he reminded her. *She's fantastic. If you let her leave the boat you're a bigger fool than you've ever imagined.* And he looked at her without speaking, wanting to hold her again. Wanting more than that.

"I don't want to be a lawyer anymore," she said. "I was thinking of something nautical."

"Katharine was never as fond of the sea as I was," he said, stepping toward her and taking one hand in both of his. "Sunshine and salt air aren't very good for the skin."

"Are you suggesting that I avoid the seafaring life?" Nicole had never before felt so close to someone while feeling so far away. What was he thinking? Why did he hesitate?

"No," he said at last. "I'd only suggest that you think twice about it." He smiled wanly, squeezing her hand. Then the smile died, replaced with serious concentration as he gazed into her eyes.

"Nicole," he said tenderly, capturing her other hand and squeezing both of them. "I didn't want to feel this way about you. But it seems that no matter what I thought I wanted, my heart had other plans. I've spent all my energy avoiding life since Katharine died, and now I want to rush back into it with you. I've been so afraid that we wouldn't succeed and I'd lose you like I lost Katharine that I kept drawing back and trying to stay clear of you. Then last night—well, that wasn't just a fluke for me. And now that the danger is over, I don't want to pretend that it was. I want to live again with you. But if you don't feel the same way about me now, I'll understand. I mean, the strain of everything had us both on edge, and maybe a bit more lonely than we might normally be."

"Oh David," she said. "You don't have to worry about how I feel. Last night was wonderful, and I haven't changed my mind about anything." There was nothing in the world but this man's eyes and his shy, happy smile. Nothing but his hands on hers.

"I love you, Nicole," David said, quietly. He stared into her rich hazel eyes, not quite able to believe that it was coming to this conclusion. He couldn't lose her as he'd lost Katharine, not now or ever. Such cruel fate did not exist in the world he knew.

"I know why this all happened to us." Grasping his hands as tightly as she could, she wanted to savor this moment even as she wanted to move on to the next. "It wasn't to save my life or yours. It was for *our* lives, David. Our love. That's why it felt so urgent that we stick together. It was our love that was fated, and time held itself in check to keep us together. That's our fate."

"It does feel that way," he said. "We're both alive again. And I love you so much that it hurts to even think of parting."

"Then let's never part," she said. And she raised her face to his, letting him savor her lips as though his life depended on it.

Nicole threw her arms around him as though trying to fuse their bodies into one. Her lips lingered on the edge of the kiss, tasting his sweet warmth and hungering for more. His muscles were taut and alive, making her ache for him more. She could have screamed out in joy had she been willing to break away for even a moment, but she clung to him with frantic urgency, too overpowered by this sudden release of feelings to say a word.

David trailed kisses to the base of her throat, sending delicate ripples through her body like laughter. His capable hands pulled her even closer.

The restraints they'd felt before were gone now. And, tonight, they were free of the anxiety that had colored their every thought and emotion.

Nicole had no memory of how they managed to descend the spiral staircase to his private quarters. There were only his arms around her and the burning, impatient need in her heart. Everything was motion and startling peaks of joy, ending in a euphoric fog of happiness and sated desires. They nestled together in sleep, his arms circling her waist protectively, possessively. As dawn began to creep across the sky, Nicole fell asleep with the secure feeling she'd always have his love.

Nothing could go wrong for them now.

WATER GLASS. ASHTRAY. CIGARETTE BUTT. Nicole was too tired to reach out for them as they floated before her in the warm, dark void. It wasn't a vision or a déjà vu experience; her subconscious mind knew that this was only a dream and there was no urgency in it.

Ashtray. Cigarette butt. Missing gun.

They didn't matter. Lance was dead while David was alive and holding her close. She was aware of him, firm against her back even in sleep. This was only a dream and made no difference now.

Ashtray. But what about that ashtray, and why had she felt it was strange when she first saw it? What was wrong with the scene but had been overshadowed by the sight of Clint Forrester, slumped, quite dead in his chair? It didn't matter. Stop dreaming about it.

But the dream wouldn't go away. A simple progression of images floating unsupported just beyond her reach, if she'd had any desire to reach for them.

Instead of reaching, Nicole rolled in her sleep to hug her lover to her. No dream was important when her most fervent dream had already been realized.

"THERE WERE NO ASHES in the ashtray."

"What?" David turned to look down to where she rested her head on his chest.

"The ashtray." Then Nicole laughed, stretching up to kiss him as he lay contentedly beside her. "But then I should have said good morning first, shouldn't I?"

"I don't think it's morning anymore." He laughed. "Do you always wake up thinking about ashtrays?" He twined his fingers through her hair, studying the strands in the sunlight that flooded the stateroom.

"I was dreaming about it," she said. "I just couldn't get away from the ashtray and the water glass."

"Sounds like a dull dream."

"It was. But there was something very compelling about it, too." Nicole twisted to rise on one elbow and look at him earnestly. "And now I know what seemed so strange about the ashtray. There were no ashes in it."

"The one in Forrester's office, you mean?"

"Right. Why would there be a cigarette stubbed out in the ashtray but no ashes?"

"He'd smoked it down before going in and put it out right away," David suggested.

"But the bottom of the ashtray was clean, David. There was no smudged ash on the glass like there would be if he'd put it out there."

"He might have stubbed it out on the sole of his shoe. Out in the hallway, I suppose," David mused, scraping his fingers back through his tousled hair. "But Lance was never the neat type. He would have thrown the butt wherever he put it out rather than carrying it to an appropriate place."

"So, why wasn't the ashtray dirty?"

They looked at each other silently for a moment, both reaching the same shocked conclusion.

"David," Nicole said, slipping her legs out of the bed to stand. "What time is it?"

"Twelve-twenty," he said, reading the bedside clock. "But you don't think that..."

"Yes, I do." Nicole gathered her clothing unmindful of her nakedness as she hurried to get ready. "I think that Lance Decker was just the patsy. He was supposed to be blamed for everything while the real perpetrator got away with it.''

"But who is left that might benefit?" David was infected by her urgent manner, but was having less success in finding his clothing, finally going to the dresser.

"Who's left?" she asked seriously. "There must be someone. Unless—'' But she let her words trail off, unwilling to voice the thought.

"What?"

"What about Robert's mother? I got the impression that it was she who was pushing hardest for him to win your fights. And she was the one who tried to take this boat away. What if she arranged all of it?"

David didn't answer at first, but stood at the dresser gazing pensively into space. "I don't know," he said at last. "I'd say she wouldn't stoop to murder, but then I couldn't be sure. Not sure enough to stake my life on it, anyway."

"She'd want her son's deal to succeed, wouldn't she? How far do you think she'd go for that, and to get revenge for the supposed injustice in your grandfather's will?"

"Like I said, I wouldn't stake my life on the answer," he answered, buttoning his shirt. "And, if you're right about that cigarette, it stands to reason that someone else was in on it."

The dark feeling within her told her that her intuition was right. They weren't out of the woods yet.

"I'm going up to call Lieutenant Potter," she said, leaving the cabin. Impulsively, she put on her wristwatch as she walked down the hall.

Nicole picked up the phone in the main cabin and dialed the number the Manhattan detective had given her the day before. While she waited for him to come to the phone, a movement on deck caught her eye and she flinched involuntarily, tensing in readiness for flight. But it was only Connie coming aboard. She paused to stare down where the police had chalked the outline of the fallen body. Breathing easier, Nicole sat at the table and waited.

"Detective-Lieutenant Potter," the man said at last.

"This is Nicole Ellis," she said, quickly. "I think there may have been another person involved with Lance Decker."

"Why?"

"Because the ashtray wasn't dirty," she said. "I think someone planted that cigarette butt there. Probably the water glass, too."

The detective paused a moment, the sounds of busy people replacing him on the line. Connie came through the door then, her face ashen with worry and fear as she approached Nicole.

"What is that?" she asked.

"We had some trouble last night," Nicole said. She was thinking, inappropriately, that she must look a fright with her blouse not quite tucked into her skirt and no stockings. Connie would have little trouble figuring out some of what happened to her the night before. "David is fine, though," she reassured her.

"That's good," the woman answered vacantly.

"Okay, I do have a note here from the lab that the ashtray held no ash or combustion residue." The officer broke his silence with a thoughtful tone. "That's how they worded it, but it sounds like you both have the same thing in mind. And that is the only water glass in the office of that style. It's plain while the others have an etched design that matches the pitcher."

"Did you check the inside of the glass for prints?" Nicole asked, suddenly. "You know. Someone may have picked it up with a couple of fingers inside and brought it to leave at the office."

"I'll have it checked out. If they didn't put too much water in it, there might still be prints," he answered, his growing excitement showing in his voice. "Anything else?"

"No, I don't think so."

"Okay. You two batten down the hatches and stay safe. If you're right, then the mastermind who left the cigarette has Forrester's gun."

"Don't worry," Nicole said, glancing at her stopped watch. "We'll keep a low profile." She hung up, taking a deep breath to fight off her growing fear. "It was Lance Decker," she said, trying to push her hair into order. "He tried to kill David."

"I know," Connie said, calmly.

"You what?" Nicole turned to look at the other woman and found herself staring at the snub nose .38 from Clint's drawer. "My God!"

"Couldn't you have just taken the hint and gone away?" Connie spoke in a calm, level voice, like someone lost in thought. "You didn't have to die."

"Please, Connie," Nicole said, frantically. "Stop now and you'll be all right. Everyone thinks Lance was working alone."

"No, they don't. Not now." Then Connie smiled. "But they won't find any fingerprints inside the glass. I wore gloves."

"Why are you doing this?" Nicole stood carefully, gauging the distance between them as she watched the gun.

"I deserve my share of things around here," she said. "It's only fair."

"What's fair, Connie?" David called to her from the hall but didn't approach. "What's fair about killing us?"

The woman didn't take her eyes off Nicole, but stepped back and turned slightly to face the galley wall and include David in her field of vision.

"It will even things up, David," she said, seriously. "After you married my sister and spent all those years using me like a dog to fetch sticks for you, I think it's time to even things up."

"You were my paid assistant," he said. "Fetching sticks is pretty much what assistants do."

"But I could have been more than an assistant," she snapped. "I was there at your side after Kate died, but you never once turned to me. You acted as if I didn't exist. But I was there, David. And I worked just as hard on the *Crab* as you did. I lost just as much sleep. But you didn't care for me and you didn't worry about my share when you decided to give that thing away. It's just like when you used me to meet Katharine," she said, smiling grimly. "Once you had what you were after, you dumped me fast enough."

"I had never seen your sister before you introduced us," David protested, taking a step to close the seven-foot gap between him and Nicole. "So how could I have used you to meet her?"

"That's what you say now, isn't it? Sure, when it's time to pay your debt, you try to make it all seem like some strange coincidence. It won't work." She stepped back, sliding her hip along the edge of the table and watching Nicole standing at the corner of it. "I'm tired of being ignored and tired of being poor. They both end now."

"How?" Nicole distracted her from David's movement with her question.

"It's all in the will," Connie said, smiling.

"I don't leave you anything in my will, Connie," David said. "A small stipend is all."

"No. Katharine's will. And you can stop sneaking toward your girlfriend now, Dave," she said, coolly moving the gun toward him.

"What about Katharine's will? I was there when they read it and don't see how it gave you any of my estate."

"You and I were both her heirs, David," Connie said. "We both inherited a piece of nothing. But, as Kate's heir, I'm entitled to quite a bit of your estate. Almost all of it, as I recall."

"You . . ." Then he smiled, ruefully. "Because my will leaves everything to Katharine or to her heirs," he said.

"Right. You meant children, I guess. You thought you had it covered if you and she had died together. But you see what you did, don't you? You put me in line before your family, David."

"Robert will bleed you dry in court contesting it, you know," David said. "And, if he doesn't, his mother will. It's just a technicality."

"A very important technicality, dear. And I think it's enough. Besides, Robert will be happy to accept a discount price on Albany Manufacturing to buy him off. The *Crab* will cost extra, however."

"You planned everything very carefully, didn't you?" Nicole asked. "Did Lance think he was going to live a life of luxury with you after he took care of us?"

"He was a sweet boy, but stupid and lazy. Quite perfect for my use."

"And you can accuse me of using people after the way you used Lance?"

"This isn't easy for me, David." Connie lost a bit of her calm then, a tear streaking one tanned cheek. "I loved you for years. Even when you were married to Kate, I loved you. But I finally grew up and faced facts. You aren't going to give me anything. I'll have to take it myself."

Connie tensed her arm, swinging the weapon between the two of them. "I'll have to arrange things a bit to throw them off the track," she said. "So I'd better get on with it."

"Wait, Connie!" David called, taking another step toward Nicole. "You can still stop."

"No. I killed the lawyer, after all," she said. "They can't punish me any more for three than one, so I might as well try to get away with it. And, David, I think it's only fair that I kill your girl first."

The gun snapped into alignment with Nicole's chest, and she could see Connie's finger tensing on the trigger. But David jumped with a shout, knocking Nicole to the side just as the gun went off.

"No!" Nicole shouted, seeing David spin back from the impact of the bullet. "No!" And she leaped past the table, avoiding the aim of the gun when it spoke again. She dashed through the door to the deck.

Nicole's only impulse had been to get the woman away from David at any cost, but now that she'd done that she had no idea how to stop her. She couldn't leave the ship for help and no one would be able to come in answer to a shout for help in time to do any good. She ran toward the stern, the other woman moving quickly behind her. There was no place to go but over the edge. What could she use as a weapon against her? The *Crab*! Yes.

Nicole stopped just past the bulk of the submarine lab where it was resting on its wheeled cart under the boom of the winch, the deck rail near it open to allow access to the sea. Taking a deep breath, Nicole turned and watched as Connie stopped on the other side of David's machine and just past the last stretch of railing. The woman stood directly in the path of the research machine, which hugged the deck like a torpedo.

"You can't shoot me out here," Nicole said, mustering as much authority as she could as she rested her hands on the *Crab*. "There'll be witnesses."

"No, I suppose I can't." The woman glanced toward the boats anchored along the docks. "But if you don't come inside, I will." The look in her eyes told Nicole that she would, too.

"Stop now," Nicole said, surveying the length of the *Crab* quickly. She'd remembered correctly; David hadn't tied it down. "Give yourself up, Connie. Please. I don't want to see anyone else harmed."

"Especially yourself, right?" Connie laughed abruptly, moving closer toward the edge of the deck as she motioned for Nicole to move. "Get inside," she commanded.

"No." And Nicole ducked quickly and threw herself against the smooth metal skin of the machine, putting every bit of strength she had into one convulsive push. The cart rolled easily beneath the heavy vessel, gaining momentum quickly as it rushed toward Connie.

Connie fired wildly as she jumped away from the rolling machine, the bullet pinging off the *Crab* just above where Nicole crouched. She didn't have time for another shot, for her startled leap had carried her to the edge of the deck where the railing was gone. She flailed to maintain balance, and only managed to grab the last railing standard by letting the gun drop to the deck.

The *Crab* continued rolling until it slammed against the wall of the cabin. Nicole grabbed up the gun, then turned to watch her would-be murderer struggle back on board to crouch like a caged beast before her.

"Please don't be foolish any more," Nicole said, holding the gun carefully but resolutely at the woman. "I don't have the faintest idea how to use this thing, and it might go off."

"You ruined everything," Connie whispered. The fight had left her, and she sat down with defeat shrouding her features. "I knew you would. I knew it when you first came on board."

"Come on," Nicole said, nodding toward the cabin. "I've got to find someplace to put you."

"Lock her in the pantry," David suggested weakly from the door.

"David! Thank God you're all right!" Nicole almost ran to him, but checked her movement to motion for Connie to stand up. "You heard him. Get moving."

She locked her up quickly and ran back to David, who sat on the floor just inside the door to unbutton his shirt. Grimacing he examined the wound on his chest.

"Oh, David. That must hurt horribly." She knelt beside him, gingerly pulling back his shirt to expose the bullet hole in the lower right side of his chest. Quite a bit of blood had soaked into the fabric. "Can you breathe all right?"

"I'll live," he said, smiling. "She could have hit me in many worse places. I wasn't much help though, was I?"

"You saved my life," she said, kissing him tenderly. "I wouldn't ask you to be any more help than that. Now lie down again while I call an ambulance."

"I guess I don't feel much like moving at the moment," he admitted, letting her lower him back to the floor.

Nicole hurried to the phone and dialed 911. While she spoke to the operator, she looked at her wristwatch with satisfaction.

12:44. The watch was back in motion again, its little numbers counting the seconds as they passed by. 12:44:33 . . . 34 . . . 35. She was already three minutes into her new life.

Epilogue

The sun burned hot in the clear blue skies over the south Pacific as the *Katharine* cut a northward course through the gentle waves. The crew of oceanographic students sat under the canopy behind the salon playing a casual game of gin and laughing the tropical hours away. In the main cabin, Jerry Brunsvold was busy at a computer terminal examining the data he'd gathered on the Barrier Reef. He was every bit as happy as the card players.

Nicole stood at the wheel on the flying bridge over the enclosed wheelhouse. Her hair billowed about her in the gentle breeze, sun-bleached to a dark golden hue. Except for three weeks when she and David had flown back to New York for Connie's trial, they had lived the last year on the boat. She'd learned the ropes of shipboard life and had taken on the duties of navigator. When they reached Los Angeles, she planned to take a licensing exam to get her certification for the job. It had been a wonderful year working beside her husband as they dived in the warm waters off Australia. She couldn't imagine now how she could have survived a life spent indoors with musty law books for company.

She knew she was making the right use of her secon
chance at life.

"Refreshments, m'lady." David bounded up the ladde
with two cans of soda clasped under one arm. "We sti
going the right direction?" he asked, kissing her chee
lightly as he put her can on the console before her.

"No," she laughed. "I'm lost." Nicole turned and cir
cled his bare shoulders with her arms, claiming a better kis
than the peck he'd just given her.

"Then maybe I'll have to find someone more compe
tent to handle the helm while we go below and try out som
more of those great kisses of yours." He slid his arm
around her easily, patting her bottom. "Or have we bee
married too long for that sort of thing?"

"No, I wouldn't say that," she answered, smiling de
murely. "But it's broad daylight, mister."

"I'll close my eyes. Promise."

"Should I take this energy of yours to mean that yo
don't regret marrying me?" She slipped away from him
hoping to cool her desires with distance, and popped ope
her soft drink.

"Not for a moment. And you?"

"Never." Watching his eyes, she could see the ligh
burning for her there as she knew it always would.

"Good." He sipped on his soda, looking out at the ho
rizon.

"Isn't Robert supposed to contact us soon?" Nicol
asked.

"When we dock. I don't want to find out any soone
than necessary what a mess he's made of my company."
But he smiled as he spoke, quite satisfied with the in
creased work his cousin's restructuring had brought t
Albany Manufacturing.

"He's doing just fine, and you know it," she said. "He's actually a nice guy on a personal level, isn't he? Paying for Connie's lawyer was awfully nice of him."

"Sure, but it's partly his fault. Whenever he couldn't get me he'd pump her full of malarkey about the company. That's what started her thinking about the wills."

"She wasn't thinking straight for a long time, David. No matter what he might have told her."

"I suppose not. I can't help feeling sorry for her," he said.

"At least now she'll get treatment if she needs it," Nicole replied. "She'll be all right."

"Yes she will. Meanwhile, we've got our own business to do. I've been toying with the idea of renaming the boat," he said seriously. "What do you think?"

"No. I like the name it's got."

"Really? It's not uncommon to rename ships when they come under new management, so to speak. Wouldn't you like to call it something else?"

"No. I have no problems with retaining Katharine's name. You don't want to sweep the past away, David. And I'm quite secure in our relationship. We're fated to be together, remember."

"I know. And I didn't want to sweep anything away, Nicole. I wanted something that might reflect our new beginning," he said lightly. "Maybe call it the *Twelve Forty-one*, or something like that." He slipped his arm around her again, standing beside her at the wheel.

"That's silly." Nicole laughed, settling back against him comfortably. "And you're silly, too."

"Them's mutinous words, matey," he growled. "I'm going to have to confine you to quarters."

"Really?" She leaned forward to set the autopilot on course, then turned with a laughing gleam in her eyes. "Well, you're the captain," she said, hugging him to her. "But I want the record to show that I'm going of my own free will."

"I'll make a note of that."

They kissed as though the summer sun didn't provide enough heat, and the passion that time had saved from destruction lived on in the eternal flame of their love.

Harlequin Intrigue

REBECCA YORK

Labeled a "true master of intrigue" by *Rave Reviews*, best-selling author Rebecca York makes her Harlequin Intrigue debut with an exciting suspenseful new series.

It looks like a charming old building near the renovated Baltimore waterfront, but inside 43 Light Street lurks danger . . . and romance.

Let Rebecca York introduce you to:

> *Abby Franklin*—a psychologist who risks everything to save a tough adventurer determined to find the truth about his sister's death. . . .
>
> *Jo O'Malley*—a private detective who finds herself matching wits with a serial killer who makes her his next target. . . .
>
> *Laura Roswell*—a lawyer whose inherited share in a development deal lands her in the middle of a murder. And she's the chief suspect. . . .

These are just a few of the occupants of 43 Light Street you'll meet in Harlequin Intrigue's new ongoing series. Don't miss any of the 43 LIGHT STREET books, beginning with #143 LIFE LINE.

And watch for future LIGHT STREET titles, including
#155 SHATTERED VOWS (February 1991) and
#167 WHISPERS IN THE NIGHT (August 1991).

Harlequin Superromance®

A powerful restaurant conglomerate that draws the best and brightest to its executive ranks. Now almost eighty years old, Vanessa Hamilton, the founder of Hamilton House, must choose a successor.
Who will it be?

Matt Logan: He's always been the company man, the quintessential team player. But tragedy in his daughter's life and a passionate love affair made him make some hard choices....

Paula Steele: Thoroughly accomplished, with a sharp mind, perfect breeding and looks to die for, Paula thrives on challenges and wants to have it all ... but is this right for her?

Grady O'Connor: Working for Hamilton House was his salvation after Vietnam. The war had messed him up but good and had killed his storybook marriage. He's been given a second chance—only he doesn't know what the hell he's supposed to do with it....

Harlequin Superromance invites you to enjoy Barbara Kaye's dramatic and emotionally resonant miniseries about mature men and women making life-changing decisions. Don't miss:

- CHOICE OF A LIFETIME—a July 1990 release.
- CHALLENGE OF A LIFETIME
  —a December 1990 release.
- CHANCE OF A LIFETIME—an April 1991 release.

SR-HH-1

Harlequin Historicals®

CELEBRATE THE SPIRIT OF
1776

If you enjoyed the story of Merry Morgan and Darcy Montour in FREEDOM FLAME, then you'll want to see how intrepid newspaperwoman Libby Morgan and Tory aristocrat Cam Gant fell in love in Caryn Cameron's first American Revolution book, LIBERTY'S LADY (Harlequin Historical #39).

As the American colonies rose up against the oppression of mother England, spirited journalist Libby Morgan fed the fires of rebellion—and clashed head-on with the prime target of her rabble-rousing. Dashing New York aristocrat Cameron Gant was an avowed Tory, a spy—and her sworn enemy. But Cam Gant was not what he seemed, and in his arousing embrace, Libby's contempt quickly dissolved as passions flared.

If you missed LIBERTY'S LADY the first time around, order it now!

COMING SOON

In September, two worlds will collide in four very special romance titles. Somewhere between first meeting and happy ending, Dreamscape Romance will sweep you to the very edge of reality where everyday reason cannot conquer unlimited imagination—or the power of love. The timeless mysteries of reincarnation, telepathy, psychic visions and earthbound spirits intensify the modern lives and passion of ordinary men and women with an extraordinary alluring force.

Available in September!

EARTHBOUND—Rebecca Flanders
THIS TIME FOREVER—Margaret Chittenden
MOONSPELL—Regan Forest
PRINCE OF DREAMS—Carly Bishop

DRSC-RR